7/1/90

To Scarlet

Something about
this book had your
name all over it.
I heard it through
the grapevine that it
was good.

Love,
Kate

BY SUSAN RICHARDS SHREVE

A COUNTRY

SIMON AND SCHUSTER

New York · London · Toronto · Sydney · Tokyo

OF STRANGERS

Susan Richards Shreve

Simon and Schuster
Simon & Schuster Building
Rockefeller Center
1230 Avenue of the Americas
New York, New York 10020

SIMON AND SCHUSTER AND COLOPHON ARE REGISTERED TRADEMARKS
OF SIMON & SCHUSTER INC.
DESIGNED BY SYLVIA B. GLICKMAN/LEVAVI & LEVAVI
MANUFACTURED IN THE UNITED STATES OF AMERICA
10 9 8 7 6 5 4 3 2 1
LIBRARY OF CONGRESS CATALOGING IN PUBLICATION DATA

SHREVE, SUSAN RICHARDS.
  A COUNTRY OF STRANGERS / SUSAN RICHARDS SHREVE.

    P.   CM.
  I. TITLE.
PS3569.H74C68   1989   88-28735
813'.54—DC 19   CIP
ISBN 0-671-64409-2

FOR TIMOTHY SELDES

Contents

BOOK ONE

Skunk Farm, 1942

*August
Eleventh,
1942*

In the evening, along Route 7 south of Washington, the farm—still called John Spencer's place in spite of what had happened—filled the sky. It had been built by the Spencers before the Civil War on a high rise above the Potomac, white and colossal, inappropriate to the gentle watercolor landscape of the Virginia hills. Along the front, the land had been planted in great elms to name the place; *Elm Grove, 1803* was painted in calligraphic letters on the sign which marked the entrance, and for a century after a blight killed many of the elms in North America, the Spencers had kept the huge black skeleton trees. If you happened to be driving south, even familiar with the road after the curve at Tyson's Corner, there was something terrifying, especially at dusk, about the sudden and luminous appearance of what the natives of northern Virginia called Dead Elm Grove.

On this particular summer evening, thick and sultry as evenings get in the swampland surrounding Washington, D.C., a caravan of automobiles, full of citizens, with the windows down, the heads of the occupants hanging out, traveled along Route 7, past Tyson's Corner. At the Spencer Farm, they slowed down to five, ten miles per hour, or stopped to watch in silence the life behind the brightly lit lace-curtained windows. The carloads started to arrive after eight, when the sun fell, so they wouldn't be noticed, but by nine o'clock there were more than twenty cars parked along the side of the road, on the field across the way—people sitting on the trunks drinking beer, on the hoods, lying on the tops of their cars under a perfect moon. Even the Fairfax County police had been called with a warning that there might be trouble afoot at the Spencer Farm. Two patrol cars had arrived at nine-fifteen, parked in the driveway and joined the assembly.

The chief of police had been born in Vienna, just down the road from the Spencer Farm, in fact, but he had spent enough of his working life in Philadelphia to have a perspective. He knew his home territory, however, and wandered through the parked cars testing the temper of the crowd.

"So?" his fellow officer asked when he climbed back into the car.

He shrugged. The crowd was certainly uneasy.

"Are you going to check for guns?" the one officer asked.

"There's no reason to check for guns at the moment," the chief of police said.

The young officer put his feet up on the dashboard. His voice was blistered. "If I weren't an officer of the law, I'd take my gun and empty it out straight in the center of that bay window on the second floor."

In the bay window on the second floor of the Spencer Farm, Moses Bellows stood naked above the waist, blue-black and splendid in the bright light. He cupped his huge hands, leaned against the window and looked out.

"Why Miracle darling," he called to his wife. "We have an audience." He had named her himself—Miracle Bellows—on their wedding day. Miracle for the Miracle at Cana, though she'd been May for John Spencer's mama for the first sixteen years of her life, but he didn't want a woman in his bed carrying the name of any blue-veined white woman with spun-cotton hair. And that was before he knew of any trouble with John Spencer, whose name made his blood boil to this day.

"Turn out the light, Moses," Miracle Bellows said, and she called to her niece Prudential, who was playing music on the Victrola in the living room, dancing around the room wild as a drunk cat, "Turn out the lights in the living room."

"And keep these nice people from their moving-picture show tonight?" Moses asked.

"Someone could shoot us," Miracle replied, emptying the linen closet of towels and sheets. "Gladly they'd shoot us, as you very well know." And she turned out the light which illuminated Moses Bellows with his great bare chest to the citizens in the fields across the road who were watching him, stirred by an ancient unsettlement, primitive, akin to fear.

"The reason I don't like the colored," one little boy broke the silence along the parked cars, "is that they smell bad and they been smelling up that big house."

"Hush," his mama said, but people heard and there was an uneasy rush of laughter through the crowd just as the lights of the Spencer Farm went out.

The facts about the Spencer Farm were these, reported in full on the second page of the *Washington Post*, August 11, 1942.

Elm Grove was built in 1803 as a summer place by Jeremiah Spencer, who was an attorney in Washington and later Democratic Senator from Virginia. It was built along the lines of Italian Palladian architecture—large and square, with columns, floor-to-ceiling windows, a veranda and no porch—built high for the view, and lived in by Spencers from the beginning of the nineteenth century until January 12, 1935, when John Spencer fell off the world, as Moses put it. The Spencers kept slaves and had a reputation for humane consideration and generosity, particularly to the women in the house. The Spencer men did not as a rule take advantage. The slaves were emancipated after the Proclamation of 1861 without event, and only the Bellows family remained in a relationship agreed on by both parties much the same as had existed before the war. The Bellows women worked in the house, cared for the children; the Bellows men and boys worked in the fields. They lived in three clapboard houses, down a dirt road behind the main house, still unheated in 1942 except by wood stoves. The Bellowses increased in number. Some moved off the farm, into the community, moved north or into Washington, D.C. The Spencers decreased. By 1935, John Spencer, a direct descendant of the lawyer Senator, was the only heir to an estate which had dwindled over the years to the main house, a large barn, three tenant houses and twenty-five tillable acres. There was at the time of his disappearance a checking account at First Virginia Bank with $456.89 and a savings account of $3,200, which is all he had managed to accumulate since he'd lost about $100,000 in the depression.

Little was known about John Spencer. He had been born at Elm Grove and lived there except during his early twenties when he was at Oxford for two years. He commuted to the University of Virginia, undergraduate and law school; he kept the house in beautiful condition after his parents were killed in a head-on collision with a county school bus empty of children, during his last year in law school. He never married but had a variety of attractive women who arrived in their smart gabardine suits and felt cloches and left with him the following morning for Washington, where he had his law office and did something—no one knew what—with the government. He was exquisitely polite, handsome in an overly defined way, and a bit taciturn, according to people who invited him to supper or cocktail parties. During the last year of his physical presence in Virginia, he stayed home more often than he went to work. There was conversation in the community that he had developed cancer, although when he came into Vruels' market on January 12, 1935, Doc Vruels, who owned the shop, told the police that he looked wonderful, relaxed, at ease, even youthful for what turned out to be a fifty-year-old man.

On that day in January, John Spencer arrived at the market about eight-thirty on his way to work. He bought the paper, shaving lotion, hair tonic and a package of Old Golds, one of which he lit up in the store, although Doc Vruels had a rule about smoking. He said good morning to Mrs. Hatfield, asked Mr. O'Leary whether he could purchase some piglets from him in the spring. Doc Vruels saw him walk across the street to speak for a moment with Moses Bellows, who was on his way on foot to help the O'Learys clean up after a barn fire.

Doc Vruels saw Moses get in the car with John Spencer, and the two of them drove north towards Washington on Route 7, which passed the O'Learys' at the intersection of 123 and 7. Moses Bellows got to the O'Learys' about nine-fifteen, according to Mr. O'Leary, questioned two days later on the disappearance of John Spencer and the possible implication of Moses Bellows. At five o'clock that night of January 12, police found John Spencer's Ford coupe parked by the canal with the keys in the ignition, an Old Gold cigarette burned to ash in the ashtray, a bag with his purchases at Vruels' market on the passenger seat. No one saw him again. He had a secretary at his office on K Street, N.W., who told police he had been suffering from intermittent headaches and depression. There was evidence in his room that he had traveled to England twice in December and stayed at the Savoy, but no one, not his secretary or anyone else questioned, knew anything about his business in London. According to records in the files at his office, his business with the government was personal with individuals and not official. Several women named as girlfriends were questioned. Most of them said their relationship with John Spencer was formal and social; several indicated he might be homosexual or at the very least indifferent to women. These personal details did not, of course, appear in full in the article in the *Post*.

Moses Bellows, when questioned, said he got along with John Spencer "good enough" but found him a cold and distant man on the few occasions they spoke to one another on matters unrelated to the farm.

He told the police that he had left Vruels' in John Spencer's car close to nine. They had had a conversation about piglets and painting the barn in the spring before Moses was let out at the entrance to the O'Learys'. Moses walked through the back field checking the sheds behind the barn to determine if they had been damaged by the barn fire and then walked up to the barn, where he met Mr. O'Leary and some workers who had come to help at about nine-thirty.

When the police asked Miracle, who worked in the house, she described John Spencer as tidy and a little dreamy. He read a lot of books, she said, and talked quietly and at length on the telephone. When asked did she like him, she said what difference does that make, and the officer could not think of a reply.

None of the other members of the Bellows family, busy with their own dark lives, had much to say about John Spencer except that he was nice enough.

And that was that. From time to time, during the next seven years, word would pass around especially at Vruels' that someone had seen him, but nothing was substantiated. And in time, people forgot.

They did not, however, forget what had happened to Elm Grove, although nobody took action against the Bellowses.

Moses Bellows moved into the main house of Elm Grove in early spring after the thaw. His own house—the second cottage along the path behind the wheat fields—out back, it was called, where the tenant houses stood—had fallen cold silent when John Spencer disappeared. Not that they didn't go about their daily lives. Every morning Miracle went to the main house, fluffed the pillows, vacuumed the rugs, dusted the furniture, polished the dining-room table with Old English and looked after the flowers she bought herself at Vruels' when Moses drove her there to market. Moses kept the livestock, twelve milking cows, chickens, lambs on the back field. He planned for piglets in the spring as John Spencer always did and had three pigs growing fat to be butchered in late summer. He put in eight hours at the O'Learys' and came home midday for lunch, which Miracle cooked—a big lunch set at the table by the window overlooking his own vegetable garden. They ate as they always had, face to face, across the table but without a word—Miracle looking out the window with her dark sorrowful eyes as if the rest of her life had been snatched away by the absence of John Spencer.

And as the winter passed, Moses Bellows filled with an anger finally too large for the clapboard house. In March, he packed his clothes in pillowcases tied with rope, took the picture of his parents off the dresser, put the picture of Miracle facedown on the mantel, took his knife from the kitchen cupboard, his rifle from the hall closet and a picture of Jesus, the Savior, given him by Miracle to keep him pure when she was lamb-innocent and twelve years old and he was twenty, raging with sex and fury at being too long boxed in on one farm in a small town without a future.

"You must be moving to a hotel," Miracle said that day at lunch, wiping her hands wet from the dishes on her round hips.

"I am moving to the Mayflower Hotel in Washington, D.C., this very afternoon. You can reach me by telephone if you've a mind to speak again in your life."

Moses put on his red-and-black jacket and a broad-brim hat he very much liked and had stolen from the Klingles when he was ten years old, slung his pillowcases over his shoulder, walked down the road half a mile to the main house and moved into John Spencer's bedroom. He pushed John Spencer's clothes to the back of the closet and hung up his own blue jeans and overalls and church pants, though God knows he never went to church—that was Miracle's social life. It was the first time in his life he'd hung his clothes in a closet. He slept in John Spencer's double bed, a four-poster with a canopy and a velvet bedspread. The next morning when he woke up to feed the animals and go to work at the O'Learys', he left the bed unmade and wrote a note to Miracle as John Spencer used to do. CHANGE THE SHEETS, PUT ME SOME SUPPER IN THE OVEN, BUY BRILLO PADS AND DISH SOAP AND TOILET PAPER. DO MY WASH.

Miracle was there when he came home for lunch that day, looking so warm and soft his heart sank to his stomach and he wanted her there on the four-poster with the velvet bedspread. But he restrained himself.

"Lunch is ready at home," she said, not a bit surprised to see he had moved into the main house.

"I live here," Moses said, going into the larder to wash his hands. He opened the cupboard and got out plates and a glass.

"I got my own lunch at Vruels', " he said.

Miracle's sweet face turned cross.

"You can't eat on those plates, Moses."

He made a large cheese-and-liverwurst sandwich, poured a glass of milk, cut the sandwich in half, put it on the plate and sat down with his lunch at the dining-room table.

Miracle followed him.

"What do you think you're doing?"

"I'm doing what it very much looks like I'm doing, Miracle darling," Moses said, flushed with pleasure for the first time since August 1934, when he'd had suspicions about John Spencer and his beloved Miracle.

"I don't want you to live in the house and use these things and sit on these chairs," Miracle said quietly, but he could tell by the tremor in her voice that she knew she had lost.

"I am sorry, but this is the house I'm living in." He finished his sandwich and got more milk, sitting back down at the dining-room table to drink it.

"What if Mr. Spencer comes back?" Miracle asked.

"Mr. Spencer won't be coming back," Moses said.

And Miracle spoke, so under her breath as to lose the words in her throat, so quietly only a man who knew her well as Moses did could have heard what she said.

"He won't be coming back because you killed him," was what she said.

"They haven't found his body yet," Moses said. "Until

20

they find his body, he isn't dead. And if he isn't dead, I didn't kill him. He just disappeared because that's the kind of white man he is. A disappearing white man."

Life at Elm Grove went on that way all spring, and there was talk about it in Vienna and Falls Church and Langley. Moses Bellows had moved into the main house. People would drive by in the evening, slow down as they passed, look up at the bedroom window to see a colored man in a white man's house.

"They could lynch you, Moses," Miracle said. She took to making his bed every day at the main house, cooking his lunch for him, although she wouldn't sit down at the dining-room table but stood in the door to the kitchen and watched him eat, doing his laundry and hanging it in John Spencer's closet. She was even pleased to have Moses there to do for.

"They're not going to lynch me—not in Fairfax County —and besides, they're afraid," Moses said. "What you should do is move in here with me, Miracle."

That night at home, Miracle asked her sister-in-law, Aida, married to Guy, Moses' brother, who lived next door, "You think the reason nobody in town has moved Moses out of the farmhouse is because they're afraid of him?"

"Sizzling with fear," Aida said. "Moses Bellows could make a grizzly have a heart attack on the spot if he'd a mind to." Aida sat on her front porch, as she did most evenings after day work in the community, her skirt up to her thighs, her legs apart, a cigarette dangling from her full lips. "Moses Bellows makes me burn right through my blood," Aida said. But nobody paid much mind to Aida's burning, because that's the woman she was unprovoked. Hot-blooded, full of sweetness and temper and trouble at the same time. She had married Guy Bellows when she was eighteen, and from the start she took charge of him, which was not difficult, because Guy Bellows had locked in step at eleven years old and did not wish to behave grown-up except when he was drinking.

All the Bellowses were good friends, the best of friends. Since Moses and Guy's parents, who had lived in the last cottage, had died, they had spent all their time together, until the business between Miracle and John Spencer got started. They were high-spirited children capable of flinging off their dark lives like winter coats, playing with abandon. Only children—and adults whose lives are so robbed of promise there is no longing possible—are capable of that kind of uncomplicated pleasure.

"It looks like John Spencer isn't coming back," Miracle said. "So Moses thinks we should all move to the main house."

"He does, does he?" Aida lit up. "I'll ask Guy about that when he comes home this evening, long as he isn't drunk or got his finger shot off like he did at Christmas."

"Ask him," Miracle said quietly, for she had been thinking maybe she should move. Maybe things were meant to be this way, and besides nights she longed for Moses Bellows by her side. But she wasn't going to give him the satisfaction of knowing.

"So you don't think Mr. Spencer's coming back, is that so, Miracle?" Aida asked.

"I don't think so," Miracle said.

"You think he's dead?"

"No," Miracle said loyally. "He's just disappeared. He's that kind of white man."

"I suppose he is," Aida agreed. "Chicken to the toes."

And that night late when Guy Bellows came back from Leesburg where he worked construction, a slow but dependable worker, Aida told him the plans.

"I don't like that plan," Guy said. "We'll have trouble. Only a man like Moses can live in Elm Grove and not be killed for it."

"Listen, Guy Bellows. I packed your clothes this very evening, because moving is what we're going to do. I didn't marry you to turn soft the second fortune stared you in the face and said, 'Mr. Bellows, my friend, my hero—I got gold for you at the other end of the rainbow if you'll just open your sleepy eyes and grab a handful.'" By late that night, Guy and Aida Bellows had moved into the guest room with white starched curtains and matching bedspreads and pretty trinkets on the dresser and a fireplace just for show since the main house had central heat and a bathroom attached with a sunken tub and a double sink and begonias filling the windows with bright yellow.

"So, Guy," Aida said that night from her twin bed. She'd never slept alone in her life—first with her sister and then with her mama after her papa died and then with Guy. She stretched out and wiggled her thin toes under the sheets. "Isn't this the cat's meow."

Guy grumbled.

"I liked it better in the same bed," Guy said.

"I wonder who slept in this bed before. One of those pale-haired girls with no flesh and perfume Mr. Spencer used to bring home."

On September one, Miracle packed her sleeping gown, a work dress, a church dress and a picture of her mama and moved into the main house.

So by October of 1935 when Hitler was transforming Germany and President Franklin Roosevelt was pulling America out of the worst economic depression in history, the Bellows family had taken over a white man's farm in the South and were living like kings.

Years passed and John Spencer did not reappear.

The citizens were angry about Elm Grove, deeply angry. But there was something about the brashness of the Bellows family packing up and moving in which stopped everyone in his tracks. No one mentioned it to Moses Bellows at the O'Learys' nor to Aida where she did day work. Occasionally someone at Vruels' would make a comment to Miracle when she did the marketing, but she'd just smile her warm and winning smile, cluck in her throat as if the speaker didn't know the half of it and finish her marketing.

The fact was that the Bellowses kept the farm in shape. Guy painted the house so it glittered in the winter when the trees were bare. The gardens were kept up. Even the wheat fields and animals stayed exactly as they had been when John Spencer was around.

In 1939, the townspeople formed a committee to determine whether it was possible to gain control of the farm.

They decided that the sensible thing to do would be to have John Spencer declared legally dead after seven years and then see to it that the farm was sold. Moses heard about the plan at the O'Learys' and mentioned it to Guy. But 1942 seemed a long way off, and besides, they were realists living well on borrowed time.

In December 1941, when the Japanese bombed Pearl Harbor and a reluctant America entered the war, the city of Washington filled with soldiers, and in January, John Spencer, who had been missing for seven years exactly, was declared legally dead, as a result of efforts by the committee of citizens for the protection of Elm Grove. The house and land were put up for sale in the spring, without much hope for selling a farm twenty miles south of Washington, D.C., in wartime.

However, on a Thursday night, the week the sale sign was put up, a young journalist named Charley Fletcher came out to look at the farm. He had just moved to Washington from the Midwest to help run the Office of Censorship, which had been established before Pearl Harbor. At the time he visited the farm, he was living in a rooming house on Dupont Circle until he found a place to bring his family—his wife, a Danish actress older than he by ten years, her thirteen-year-old daughter born out of wedlock and their infant son.

As it turned out, Charley Fletcher bought the house that night without even looking at the upstairs or the land out back or the barn. He bought the livestock and the furniture and the Bellows family insofar as they planned to remain at Elm Grove, which they certainly were going to do, since Guy and Moses had been born there and did not imagine alternatives.

"Something foolish got into the Bellowses when John Spencer disappeared," the real estate agent said to Charley Fletcher. "But I wouldn't worry if I were you. They know their place."

"I don't worry about the Bellowses," Charley Fletcher said. And the real estate agent could tell and so could Moses, who met Mr. Fletcher for a moment just after he bought the farm, that this young man from the middle of the country had some kind of purpose in mind.

Moses broke the news to his family that night at supper, and they all got drunk. Even Miracle, who didn't drink at all, danced on the kitchen table to the music on the radio.

"So. What's life going to be like under the new management?" Guy asked his brother. "You met him. You got a nose for people."

"He's young," Moses said deliberately. He had had a reaction, certainly. Something about Charley Fletcher made his hair rise straight up on his back.

"I don't know why a young man with an important job in Washington would want to be on a farm twenty miles in the sticks unless there's something fishy," Guy said. "That's my considered opinion. There's something fishy."

Moses was pensive. He'd drunk too much, and people, his family in particular, listened to him. He didn't want to give a false impression and set them all thinking down the wrong path.

"He's got ideas. That's the sort of man he is," Moses said. "What's more, I don't think John Spencer in all the years I knew him ever shook my hand."

"Are you telling me that Charley Fletcher shook your hand, Moses?" Aida asked.

"He did," Moses said. "He shook my hand like this." And he shook Aida Bellows' thin hand firmly in his own.

Miracle knew that Moses was worried.

"What do you mean, ideas?" she asked him that night in the four-poster bed with a light spring wind blowing the curtains like canopies. She lay naked up against his fine firm body.

"Just a feeling I had about him. He's a man who fills a room up—and I thought trouble when I met him written in pig's blood on his forehead."

Pig's blood was spilling in the pantry of the main house on the night of August 11, 1942, when the citizens of Fairfax County had come to witness the Bellows family move out back. Guy Bellows had butchered that afternoon so they'd have a hog for winter in case the new owner wanted to give up the livestock. When Miracle ordered the lights out, he and Aida were working against the night to finish up the job. The pig hung head down from the rafters—actually the head was off by the time Moses came to check on his brother—split down the center. A large bucket caught the spill of blood, which smelled too sweet in the hot night.

"She's going to be spoiled," Aida said crossly. "I can smell her going rotten while we work."

Guy did not speak. He worked slowly but with care and precision, indifferent to Aida or the hot night until Moses came down to tell them that Route 7 had a few cars come to watch the Bellowses move out and therefore Miracle thought it best to turn out the lights in the front of the house.

"Gawkers," Guy said. It was a statement of fact. He cut the left flank off the hog and flung the heavy slab on the butcher-block table. "If they don't quit, I'll kill them for looking," he said evenly.

Moses didn't engage his brother in conversation.

At thirty, Guy was younger by eight years than Moses—a simple man, easily led, essentially sweet and without complication. He wasn't even deeply bothered by the inner plight of being born colored in northern Virginia as Moses was. He had only one golden rule—a single moral position in his small bag of tricks. He would not tolerate ridicule. That was that. Not of himself or of his wife or Moses or Miracle.

People could call him lazy or tell him what to do or how to do it or criticize the way he went about his business. But he had told Aida the first time they went out and were lying in the shed behind her father's place, "If anyone in the world, even my brother Moses makes fun of me, I'll kill him. I got my shotgun on the spot just in case."

Which is why Moses had come downstairs to check on his brother. He knew very well that if that soft bruised spot on Guy Bellows' heart was touched, he'd go crazy.

People were careful. Even Aida, flushed with sex as she seemed to be without stopping, was careful.

Moses pretended to be checking out the pig. "Big one," he said, "and fat." He laid his hand on his brother's shoulder in case there was a temper rising. Then carefully he slid the shotgun off the table while Guy's back was turned.

"Miracle says we ought to be out of here by midnight." He gave Aida a confidential look.

"I'll be out of here when I finish this hog," Guy said.

Moses took the shotgun into the living room. Perhaps Guy was sufficiently preoccupied not to notice. Perhaps the night could just slide by without incident.

Prudential watched him put the shotgun behind the couch.

"So what's going on now?" she asked her uncle.

"People come to watch us move, darling." The lights were out but the night was silver and they could see each other clearly. Moses walked over to the living-room window and looked out across the front lawn, across the road. He lifted the curtain and let it drop so it closed softly.

Prudential Dargon, named from the Prudential Life Insurance sign in front of Mr. Owen B. Snaffer's house in Okrakan, South Carolina, was thirteen, high-tempered and bone-thin with a gentle round belly that was a baby growing into its sixth month of incubation. Not that Prudential hadn't tried. She'd used coat hangers and ridden the pony bareback over the fences and drunk some terrible brew her grandmama concocted, but the baby stuck, and so she was sent out of South Carolina before she showed to stay the summer with her Aunt Miracle. And then she'd plans to leave the baby with Moses and Miracle, who couldn't seem to get a baby of their own started.

"I send you Prudential, Miracle sweetheart," her mother had written. "See if you can tame her."

"I can't be tamed ever," Prudential said and danced through the house to the music on John Spencer's Victrola lifting her summer skirt high in the air, turning her bare feet so fast you couldn't tell one from the other, hugging and kissing the lamps and banisters and mantelpiece, pretending they were boyfriends.

"That baby's gonna drop, Prudential, if you don't stop carrying on," Miracle said.

"Babies don't drop, Aunt Miracle," Prudential said. "They're glued to you till your time. Besides," she said, "I may want to keep this baby stuck in there until I'm twenty so he won't ever have to see his daddy."

"And who might his daddy be?" Moses would ask from time to time. "You can tell me. I'm not going to make a federal case."

But Prudential wouldn't tell. Not even her mama or her next sister, Holiday, or Aunt Miracle, whom she truly loved better than anyone in the world.

All she ever said and that once to her own mama was: "I can't tell you anything at all because you know him."

"How well do I know him?" her mama asked.

"Well enough that there'd be no Sunday suppers around the kitchen table if the news is out."

Prudential stood next to her uncle, leaned her head just so against his chest. Moses Bellows was the only man she'd ever known strong enough to rest her head on, and that was bad news for the future of a girl still mud-deep in childhood.

"Who do you think Guy's going to shoot that made you hide his gun?" Prudential asked. "I always thought he was a pussycat."

"Mostly he's a pussycat," Moses said. "But once when he was small he got hit over the head and since that time he's got a doorbell in his brain and if you ring it, he's gone to the world."

The story was this, and Moses told it to his niece while they watched the policemen across the street angle on foot through the crowd.

Guy Bellows was eleven years old and lived where he still lived, out back in the middle tenant house on Elm Grove. But this afternoon he'd gone across the road to set up Mrs. Albright's garden for planting and Bobby Albright, Mrs. Albright's grandson from Alabama, sat on the tractor and watched him. They didn't talk, and Guy wasn't even bothered by Bobby Albright's staring at him while he worked. Guy wasn't bothered by much in the world except hay fever.

"So," Bobby said finally. "Bet you don't know what's black and white and smells bad when he's scared."

"A skunk," Guy said proudly, down on his knees breaking up the dark red Virginia clay with his hands.

"Not a skunk," Bobby Albright said.

"Sure, it's gotta be a skunk," Guy said, very pleased with himself for guessing a white boy's riddle.

"It's a nigger. Doncha get it?"

Guy stood up and looked straight at the younger smaller boy.

"A nigger's not white," Guy said quietly.

"Part white," Bobby Albright said. "Chocolate milk is what he is from colored women screwed by white men for their pleasure to make skunk babies who smell bad, scared or not."

Then Bobby Albright leaped from the tractor seat and bopped Guy Bellows on the head with a small iron pipe, leaving him unconscious in the red clay of Mrs. Albright's garden.

"Our mama always said that accident made Guy simple-minded, but she was wrong," Moses said to Prudential. "He's single-minded and sweet-tempered but not simple."

"That's a terrible story," Prudential said.

Moses took her hand.

"What do you think happened to Bobby Albright?"

"I suppose he went back to Alabama."

"And died?"

"I doubt he died," Moses said. "He's young as Guy."

"He should have died," Prudential said. "He should have died on the spot."

"Things don't often happen the way they should." He started up the stairs. "Even now when Guy talks about the colored, he calls us skunks," Moses said. "Now you come on upstairs and help Aunt Miracle carry out the rest of our things."

Prudential followed. She took one load of sheets and

towels which had belonged to John Spencer in a laundry basket out back to the tenant house where she was going to live with Miracle and Moses until the baby came. Then she followed Moses back to the main house.

"There'll be a girl your age moving into the house," Moses said. "Did Miracle tell you?"

"She told me," Prudential said. "A girl thirteen and a newborn baby."

"It'll be nice for you to have a playmate."

"I don't need a playmate when I got myself," Prudential said crossly.

"Suit yourself." Moses reached down and took her hand.

"I'm not a child," Prudential said.

In South Carolina, Prudential was well known for her tough hide. She was the eldest of eleven children, one born after the other, Holiday next to her, then Mercury and General Lafayette, who was born with clubfeet and a lot of his brain gone—and on down it went with Prudential in charge because her mama was always busy with General Lafayette or having another baby and her papa worked days on a tobacco farm and nights in a filling station and Prudential very much wished he'd move to Georgia so he wouldn't be after her when he came home nights to find his wife full up with child had fallen exhausted into bed.

Prudential Dargon was very smart, and she had plans surprising for a country girl who was growing up without a sniff of promise in the world. What she had learned came from magazines at Willoughby's country store and the library. She took out two books a week and read by candle in the bed. Once a week, she went to Willoughby's and sat behind the counter where no one could see her and read *Glamour* and *Cosmopolitan* and *Time* and *Vogue* and *True Romance* and *Good Housekeeping* cover to cover. She studied how to dress and put on makeup and look sexy and how to manage your money and find a career and where to go to college and how to decorate your house—plans that had no place even in the dreams of her house, which like most of the houses in Okrakan was dominated by dreams of Jesus and salvation. But Prudential planned to leave South Carolina and go north. She hoped her mother and the babies which kept coming would survive without her, but finally, she was a practical girl who knew a great deal about matters of the world for someone without a whisper of sophistication. Besides, if she didn't leave home soon, something terrible was going to happen with her father and she would be responsible.

Those were the thoughts charging through her mind as she walked with Moses back into the main house, conscious of the hardness of her baby, of the sharpness of exchange between Guy and Aida, of Miracle's soft shoes back and forth, back and forth on the floor above them and of a company of strangers just outside the front door invading the last hours of the Bellows family in the Kingdom of Heaven.

She looked out the window. A few cars had driven off, but there were still ten or fifteen of them in view, and two patrol cars in the driveway. It was probably fifty yards from the front door of Elm Grove to the bottom of the driveway where the sign *Elm Grove, 1803* hung on a wrought-iron post.

Barefoot and quiet, Prudential tiptoed across the living room and across the hall and opened the front door, careful that Moses and Guy not hear her. Then she walked down the hill towards the road, swinging her arms, sashaying, her head cocked to one side as if it were the most normal thing in the world to walk directly into the arms of an angry crowd of white men.

"What's up?" someone shouted.

"Come on over and have a beer," another said, and then there was a hush. The policemen, smoking cigarettes in their cars, got out, walked across the road and stood in front of the field where most of the cars were parked.

Prudential knew exactly what she was going to do. She kept her head up, looking at the stars, at the full moon, and hoped the furious citizens would think she was praying to almighty God and be respectful—although not for a minute in her young life since she could remember had she believed in almighty God. Just the devil and all his works on earth, which she had in mind stopping for good when she grew up.

She walked down the hill, lifted the Elm Grove sign off its stand, tucked it under her arm, turned around and walked back up to the main house. This was the hardest part, she thought, walking with her back to the silent crowd, and she walked quickly, her heart beating in her chest and belly as well.

Once inside, she listened for a moment upstairs to the steady hum of Miracle and Moses talking. They must not have noticed she was gone. Then she went to the back of the house to a room off the kitchen next to where Guy and Aida were working and where tools and paint were kept. She put the sign facedown on the work table, looked through the paints on the shelf and took down a quart of black enamel and a brush sitting in a mayonnaise jar of turpentine.

She painted carefully in large-scale block print on the wood surface of the sign.

SKUNK FARM, 1942

She wanted to show Guy, but she didn't. He would either be very pleased or else he'd go crazy and rush around the house after his shotgun and blow somebody's head off, maybe his own. In fact, she decided she wasn't going to show anybody, because she was sure Miracle and Moses would not think it funny to change the name of Elm Grove in a public ceremony, but that's what she had in mind doing.

She put the sign under her arm, careful not to smudge the paint, opened the front door and slid back outside into the moonlight and the rush of voices from the field.

The policemen still stood across the road. A few cars had turned their lights and engines on and were pulling back onto the road as Prudential Dargon, proud and straight, marched down the hill, turned her back to the crowd and hung the newly painted sign so SKUNK FARM, 1942 faced the road.

It was at that moment Moses looked out the bay window on the second floor to check the activities and noticed the chicken-bone figure of his young niece.

"Miracle," he called softly.

Miracle slid under his arm. "What is that child doing?" she asked. "You get her in here before she's hurt."

Prudential had started back up the hill. The headlights from the cars turned on to see the sign made light paths in front of her, and as Moses rushed down the stairs of the main house unaware of the growing confusion on the field across the road, Prudential sensed trouble behind her.

The shot came then—just as she reached level ground, ten yards from the house. A single shot, and Prudential went facedown on the soft grass.

"Sweet Jesus," Miracle whispered from the bay window and followed Moses down the stairs.

In the back of the house where Guy was butchering, the sound of the shot was clear enough to make him jump.

"Where's my gun?" he shouted to Aida. "I left it here." He looked under the table. "Did you take it? Did you hide it, Aida, like you're always doing?" But Aida had flown into the kitchen already and slid into the broom closet with brooms and mops and the smell of Lysol thick in her nostrils.

"Moses," Guy called as he ran out of the kitchen and down the hall to the living room. "Moses."

In the field, the chief of police had taken Tom Sales' pistol and handcuffed him. The rest of the officers faced the crowd with their guns raised.

"Everyone get back in your cars and go home," the police chief said in his large even voice. He put Tom Sales in the back of the patrol car and headed up the hill to where Prudential was lying covered by her wide skirt just as Moses burst out the front door and headed towards his niece.

Moses knelt down.

"Prudential?" he said.

"Uh huh," she whispered.

"You hit?"

She turned over and sat up.

"Nothing hit me," she said. "I just heard the gun and went down."

The chief of police had reached the crest of the hill.

"Moses?" he called.

"Yes sir."

"Is the child hurt?"

"She wasn't hit," Moses said.

"That's very lucky. You know that, don't you?"

"Yes sir."

"Move out of the house quickly, Moses. I don't like the feel of things tonight."

"We'll be out by midnight," Moses said.

Inside the house, Miracle got ahold of Guy.

"Prudential?" she asked.

"I'm fine," Prudential said.

"Guy can't find his gun," Miracle said.

Moses took Guy hard by the shoulders and held his arms down. "Pull yourself together, Guy. Finish up the hog and let's go home."

"This is my home. I lived here seven years and that's long enough to call a place your home."

Moses put his arm firmly around his brother and walked out to the kitchen with him.

"Aida?" he called.

"The stupid woman hid herself in the broom closet," Guy said. "She may as well be a broom for all the sense she's got in emergencies."

"Well, get out Aida and let's finish up this pig before she spoils."

At midnight, the Bellowses left the main house for good. The hog was done. Miracle had packed what of John Spencer's she wanted, including the china and the sterling silver and a few candlesticks. The place was sparkling clean for Charley Fletcher, who at that very moment was driving with his family through the night to be in Virginia by dawn. Arm in arm the Bellowses walked down the path headed out back, headed home.

"So what did you write on that sign worth risking your life for, Prudential Dargon?"

Prudential smiled. She tiptoed and whispered in Moses' ear.

" 'Skunk Farm' is what I wrote," she said.

"You did, did you?" And Moses Bellows laughed so hard he thought he'd break in half.

By midnight the patrol cars had pulled away, and along Route 7 the wet black paint of SKUNK FARM, 1942 shimmered in the pale light of a full moon, to welcome Charley Fletcher and his family at dawn.

August
Twelfth,
1942

Charley Fletcher loved to drive, especially at night on back roads with Lara beside him—conspiratorial travelers on the road between where they had been and where they were going. Only tonight, in a tunnel bored through the Allegheny Mountains of Pennsylvania, the silence between them was peopled with demons.

"Lara." He spoke under his breath so as not to be heard by her daughter, Kate, stretched out in the back, her young giraffe legs filling the seat. "Speak to me."

Lara had not spoken since Minneapolis—not to him, at least—only soft sounds to their infant son, whom Charley still could not identify as familiar—or to Kate, who said she'd like a horse for the new farm and hoped there were a great many animals and that the farm wasn't close to a school.

"Of course you'll go to school," Lara said.

"Not necessarily," Kate replied. "You'll need someone to stay at home with you, because the farm is miles and miles from anywhere. Isn't it, Charley?"

"It's twenty miles from Washington, D.C., which is somewhere as you very well know," Charley said.

"What about gas rationing?" Kate went on. "We'll only have enough gas to go to Washington once a month. That's what Mother told me."

"Once a week, Kate. I told you once a week. We'll make arrangements. You can go in every day if you wish. Lara?"

But she was looking out the window into the blackness as if the night were full of entertainment.

Charley Fletcher ought to have been on top of the world. He was young, thirty-one in September, high-spirited and irreverent, with dark Celtic good looks and a rare energy as if he had been arrested in a state of permanent boyhood. His father, dead for years, had been a coal miner first in Swansea, South Wales, and then New Philadelphia, Ohio, where Charley grew up in a family too large for individual conversation. His mother, who with any chance to slip through the cracks of their small lives in New Philadelphia would have been something—a dancer, a musician, a stage actress—something that stirred her heart—filled the Fletcher house with music played on the radio or sung herself over the dishes and the cleaning and the gardening. She put her soul into Charley Fletcher. By fifteen, he had galloped out of New Philadelphia, Ohio, to college and beyond.

When he was very small, she'd kneel beside his bed with him for prayers. She was a deep believer in something, perhaps God—and every night she'd end the ritual with the repeated grace "Thank you dear Lord for my great gift which I will give the world when I grow up."

"What is my great gift?" he asked her sincerely when he got older, discovering that he was quite good in school and baseball and too small for football and that people were inexplicably drawn to him. Nevertheless he did not notice anything he could point to as a great gift.

"We don't know yet," she said to him as if the discovery were going to be collective. "Someday it will show itself like gold."

"Don't delude him," Thomas Fletcher would say crossly to his wife. "The world is a hard place to get by in and he oughtn't think he has wings."

"Oh, Thomas," his mother would say sadly to his father.

"The only chance you have even for the stumps of wings is to believe in them."

Which Charley Fletcher did. From his earliest memory, he felt a sense of destiny.

Kate sat up and stuck her head over the front seat.

"What is the matter up here?" she asked.

"Nothing is the matter, darling," Lara said.

"It feels the matter," Kate said. "Bad-tempered is what it seems like. I'll go back to Denmark as soon as the war is over if it's going to be so difficult between you two."

"We'll not go back to live," Lara said.

"I said me. Not you. You'll stay here with Charley and I'll live with my father, maybe in Milan."

Kate was going to be beautiful like her mother, dark with high cheekbones and full lips, an attentiveness in her wide hazel eyes. But at thirteen, she was out of proportion. Everything was too large—her lips, her classic nose, her long long legs and hands. She was like collapsible furniture that fell one way or another every time you set it up. And lately she'd rushed after her mother's life like a young arsonist, setting brushfires which blazed out of control.

"You are making life difficult for Charley," Lara said.

"Mother says I'm making life difficult for you, Charley," Kate said.

"I heard."

"Well." She flopped over onto the backseat. "It was so much better when you loved each other passionately like you used to do before Mama was pregnant with Sam."

Kate was right, of course, but neither Lara nor Charley replied.

Evenings in St. Paul, especially winter evenings when the large apartment on the second floor smelled of wood burning in the fireplace, Kate would lie in bed, her door ajar, and listen to the soft private conversation between Charley and her mother sitting at the round table in the window at the end of the dark living room eating supper by candlelight.

Charley came home late from the paper, sometimes as

38

late as ten. Lara would always pretend to eat dinner with Kate, but Kate knew better—knew her mother was waiting for darkness to settle and the strange and secret life of grown-ups to begin.

When Kate was under the covers, reading in Danish, Lara would bathe and change to a loose silk blouse and pearls, put her hair up, pat her wrists with lavender.

"Are you and Charley going out?" Kate would always ask when her mother tucked her in, kissed her good night, although she knew the answer.

"No, darling." Lara would turn out the light. "We're in as usual."

Always Charley's arrival woke Kate if she was sleeping, and she would lie in bed, melancholy because she was left out of their lives, but thrilled to be a silent visitor to what certainly seemed to be as they whispered back and forth the sounds of wonder and mystery between men and women.

"You used to eat supper by candlelight in the living room before you got pregnant with Sam," Kate said from the backseat. "Do you remember?"

But Lara was silent.

Lara Fletcher was a woman whose presence suffused a room. "A slow-growing beauty" is how she had been described in a Danish magazine story which came out in the early thirties at the beginning of her career in film. She was soft, not fleshless like so many film stars, with a lovely face whose expression was at once warm and tentative. She had large, olive-green eyes, oddly shaped, and it was the eyes that a person noticed first as extraordinary. Then the unexpected softness. "Sensual not sexy" is how she was described in an American magazine after her first film with English subtitles was released.

She had met Charley Fletcher in Berlin at the 1936 Olympics, to which he had gone as a journalist to report on the games. But the far-sighted editor of the *Minneapolis*

Tribune for whom he worked was interested as well to learn what was actually going on with the Nazis in Germany. And Charley came back with a story. The story was about an unexceptional woman in love with Adolf Hitler whose death Charley had witnessed at the games. And when the story, syndicated as an innocent feature in September 1936, was read years later, after the Nazis' devastation of Europe, after Pearl Harbor and the murder of the Jews, people realized that Charley Fletcher with his sense of the truth at the heart of things had actually anticipated the horror simmering in Germany.

Lara, full of the windsongs of summer, was in Berlin for a film on a long-distance runner. She spotted Charley first on her way to the opening ceremonies and was, as she told him later, compelled by his presence. She had followed him up the hill and sat down just behind him at an angle so if he turned slightly, he would see her. And she would smile her wonderful smile. The day was warm and bright, the spirits in the crowd sprinkled on the hill were high, and there was a sense of triumph in the air as they waited for Hitler and the storm troopers to open the game.

The old German woman arrived late, scrambled up the hill molelike, low to the ground, and sat between them, obstructing Lara's view of Charley.

Later, Charley remembered her exactly. She was a warm-faced, gentle Bavarian woman with round eyes, soft loose flesh and gray hair braided in a cap around her head with wilted wildflowers pressed in the braids. She wore a wool skirt even in the heat and a gray work shirt. In the pocket of the work shirt was a triangle of lace handkerchief, wide intricate lace, perhaps a wedding handkerchief from her grandmother, Charley thought. He was struck by her intensity, a woman so old, whose life by all rights ought to have spilled out to almost empty.

At once after the woman arrived, the music began and the heavy drumbeat of Hitler and his storm troopers sounded gunfire in the distance. As soon as they were visible at the entrance to the amphitheater, the crowd stood and cheered. The old woman, her head shaking back and forth, held on to Lara. *"Der Fuehrer,"* she murmured. *"Der Fuehrer. Der Fuehrer. Der Fuehrer."* She was weeping and weeping. And as the new leader of the German people marched past the grandstand below the hill where they were standing, the old woman fell facedown in adoration. Or so Lara and Charley Fletcher and the crowd who saw her thought. They did not investigate immediately.

When the storm troopers stopped at attention and Hitler mounted the podium to open the ceremony, several people close to the old woman, including Charley, realized with a start the stillness of the woman and knew that she was dead.

That afternoon, in a crowded restaurant, Lara and Charley Fletcher sat across a dime-size table and drank dark German beer.

"It's not her dying that surprised me," Charley Fletcher said. "It was her weeping when she saw Hitler."

"She was weeping for joy that he will save them," Lara said.

"And you?"

Lara shook her head. Her father, a physician with whom she had almost always lived, an only child after her mother died when she was eleven, was a strong anti-Nazi in Copenhagen.

"I don't know about saving," she said. She could not speak of her father's sentiments in public, of course, and she did not have a sense of Americans. They seemed innocent in general. There had been jokes about their foolishness when she was growing up in school. "If you get saved, it is because you do it for yourself. That is how I have been brought up, so I have no belief that Hitler will save the Germans."

They saw each other the next day and the next before she left to go back to Copenhagen. He did not even kiss her, but on their last afternoon together, she took his hand, put his fingers between her lips and kissed them so sweetly it took his breath away.

"If you're ever in America," Charley said and gave her his address and telephone.

At home, Lara put herself to sleep at night with Charley Fletcher's face behind her eyelids.

That was the summer of 1936. In the fall, Lara did a film at the orphanage in Odessa in which she played the guardian mother to the young orphans. She took Kate with her, and they were gone from Copenhagen until Christmas. When she returned, her father's life had changed. He was involved in meetings almost nightly after work and had grown secretive and somehow old. He was fiercely against the Nazis—crazily, it seemed to her—and sometime after the first of the year, he began to travel and would be gone days at a time. His medical practice deteriorated, and he seemed unwell.

"I will not be myself again as long as the Nazis are in power in Germany," he told Lara. "I must do what I must do."

So Lara lost herself in her work and her life with Kate and noticed less his frequent absence, his distractions and ill temper. And then one evening she came home for dinner as usual and he was dead on the couch in their living room. He had been shot.

There was no investigation, simply the assumption that he had become too involved.

"You should probably leave Denmark for a while," the police told her. "As a film star, you are too much in evidence."

"Go to England or perhaps America," her friends told her.

And so, four days after her father's death, she packed up her clothes and Kate's, took a train and boat to England and waited there for the next ship to the United States. She arrived in New York, took a train to Chicago and then to Minneapolis. In the train station, she called Charley Fletcher, and when he answered, she hung up. She wanted to surprise him. It never occurred to her that he might have a girlfriend or a wife or simply not wish to have Lara Bergmann and Kate move into his apartment on the second floor of a Victorian house on Quincy Street with one bedroom and a kitchen and a parlor.

42

Even Kate wondered.

"Why do you think your friend will be glad to see us, Mama?"

"He will be delighted, darling," Lara said. "He is very fond of me and will be so of you as soon as he knows you."

And she was right.

She arrived by taxicab on the evening of April 7, 1937; it was still winter in Minneapolis. Charley answered the doorbell in a robe just out of the shower.

"You said if ever I'm in America." She smiled. "And here I am, although America is farther from New York than I had thought it would be."

They stopped at a truckers' stop under high bright yellow lights which turned their faces pale and sickly orange.

"How far is it now?" Kate asked from the backseat.

"We're halfway there," Charley said.

Lara handed Sam to Kate, got out and walked across the parking lot to the rest rooms.

Charley followed her. "Lara." He took her elbow. "If you'd just say something. Good morning. Good night. I hate you. I'm in love with Mr. Roosevelt. Anything. Just speak in remembrance of our onetime enchanting love affair."

She unlocked the rest room and pushed open the door. He held his hand in the door so she couldn't close it.

"Please." She fumbled for the light.

"Would you speak to me?" He stepped inside with her. "I don't want to make a scene in the car in front of Kate, so I followed you here. I'm being perfectly reasonable and fair and humane. Just speak to me."

They stood in darkness.

"Say something, darling." His voice though soft was on the edge of desperation.

"Will you please leave the bathroom?" Lara asked.

"I will leave. Of course I'll leave. If you'll talk, I'll fly out of here in a second."

Lara found the light. The room was bright green, papered in graffiti. KILROY WAS HERE. JOHN LOVES MEN. MEET ME IN ST. LOUIS BABY, WITH YOUR FOUNTAIN PEN.

"Sometimes I hate America," she said.

"I know." He took her wrist.

"I don't want to move to the farm, Charley," she said evenly.

"It is a very beautiful farm." He leaned against the door so she could not bolt if she'd a mind to and take the car and flee somewhere with Kate and Sam. That was his state of mind, almost delirious lately, with imaginings of her departure. He wanted to freeze her temporarily, lock her away in a box or a closet, bury her not to death but for a time until she was his again. "There is no housing in Washington because of the war. I have told you that."

"I don't believe you."

"You'll see," he said. "Give it a try, Lara, please. We'll move if you hate it, of course."

"You said you would leave the bathroom if I spoke to you, and I have spoken."

He covered his face with his hands.

"I'll leave," he said, but he could feel the heat rising homicidal in his groin. "We are killing each other, Lara." He grabbed her arms and tried to pull her towards him, but she had stiffened and held her place.

"It is certainly a kind of killing to put me on a farm twenty miles from the world," she said. "For punishment, isn't it?"

"No, it's not for punishment," he said.

"It is not for love," she said.

"Mama," Kate called, banging on the bathroom door.

Charley opened the door.

"I gave Sam to the gasoline attendant, who heard the shouting and thought you were having a terrible fight in here so I said I'd look into it." She stepped into the bathroom. "I didn't tell him that Sam throws up."

"Please leave, Charley," Lara said. "Get Sam."

So Charley left, closed the door behind him and walked over to the building where he could see the attendant standing in the picture window with Sam.

Kate took her mother's large purse and fumbled in the bottom.

44

"I think I look pale." She looked at herself in the mirror.

"You are meant to look pale, darling. It is your natural color and it's lovely. Like porcelain."

"But Charley likes color in cheeks. He said that to me. He said you have wonderful color in your cheeks." She found a tube of lipstick. "May I?" She drew two peach circles on her cheeks and rubbed them in. "He used to like everything about you. Every tiny thing, even your mind, he said." She tried the peach on her long thin lips. "He said your mind is like a spider's web. I heard him say that to you myself when we were living with his mother." She put a dot of peach on her forehead. "Fine threads and mysterious is what he said. Very nice, I thought to myself. I don't have a mind like a spider's web even though we're closely related. It's too bad. Mine is like dandelions."

"Hurry, darling. We don't want to stay in this dreadful room because of the smell."

"Don't you think mine is like dandelions? Sort of an ordinary mind flying all over the place. I'll ask Charley."

"I doubt he thinks you have an ordinary mind." Lara splashed her face with cold water and brushed her thick straight hair, which she wore long and loose and parted at the side like a schoolgirl.

Kate sat down on the closed toilet seat.

"Do you love Charley anymore? I need to know that," she said. "Before Sam you used to love each other so much, it was like Christmas every day to be with you." She took her mother's brush and brushed her bangs. "I'm going to cut off my braids. I think I could be quite good-looking with short hair." She unbraided her braids. "And I actually thought it would be wonderful to have Sam. A real brother or sister, though I wanted him to be a girl with Charley's hair. I thought that would be nice."

Lara opened the door and turned out the light. "What happened is not Sam. Or not because of Sam. The lives of grown-ups are not simple and do not always have to do with children."

"I know that, of course. I wasn't born yesterday," Kate said.

She loved her mother too much, she thought. She believed she was the most beautiful and remarkable woman she knew. She wanted to fix her in time now at forty years old with the soft lines of age just appearing around her eyes and gray sprinkled in her chestnut hair and an imperceptible mound of belly left over from where Sam had been.

"You can tell me what the real trouble with you and Charley is," she said. "I wouldn't tell anyone and I'm quite mature enough to know. Even the seventh-grade teacher at Merseyside said I'm precocious about sex. I didn't tell you that, of course, because I didn't want to worry you. But Miss Allen actually said I was very knowledgeable about sex probably because I'm Danish and she said Danish women are forward-looking and experienced and she knew that because her brother went out with a Danish girl once and told her."

"That was inappropriate for a teacher to say," Lara said.

"She wouldn't have said it if she didn't think I was very grown-up. I only told you so you'd know it was perfectly safe to explain to me about you and Charley."

Lara laughed and kissed her daughter's fingers. "I know you very well. Even that you are so knowledgeable about sex. But the fact is I don't know what's the matter with Charley and me. Something mysterious so we've fallen off track."

"You've fallen into civil war. That's what's happened. And there's going to be a catastrophe, I can tell," Kate said.

Charley was irascible when they got back into the car. He put Sam on Lara's lap and turned on the engine. He drove through the parking lot too fast.

"Charley," Lara said.

The tires squealed onto the highway and he pulled into the left lane and passed the cargo trucks one after another.

"Oh you can roll a silver dollar on a ballroom floor and it will roll-oll-oll because it's round-ound-ound. A woman doesn't know what a good man she's got until she turns him down," he sang in his low blues voice.

Kate in the backseat and giggling sang Danish love songs.

46

"Please, Charley. Slow down. Pull to the right," Lara pleaded.

"A man without a woman, is like a ship without a sail, is like a boat without a rudder, is like a kite without a tail."

Louder and louder, they sang their songs in different languages until Sam began to whimper in his mother's arms and Lara wept silent as summer rain into his soft kimono.

The first night Lara arrived in Minneapolis, Minnesota, to live with Charley Fletcher, he had taken her into his sparsely furnished bedroom, into his narrow pine bed, overwhelmed by such a flood of feeling he could not make love. At dawn, he woke first, with a high excitement to see her there, silver in the morning light and lovely. He could not believe his good fortune.

"Did you want me not to come?" she had asked him, opening her eyes to his.

"Of course," he said, laughing. "Of course I wanted you to come and stay forever."

She was confused.

"Then why did you not seem to want me to be here last night?" she asked.

He had leaned back on his pillow, closed his eyes, pulled her slender naked body, smooth-skinned and clean, against his. He had covered his face and lips with her long hair and kissed her hand so gently he could not believe the quiet of the gesture was his own.

"Too much promise," he said to her.

"Promise?" she asked. "I don't understand."

He kissed her. Kissed her eyes and nose and hair, kissed her lips, folded her to him so she fit. "Don't you see?" he said, still soft against her. "We fit exactly."

"I do not exactly see," she said.

"Last night you came to me by complete surprise with too much promise." He ran his finger across her lips. "I'll recover."

• • •

For weeks, Lara slept out her grief against his body, dreaming of her father always dead, sitting upright on the couch as he had been, his eyes marbleized in her memory. And gradually her past life, her father and Denmark and the small apartment where they had lived and Kate's father the Italian producer and the smell of winter off the river and the long light of summer floated downstream in her memory, clouding the water and gradually sinking, sinking to the riverbed.

Then they married. Through the months they married, commingling their lives, sufficient to one another's longing, imprinted, as if each had been stained by the blood of the other's heart.

Kate was named for her grandmother. Caterina. Sometimes she called herself Bergmann, sometimes DeFilio, which was the name of the Italian producer with whom she spent two holidays a year. One on the Mediterranean in July, eating sweet berries and turning brown in the sun. One for the week over New Year's when the Italians took noisily to the streets and she stayed in a flat with her father, who drank too much, and his wife, an actress down on her luck who did her face in different colors and changed costumes. Kate did not know what to make of her father. Her mother had told her he was brilliant and exciting and difficult. But he seemed to her to be a pudgy, ill-tempered man whose eyes were always turned in on a scene in his mind.

"Papa," she would say. "What are you thinking about now?"

"Now," he'd reply. "Now I'm thinking of a beautiful woman in a long purple dress coming down the stairs to meet the man who has betrayed her years ago. Show me, Caterina. What is the expression on her face as she comes down those stairs?"

"Some days do you think about Mama and me?" she asked.

"That is it," he said. "That is the expression exactly. You are a natural-born actress, Caterina."

48

Kate never told her mother the truth about these visits, because there was no terrible story—only small sad truths for which she braced herself every January at Epiphany and July.

When she moved to Minneapolis and went to the second grade at Merseyside Public School, she called herself Fletcher. Not officially, of course, but to the other children fascinated by her accent and the deep dimple in her chin. She was Kate Fletcher in her secret mind, Charley Fletcher's wife. In daydreams, they went out together to the German restaurant in St. Paul and drank beer and she wore a red-spotted dress, very tight at the bottom, and a wide-brimmed straw hat and black pumps with heels the width of a pencil. Lara in these thoughts stayed home and read in her cotton robe. Happy to see Kate and Charley have so good a time together at the German restaurant. Happy to see them home again.

"I like Charley better than my own father," she told her mother once.

"Actually, you know him better, darling. You can't know someone you only see on holidays, and now we've been so long in America."

Kate was pensive. Her mother had misunderstood.

"I mean I love him better," she said.

"I know," Lara said, guessing now at Kate's meaning. "You think about him."

"A lot."

"In your daydreams," her mother said. "So do I. I think about him just like you. Young girls are always looking for a father who is entirely satisfactory, all of their lives until they are quite as old as I am."

"Tell me about the colored." Kate leaned over the backseat. "Miss Allen said we'll have terrible trouble with the colored because in the South they have been treated like pigs."

"Miss Allen is wrong," Charley said. "We will not have any trouble."

"She said they probably live in sort of pens in our backyard and will call me Miss Caterina and serve me breakfast in bed."

"They live in ordinary houses and will eat meals with us and you'll play with their children who you'll find no different than you are, only more polite." He lit a cigarette. "No one but the terminally ill should eat breakfast in bed."

It was the exact middle of the night and the Pennsylvania mountains closed around them filling the car with a solitary darkness. Sam slept and Lara drifted in and out of sleep vaguely aware of Kate's persistent inquisition. "Why?" Kate asked always after definition. "Why this? Why that? Why? Why? Why?" until Lara's father called her Darling Caterina Why, but Lara, for whom the world was a capricious impression fleeting with the light, was pleased to have this exacting child.

"I have never known anyone with colored skin except in Copenhagen," Kate said. "There was an Indian girl called Dimitri who had a ruby in her nose which I quite liked, and I put a blue stone in my nose one morning but it fell out on the way to school." She leaned her head against Charley's shoulder. "Mama knows the colored quite well because of Paul Drake."

"I don't know Paul Drake," Charley said, easily angered by Lara's past, by the Italian producer and Lars Groener, now dead, killed in a raid in London. He wanted to possess her history.

"Yes you do. Mama told you she played Desdemona to Paul Drake's Othello in Copenhagen for a long time. Didn't you, Mama?" Kate asked. "In the second act, he would kiss her from her fingers up. Like this." She kissed her own arm. "Paul Drake was light black and had a booming voice. Remember, Mama?"

"Lara?" Charley said. "You never told me you played Desdemona."

"I forgot," Lara said.

"My grandfather thought Paul Drake loved Mama," Kate said. "Once we went to the matinee and we could see just behind the curtain because we were in the front row and after the first act, we saw Paul Drake fall on his knees and kiss Mama's ankle. Remember, Mama? And grandfather was cross not because Paul Drake was colored, of course, since no one in Denmark ever kept slaves, but because Mama is soft. That's what he said. 'Soft as silk,' he called her."

Since Sam, Charley Fletcher was possessed. Sometimes he honestly thought he would lose his mind, and now the car was filled with furies taking up the air.

"Was Paul Drake someone in your life?" He could not help himself.

"He was Othello in my life." Lara leaned her head against the window. "Please, Charley, stop all of this."

The car fell silent. Lara adjusted Sam in her lap, opened her blouse to his tiny mouth and closed her eyes. Kate slid down into the backseat and Charley Fletcher drove on and on through Pennsylvania, uncertain in the long darkness. What he wanted was to take off over the mountains with his small charge, sail into the heavens and put down in a new land where his enormous hopes floated within reach.

Lara had a recurrent dream when she was small which her mother called her dancing dream.

"I had my dancing dream again," she'd tell her mother the last year of her life when she came in at dawn with a cup of tea and sat in her robe at the end of Lara's bed.

In the dream, she was in a wide skirt with a sash around her neck, bare feet and bare small breasts and her hair fanned like a kite in her sleeping mind while she danced, around and around in a small circle, faster and faster, finally propelled into the sky by the spinning skirt, into the warm soft cushion of air where she slept waking into the real day entirely satisfied.

"Why such a dream again and again?" she'd ask her mother.

"Because you'll be a woman," her mother would reply. And Lara never inquired further, thinking certainly she ought to understand her mother's explanation. After her mother died, the dream disappeared. In fact, for years, sleep was a long dark airless tunnel without dreams and she would get up weary in the morning.

When she moved into Charley Fletcher's apartment, the dream came back. But then she'd wake in the middle, during the dancing or just after her feet had left the ground, and reach over for him, pull him against her, press her face into his chest.

"I'm having a nightmare about my father's death," she'd say to him. She never mentioned the dancing or understood why she had lied to him, since the vision of her father dead had left her in the early weeks in America.

He would hold her, stroke her head for a moment and fall immediately asleep while she lay awake, staring through the bedroom window at the dawn.

In the apartment in Minneapolis, Lara and Charley settled into a life as if they had always known each other, familiar as blood.

"We belong together," Lara said to him. They were lying face to face, their lips touching, their eyes filling the other's vision. "I have not known this before except when I was small and the world seemed entirely safe."

And she would roll over on her back, fling her arm over her head, her long and perfect olive body strong as a dancer's, her cheeks flushed, her hair across her face as if windblown.

"Aren't we beautiful," she would whisper in his ear. "Aren't we so beautiful lying together, it breaks your heart."

And he would make love to her until, both deeply spent, they would fall asleep in one another's arms.

Perhaps, she sometimes thought, it was only the dailiness of their lives which had overtaken them, the slow tedium of ordinary hours.

"Tell me a love story," she used to ask her mother when she came in to kiss her good night. Her mother told wonderful love stories with horses, and handsome men and narrow escapes, cascades of yellow hair.

"I would like that love story in my real life," Lara would say happily after the story was done.

"Of course, my treasure," her mother would say. "That is why we have stories. In real life men and women come from different planets, you see, which only occasionally, and then by accident, collide."

She had collided with Charley Fletcher. They had a real love story, and whatever had happened between them which cost him desire was so strong that she was inextricably bound to its memory.

Light had just begun to streak the bottom of the horizon when she reached over and put her hand on him.

"Will we ever fit together perfectly again?"

"I have told you that, Lara," he said. "I have promised."

But he took her hand away and laid it on her belly. Just the gesture, which was gentle and not unkind, made her unbearably sad.

The rain started in Maryland, heavy at first and then in fits and starts as if the heavens were coughing. By morning, it was hot.

"How can it be raining and so hot?" Kate asked, sticking her head out the window so the wind from driving chilled her wet face.

"Too hot," Lara said sleepily. "Is it always so hot in Washington?"

"We're quite far south," Charley said. "And below sea level. It can be very hot."

Kate pulled her head back in the window.

"Miss Allen says it's common knowledge that the heat makes the colored lazy. It's too hot to work."

"The great Miss Allen is wrong again," Charley said. "I never knew you to be so mindful of authority, Kate."

"She knows a lot about the colored," Kate said. "Anyway, she's not blaming them. She's blaming the heat. She was simply making an intelligent observation. It's too hot for everybody." She flopped down on the backseat. "Even me."

They crossed the Potomac River into Virginia, and the landscape spread to farmland.

"Virginia," Charley said matter-of-factly.

"Where is Washington?" Kate asked.

Charley gestured north.

"Aren't we going first to Washington?" Kate asked.

"Later," Charley said.

"Years later." Lara shaded her eyes against the odd glare of morning light shining through the gray and rainy dawn.

"Tonight," Charley said.

Moses Bellows pulled on his trousers, laced up his boots and patted Miracle on the bare behind.

"Can't be six o'clock yet," she said, full of sleep.

"About six. And I'm going down to the road to catch a glimpse of their arrival."

Miracle sat up on her elbow.

"Hot." She rubbed her eye. "Too hot for clothes and raining too. I'm not particularly looking forward to this day."

Moses went into the kitchen, splashed water on his face and left the cottage, headed towards the main house. The rain was cool and felt good on his bare chest and back; it woke him up after a sleepless night, tossing in the heat, worrying over Guy and whether he was going to hurt somebody. Now John Spencer crowded his brain again as he hadn't done for years since the Bellowses moved to the main house. Just last week he'd been listening to the radio about the Germans and what they were doing in Europe and found himself wondering ever since what kind of anger the Germans must have had to do what they were doing and whether sometimes, like this morning when he felt a furnace blazing in his belly, he too was capable of terrible things. It was hard to get his breath in air so hot and steamy, so he walked slowly down the path, around the flagstone patio, around the house and to the front,

where he stood between two high black elms, leafless for
years and years, dead as doornails, as his mother would
have said. He stopped there completely still in the dense
heat and waited.

Finally, Lara Fletcher opened her eyes to Virginia, and
what she saw when the car rounded the bend after Tyson's
Corner was the dead black elms lined like soldiers or
stockade fencing or wrought-iron gates across the horizon.

"That's it," Charley said, unable to contain himself.

"It looks like a hospital," Kate said. "It looks like St.
Vincent's Hospital in Copenhagen where my grandfather
was taken when he was killed."

The sight of the place knocked the life out of Lara.

"What do you think, darling?" Charley asked.

"What are those black posts?" she asked.

"Dead elms," Charley said. "Which is why they've been
cropped."

"Why doesn't someone cut them down?" Lara asked.

"I suppose the reason they haven't been cut down is
that they name the place."

"We'll cut them down," Lara said.

"We'll cut them down tomorrow and plant birches and
call it Birch Wood, don't you think?" Kate said.

Lara, awake now, was looking at the line of dead black
elm trees definitive in the gray dawn when one of them
just to the right of the house moved. She looked more
carefully, squinting her eyes, and the tree moved, straight
out from the line of other trees.

"Charley?"

Kate saw it too. "The tree moved. Did you see it? It
moved left and forward."

"That's what I thought too," Lara said. "Do you see it,
Charley?"

"I see it now."

At the bottom of the driveway to the farm, the figure of
Moses Bellows was clear enough for identification.

"It's a man." He laughed. "Either Moses or Guy Bellows, who live out back."

"One of the colored," Kate said matter-of-factly, pleased with the dangerous possibilities which her new life with the colored promised.

"Do not use that word again," Charley said. "It's insulting."

"Why?" Kate asked.

"Because it is."

"You don't know whether it's insulting or not, do you? You should ask them," Kate said. "I plan to ask."

Lara was fixed on Moses Bellows. Something about his blackness and enormous size made her heart beat in her throat.

"Kate's right, I think," she said. "We should replace those dreadful elms immediately."

Charley Fletcher saw the new sign, SKUNK FARM, 1942, and the blood rushed from his head. His hands died around the steering wheel. He was a man accustomed to emergencies, born, according to his mother, with the kind of natural instinct for trouble that most people have for survival. "Charley can always smell a rat," his Aunt Sad used to say. And here was a rat straight in front of him dripping root tendrils of black-paint letters in the humidity and rain.

What he'd had in mind when he'd bought Elm Grove was a place where Lara would be safely out of touch as she had not been in Minneapolis, where a lovely and somewhat lonely Danish actress was irresistible, would be his alone on the other end of the telephone when he was at his office at Censorship or had to spend the night. His woman, his girl, his love floating through their house— grander than any he had imagined even visiting as a child. His house.

He had in mind as well—and this was part of the plan— to live amongst the Bellowses as friends, to sit at the same table and work side by side, play poker out back on Friday nights, have holidays. He was not an innocent man. Nor even a dreamer. In his sensible mind, he knew it was foolish to believe he could live in equal community with the colored, that he could on his tiny plot of land undo the short history of North America. But he wanted to believe. And so he did. In this, he was deeply American as only the child of an immigrant can be, who grows up poor with a future equal to a boy's dreams and sufficient to his mother's sacrifice.

"Did you see the sign?" Kate asked as they drove up the driveway.

"I saw it. It looks as though the Bellowses have changed the name."

"Does that mean something?" Lara asked, sensing Charley's unsettlement.

"I suppose it means we'll cut down the elms and get some skunks to go with the new name, my love," and he touched Lara's cheek. "That should be easy."

Moses ambled—slowly enough to seem in charge of the farm, an observer of the place, not a worker on it. He went around the side of the house closest to the large two-story barn where the milk cows and hay were kept. He didn't want to meet all the Fletchers just yet; the day was too thick for casual conversation. Just beyond the barn, he met Miracle scurrying down the path in a bright yellow dress Aida had made for her when she got plump, and an apron starched to cardboard around her waist. Her face was dotted with perspiration.

"Are they here?" she asked.

He grabbed her wrists and kissed her full on the mouth.

"Strawberry jam." He smacked his lips and kissed her again. "What are you rushing for?"

"I'm rushing to do breakfast. They've been on a long trip."

"Don't do breakfast, Miracle. Wait. Maybe they don't want breakfast done for them." He ran his finger across her lips. "Come back to the house with me for a while. We'll have breakfast."

"Don't turn cantankerous, Moses, like you do. Of course they want breakfast and that's what they'll have." She pulled the hair on his chest gently. "You do with life as it comes to you and don't waste your time on quarrels with the world." She took his hand and walked along the path with him.

They heard Guy and Aida bickering behind them, walking barefoot, their feet pounding against the soft ground.

"They here?" Guy asked.

"Yup," Moses answered.

"Tell Guy to watch his p's and q's," Aida said.

They heard Prudential running along the path, giving a little screech when her bare feet were stung by a holly needle.

"Wait up, Aunt Miracle," she called. "I don't want to miss the party."

She edged between Miracle and Moses and draped her long thin arm across Miracle's shoulders.

"I come to see the girl." Prudential shook her hips. "I want to see if she's just a baby girl at thirteen or if she's got some sense."

"You don't have so much sense, Prudential. You got a baby in your belly. You keep confusing that with sense," Moses said.

"I got both," Prudential said and stopped when she saw Kate Fletcher open the car door and climb out.

"So what are you going to say to that pretty baby girl, Prudential?" Moses asked.

"Nothing," Prudential said. "Zero. I'm going to get some black paint and stripe her tail." And she dashed into the back door of the main house.

Lara, carrying Sam, went around the front of the house. The door was open and she walked into the long hall, suffocating with the smell of furniture polish and cleaning supplies. There was no air. She opened the french doors and walked into the living room, which was furnished, had been sold furnished, in large puffy armchairs and couches, covered in shiny chintz with fat yellow stemless roses. The windows were hung in starched white tiebacks and the colored had filled the vases with bright annuals. She had never heard the word "colored" used in Denmark, nor even in Minneapolis, but since Charley had bought the farm in Vienna, everybody in Minneapolis, even Kate, talked about the colored. The name had taken on a certain strangeness and excitement, and Lara allowed the word itself to float through her mind as she used to do with the word "sex" when she was young.

Behind the living room was the dining room, which was formal and pretty with long windows overlooking a field of wildflowers and an oblong cherry table wet with polish, highback chairs and a crystal chandelier hung low and glittering.

Prudential sat on the butcher-block table in the kitchen swinging her bare legs high enough to show the white lace panties she had ordered in the Sears, Roebuck catalogue, two pairs and a pink-striped sundress she'd paid for with her own money so she'd look presentable if the baby came in a hurry.

"Hello," Lara said, holding out her hand. "I'm Lara Fletcher and this is Sam."

Prudential narrowed her eyes.

"I'm Prudential and visiting here," she said. "Miracle's my aunt."

"Charley told me you'd be here, and I'm very glad, since you're the same age as my daughter, Kate." She wandered through the kitchen opening the cupboards, full of dishes and glasses and jars of tomatoes, peaches, pears and beans and peas and strawberry jam.

"I'm very old for thirteen." Prudential wondered if the lady could tell she was pregnant, and she leaned back on the counter so her belly stuck out.

"Kate is young for thirteen, I suppose, but I hope you'll like each other," Lara said.

There was an odd familiar smell of women in the kitchen, and she sniffed.

"What you smell is blood," Prudential said.

"That's it."

"My uncle butchered a hog last night and bled it in the larder, and you can still smell the sweetness since it got so hot."

Miracle came in the back door in a rush.

"I'm late for breakfast and you must be starving," she said without introduction, rushing over to the icebox and taking out eggs and milk. "You go sit down in the dining room."

"You must be Mrs. Bellows. I'm Lara Fletcher," Lara said.

Miracle's lips turned and she shook her head.

"Mrs. Bellows." She smiled broad. "I don't know how old you have to get for a name like Mrs. Bellows—maybe dead—but my name's Miracle and that's what I'm called in this house. Now you sit down."

"I'd like to look around first. I thought I'd go upstairs to see my bedroom."

Miracle cracked the eggs with one hand high above the glass bowl and whipped them lightly with a fork.

"You will probably choose the bedroom in the back of the house with its own bath and sitting room." My bedroom, Miracle thought, not with sadness so much as a certain feeling of triumph stilled by a clear memory of sitting on the canopy bed against a mound of white fluff pillows with Moses lying on her bare lap. And then another memory of the wondrous pleasure in John Spencer's eyes the first time they'd made love and she had felt queenly because she had pleased him.

"You'll see Moses upstairs," Miracle called. "He's fixing the toilet in your bathroom."

Lara went up the back stairs into a small hall with two bedrooms, both quite sterile but bright, and then up another short flight of stairs to the sitting room Miracle had mentioned, which was cool and open with wicker furniture covered in soft blue. Sam, hungry again, whimpered in her arms and she unbuttoned her blouse and took her breast and pressed his mouth against the nipple.

The bedroom was complete. There were curtains and dresser scarves and bedspread and canopy, chintz covers on the window seats. Nothing personal, certainly. No photographs of someone else's family or trinkets from their summer holiday. But nevertheless, the room was done. It occurred to Lara that she had never had an empty room in

60

her life and here she was, forty in September, and every room she'd lived in had been completed by someone else. Her mother, her father, the producer, Charley or Charley's mother, and now a room furnished for the life of a man who had disappeared into nowhere. She sat in the window seat, leaned against the curved wood and looked out back.

Which was the still-life picture Moses Bellows had of Lara when he stepped out of the bathroom with his plumbing tools.

Her head was turned away, her long legs crossed at the ankles, her skirt loose and above the knees, her full breast, lush in the mouth of the baby, white against the rose blouse so indescribably beautiful, his heart leapt up.

Lara heard him come in and covered herself.

"You must be Moses," she said. "Miracle said you were up here. I'm Lara."

Moses Bellows cocked his head to one side, stood his full height, locked his thumb in the wide leather belt of his Levi's and smiled with very great pleasure.

"I'm happy to meet you," he said.

Behind the farmhouse, overlooking the long green expanse out back, Charley Fletcher stood on the thick stump of a fallen oak with his dead father. He often dreamed Thomas Fletcher beside him, in his overalls and plaid shirt, his hair wet under the red baseball cap he always wore, slightly at an angle, a cigarette in the center of his mouth, waggling.

"So this is it," Charley said to his father.

"It's wonderful, Charles. I have never seen so large a house or such a piece of land. In Swansea, like New Philadelphia, we used to live in rocky pockets, whatever the English left over for us. And here you are spread across a hill so everyone who passes by this road will say, 'That's Charley Fletcher's place.' "

Charley laughed out loud.

"What they'll always say is John Spencer's place, but I'll be the one living here."

"And that's a fact," his father said.

Charley always imagined his father in the flesh at victories. What he would have said had he been alive was "How much did the farm cost and who will take care of it and what are you going to do about the colored and why—for chrissake why—are you always wanting too much from this world?"

Like he'd said when Charley graduated from high school and got the collected works of Sir Walter Scott bound in leather and signed by his English teacher and the school principal.

"Don't count on books making life easy for you, Charley, whatever your mother might say. The smartest boy in my class in Swansea drowned in a lake because he had book smarts and no sense." His father was always prepared with bleak stories of his successful friends.

"He tried to protect you with bad news so you won't be disappointed," his mother said. "But that's because he was disappointed and didn't have a gift like you do. You'll prove him wrong."

Charley Fletcher was proving him wrong. At almost thirty-one, he was a man who had never failed in a worldly sense. He had graduated at the top of his class in college and had been the newspaper editor and started a humor magazine and worked full-time as a prison guard to pay his college tuition and published his first article with a byline in the *Chicago Tribune* when he was seventeen years old. He played the piano extraordinarily well—concert-level, according to his Aunt Sad, who was the Saturday-night pianist at the Grill, and he published cartoons of long-legged stick figures in empty landscapes wearing trousers and skirts—no shirts—with complicated facial features—noses and wrinkles and warts and fat pockets under the eyes. The cartoons were striking for an acerbic character and extremity which his editor in Chicago called Midwestern Gothic.

He decided at an early age that what he was good at in particular was winning.

"Charley even wins the pinwheel at the county fair," Aunt Sad said. "He's graced, Winona."

"Gifted," Charley's mother corrected her sister. "Grace has to do with fate and is subject to wind change."

But it was never his mother Charley imagined beside him. Perhaps because she was always there and believed in him from the start. Only his father, to whom he wished to prove that the hopes his mother had were possible.

"Success is not a good thing for a young man," his father had said three days before the tractor he was driving overturned and killed him. "It makes you afraid of losing. A boy I knew in Swansea, not the one who drowned, but another one, simply stopped walking at the age of twenty-one, paralyzed, we all thought, by the fear of losing."

"What's to lose?" Charley said.

But there was something to lose now.

Kate flew up behind Charley and grabbed him around the waist. "It's huge," she said. "A mansion. It's bigger than the palace in Copenhagen, I think."

"So you like it."

"I like it." Kate was tentative. "Who is that colored girl? Is she the one you mentioned to me?"

"There is a girl your age who is visiting for a while."

"This one is mean."

"Mean?"

"Look."

Charley looked. Kate's eyes blazed, her lips curled back and her teeth clamped together. "That's how she looked at me when I saw her, as if she hated me already, and we haven't even met."

Charley laughed.

"If you had seen her face, you wouldn't be laughing."

They walked across the patio and through the french doors where Miracle had set the table for breakfast.

"Have you seen your mother?"

"She was looking around upstairs."

"Lara?" Charley called upstairs. "Are you sure?"

"I know she's there," Kate said. "I'm going to look at the barn. Miracle says there are cows and kittens."

"Lara," he called again. "Are you upstairs?"

"I'm here," Lara said. "Upstairs, Charley. In the back of the house."

"I'm coming," he said and he dashed up the steps.

When Charley came through the bedroom door, Moses

had disappeared. Lara did not see him leave or hear his footsteps but he was gone.

"Isn't it a beautiful house, darling?" Charley kissed her hair.

"It is. It's very pretty, Charley."

He took her hand and pulled her with him to the bed.

"I want us to be happy here."

She buried her face in his arm.

"Shall this be our room or the one at the front of the house?" he asked.

"I haven't seen the room at the front of the house but I like this room. I think I prefer facing the back." She rolled over, putting Sam facedown on his stomach. "But I'd like to do this room myself. Do everything even though it's wartime. I can make curtains and spreads."

"Of course."

"I'll take off the wallpaper too and paint the room white."

"I want you to do anything which will make you happy," Charley said. "That's all I want."

"I know," she said.

"I'm sorry about these times, Lara."

"I love you," she said in Danish. She always said "I love you" in Danish.

And they lay side by side under the lace spread of John Spencer's canopy, their hands touching, isolated as planets whose orbits are unchanging and defined, but deeply attracted, longing to merge.

Kate went back to the kitchen where she had seen the fierce long-legged colored girl but the girl was gone. Miracle was there and the smell of biscuits baking filled the room.

"Don't mind Prudential, darling," Miracle said when Kate came through the kitchen door. "She can be bad-tempered when she's a mind to."

"Prudential?"

"My niece Prudential who gave you that look to fry an egg with when you came to the kitchen."

"My father says we'll probably be friends in time."

Miracle made a noise in the back of her throat, a sort of deep laugh. "In time, Jesus our Savior is expected back to visit. Here, darling." She buttered a biscuit. "Hot from the oven. You must be starving. Take this and go look at the yellow kittens in the back of the barn."

Kate headed out past the room behind the kitchen still smelling of sweet blood in the hot dampness from the night before.

In a black humor, Prudential sat on the butchering table and watched Kate pass the door. She had an idea in mind. She had heard Aunt Miracle speak to the enemy girl "darling this and darling that" so quiet and servantlike, Prudential wanted to spit on the girl and Miracle as well for being so agreeable when only yesterday, only last night, Miracle Bellows had been Queen of Elm Grove. She heard Kate open the screen door and watched her walk towards the barn, past the willow tree and the low-branched elm, one of the live ones, spread like a giant hoop skirt over the path, up the small hill and disappear into the darkness.

Another plan sailed through her mind, one of those plans Prudential knew her mother would whip her for. Her mother had only whipped her twice, once for stealing bubble gum and the other time for lying—and this plan was worse than either of those because it was what her Mama and Aunt Miracle would call dirty. But she acted on it anyway, and not wishing to soil her Sears, Roebuck white lace panties, she took them off and hid them under the tool table and then she ran in soft bare feet out the back door, past the willow tree, and scrambled light as air up the elm tree—eight feet up—and out on a strong limb camouflaged as she crouched in wait by a mass of elm leaves.

Kate couldn't find the yellow kittens, although she heard them mewing. The cows were out and the barn smelled so thick of manure in the heat that after a quick climb up the loft which was full of hay, she left, startled at first to leave the darkness of the barn into the hazy vermilion sun.

Prudential, on her haunches with both feet steady, her belly on her knees, saw Kate come out.

And just as Kate Fletcher walked under the low spreading branches of the elm tree, Prudential began to pee. A long thin stream, straight as a pencil through the branches. Bull's-eye on top of her silky brown hair.

Kate stopped and reached her hand up; her hair was wet. She moved beyond the line of urine and she could see Prudential's bright red dress and her bare feet hanging over the branch and her small black face looking straight down and smiling.

"What are you doing?" Kate shouted. "What is that water?"

The stream had thinned to big drops which flew down and landed noiselessly.

"What are you doing?" Kate asked. "Answer me." She wiped her hand on the back of her shorts.

"Urinating." Prudential sounded every syllable like a melody and before she'd stopped speaking, Kate was running up the tree, standing on the low branches, pulling herself as fast as she could go.

Prudential turned around to face the enemy girl and slowly made her way down on the wide thicker branches testing each one for strength as she stepped on it—until they were even, face to face, and Kate started out on the branch where Prudential was clinging.

"Don't you touch me," Prudential said.

"I will too. I hope you fall and get paralyzed." She went further out on the branch almost to where Prudential now held quite precariously since the branch was thin and it was more difficult to balance.

"Don't touch me until we're on the ground," Prudential said.

Prudential heard the crack first and then Kate heard it and screamed a long flute note which cut through the summer air straight to the kitchen where Miracle was making bacon, upstairs to the second floor where Charley and Lara Fletcher lay on the canopy bed with Sam, even out back where Guy was on his way out the front door of his cottage to work.

66

"What's that?" Charley asked. He ran to the window.

"Is something wrong?" Lara asked.

He saw Miracle run out the back door and Guy run down the path and then he saw Kate on the ground and raced through the sitting room and downstairs.

Kate landed on her back and was stunned for just long enough to get her breath. Then she grabbed Prudential around the middle and rolled with her down the small hill from the barn and into a grass gully; she turned Prudential on her back, locked her arms and spit in her face.

Prudential did not spit back. Nor did she resist Kate's hold. When Kate looked up, Miracle was standing beside them.

"Get up," Miracle said crossly. "Get up this minute."

Kate stood and looked down at Prudential, who was smaller than she and stick-thin except for a big belly which must, she decided as she looked at her closely for the first time, be a tumor. Prudential did not move.

"You all right, Prudential?" Miracle said sweetly and reached over to give her niece a hand.

"So." Charley ran up from the house. "What's going on, for chrissake?"

"One of them spit at the other," Miracle said.

"Spit?" Charley asked.

"No one spit," Prudential said.

"I saw it with my own eyes," Miracle said.

"You were mistaken."

"Then what happened?" Charley asked.

"Nothing happened," Kate said. "The branch broke and we fell out of the tree."

"You were fighting," Miracle said. "I heard it."

"You hear things in your sleep sometimes," Prudential said. "We weren't fighting. We were having a conversation."

"Well, come on back to breakfast then," Miracle said, bad-tempered, wiping her hands on her apron. "It's on the table for the Fletchers, and you, sassy child, come with me." She put her arm around Guy's waist. "You come to the kitchen too, Guy Bellows. I made you sausage and bacon and a cup of coffee strong as you like it."

"No, Miracle," Guy said. "I thought you understood last night. I am not eating sausages in the kitchen of the main house, now and forever more, so help me God." He turned around and headed down the path out back.

"Wait up for me," Prudential said. She turned to Kate. "If you got head lice," she said, "I've got a special shampoo on a prescription to clean your hair."

Kate looked Prudential straight in the eye with the same look Prudential had given her earlier. "I don't have head lice," she said. "My hair is perfectly clean."

In the dining room, Lara and Charley sat at the long table with starched white napkins and yellow dahlias, separated by miles of measured silence.

"You're too quiet, Mama," Kate said.

"Tired," Lara said. But what she felt was a bone-deep longing for home.

In the heat, Kate could smell the urine in her hair and wanted to finish breakfast and go find the colored girl out back. She excused herself and thanked Miracle and rinsed her dishes which Miracle said she certainly shouldn't be bothering with, and there was Prudential sitting on the tree stump just outside the back door with a yellow long-haired kitten in her lap. Kate leaned against the house.

She supposed Prudential was her age—that's what Charley had said—maybe a few months older. But her face looked old—grown up, in fact. A small fiercely made face, blue-black and always in motion. She looked at Kate now, her head cocked, her expression sardonic, and lifted the kitten gentle as if it were a human baby to her shoulder, ran her fingers along its tiny backbone.

"Is that a baby?" Kate asked quietly.

"A baby kitten," she said.

"No," Kate said. "I mean in you."

Prudential narrowed her eyes. "What did you think it was?" She kissed the kitten on its lips. "A magnolia tree?"

"I thought . . ." Kate hesitated. She was not entirely sure what a tumor meant except danger. Her grandmother in Copenhagen had died of a tumor, and so had the Queen. "I suppose I thought it was a tumor."

Prudential laughed out loud and long.

"Why you're very smart for a foreign girl because that's exactly what it is. A baby tumor. A newborn baby tumor due to come into this miserable world in December near Christmas Day."

"I see."

Kate didn't know what to say to this girl, this child, her age, pregnant with a baby and herself not a step out of childhood. And how did she get that way at thirteen years old when the mystery of sex only visits the bodies of young girls alone in their single beds with dreams of horses and long skirts? For her lifetime, Kate had been entirely comfortable in the world until this moment; now some terrible change had taken place which she could not understand.

She took off around the house calling "See you later" to Prudential as she went through the high grass, across the stone patio, down the hill towards the road. She grabbed the SKUNK FARM, 1942 sign to catch herself from flying into the street and slipped to the ground, lying face up to the lace-curtained sun.

BOOK TWO

Invisible Boundaries

October
Tenth,
1942

Summer was long and hot, lasting deep into September without an interruption to the heat. Without rain. The leaves were crisp-dried by a single-minded sun and the new lives of the commingling families slowed down to heavy-lidded observation. No one disturbed the uneasy peace.

Most nights the Bellowses gathered at Moses Bellows' cottage after supper.

"So what do you think?" Guy Bellows would begin the conversation, addressing Moses. "You think it's going to work us living here again?"

"You'd like to tell me what choice we got, Guy?" Moses said. "Maybe we'll go in whiteface and buy the Scutters' place for twenty thousand dollars or take a room at a *hotel* in Washington, D.C."

"They're nice people, Moses. They do their own breakfast and help with the dishes," Miracle said. "Just yesterday she cleaned a chicken. And she's lovely to look at besides."

Guy whistled.

"You do agree with that, don't you, Moses?"

"She's a pretty woman," Moses said. "And she keeps to herself."

"So," Aida said, putting her feet up on the coffee table, painting her toenails magenta. "You like to look at Mrs. Fletcher?"

"I didn't say anything about looking at Mrs. Fletcher," Guy said.

"So what is under your skin, Moses?" Aida asked. "You'd rather he didn't speak? I thought you liked the fact he shook your hand."

"What I'd rather is that he didn't ask me to play poker on Friday nights or come into my living room and set down on the couch like we've been friends for years."

"He asks Moses personal questions," Miracle said.

"You won't even let me ask you personal questions," Aida said, "and I'm your flesh and blood."

"You're not my flesh and blood," Moses said. "Guy is."

"My flesh and blood is perfectly all right," Aida snapped back. "Good as yours."

And the talk would unravel like wrapping string with laughter and stories and the small petty repetitions that kept their shackled lives intact. But always, night after night, when the Bellowses settled in the kitchen around the table with their beers, the talk would start with Charley Fletcher and the plans he had in mind to make Skunk Farm into the Kingdom of Heaven.

Charley Fletcher did have plans.

"Don't you see what we are doing here?" he'd say to Lara after supper, after Miracle had left, when they sat in the kitchen while Kate did her homework.

"No," Lara said. "I actually don't."

"We are becoming friends with the Bellowses. Real friends."

He believed with the confidence of a man who has inherited in the fabric of his genes unquestioned faith that a single person in the small experiment of his life can change the course of history.

"I like the Bellowses," Lara said. And she did, especially Moses, to whom she was driven in a girlish way. Her days had taken on a certain rhythm which was not unpleasant and she thought of herself as marooned on an island of strangers who spoke a different language, with whom there was always the chance of surprise. "I am not unhappy here as I thought I would be."

"No one in the South has actually lived with the colored and here we are," Charley said.

"I don't understand," Lara said. "We are two families living on a farm as in a dream while a terrible war is eliminating Europe. We are no more than ourselves."

"Prudential is," Kate said. "If I believed in God, I'd die of fear to be in her presence knowing she'd like me dead."

"Don't exaggerate, Kate," Charley said. "Prudential is wary of you because you're white."

"You don't understand the colored," Kate said.

"The colored are just like us," Charley said.

Kate shook her head sadly. "I don't believe you," she said.

The truth was Charley Fletcher's great plans for Skunk Farm started because he did not go to war at a time when all the men he knew were going and his hopes for Skunk Farm had unconsciously become his defense against the impotence of a failed soldier without access to weapons in a country isolated from the war zone. Although she did not understand exactly, Lara accommodated his dream.

In the evening when Charley Fletcher came home he stopped first in the hall to check the day's mail. Often he could hear Lara's voice and Kate's in the room above the stairs speaking softly back and forth in Danish. They would laugh, tumbling over each other's voices, and even now, after years together, the language seemed not so much foreign as private, arranged by them to leave him out.

"I'll be right down," she said to him.

He picked up the mail. There was the electric bill, a note from his sister in Cleveland saying she had miscarried again but otherwise life went on as usual—"ha ha." Her letters were always punctuated with ha-has whatever dark message or concealed sense of humor that implied. There was the usual long letter from his mother with clippings about the war from magazines and newspapers as if that information were only available in New Philadelphia, Ohio, and would be useful to him in his work. There was a picture of her on the front porch taken by Aunt Sad— "Winona Fletcher on her front porch: Wartime, 1942"— and another postcard from Tom Elliot, always the same ebullient message from the front: "To all the Fletchers, my love, my love. Tom E."

"I see Tom Elliot sends his love again," he said as Lara walked in the side door.

"To us all, darling." She brushed her lips against his neck.

"My love, my love," Charley imitated.

Tom Elliot was the photographer on the *Tribune* in Minneapolis often on assignment with Charley. He was a tall, lanky, golden-haired boy, untroubled, at ease with the world. And rich. He had family money and did not need to work at all but he liked taking pictures so he worked for the *Tribune* without salary. Such complacency in a man his age sheltered as Tom Elliot surely was from misfortune drove Charley crazy.

"You act as if you and Tom are competitive. I don't understand," Lara said, slipping down beside him at the supper table. "You work together on different things."

"We are competitive," Charley said.

The competition was not professional. Even Charley had not understood at first what in Tom Elliot drove his blood straight up to boiling. But from the beginning of their association he had sensed a deep and personal threat.

That night he and Lara had a fight and slept in separate bedrooms and Charley had a dream about hurdling, which he had done in high school. At every hurdle, he fell down on his knee until the knee was skinned to the bone and in the dream the hurdles never ended.

Charley Fletcher had not gone to the war because he had flat feet.

"Absolutely flat as a two-by-four," the examining medical officer had said when Charley tried to enlist three days after Pearl Harbor.

Charley had glanced down the line of young fleshless men, blue-skinned with the soft down of boyhood on their naked bodies.

"Which means?" Charley asked the physician, but he already knew he had been dismissed.

"It means you won't be a soldier." The officer slapped him on the bare behind. "Medical disability. Think of it this way," he said, moving along the line to the next young man. "If you drive carefully, you'll be alive next month and they may not."

Charley left the line, dressed quickly, collected his papers stamped 4F from the main desk, put his collar up against the harsh silver winter blowing in the streets of Minneapolis. At least, he told himself, not one downy boy in the lineup for the army physical was familiar with him and could report his humiliation. Nevertheless he was ill with shame.

He would lie. He would have to lie.

Lara had already imagined his death. At home that evening, she asked him when he would have to leave.

"Soon," Charley replied without hesitation. "The army will be in touch soon."

"Tom Elliot is going," Lara said, putting out supper. "He called to tell me."

"Why?" Charley asked. "Why would he call you?"

Lara laughed lightly.

"We're friends, darling. He'd be bound to call with such important news."

"Maybe we'll be together in England," Tom had said to Charley the next day at work, flushed with the thrill of war. "Taking pictures from an airplane low over the enemy." He aimed his camera at the city desk floor. "I can't wait to go."

"They're using real guns in Europe," Charley said sharply. "I ought to warn you."

Tom was taken aback. "Don't *you* want to go?" he asked. "I thought everybody did."

"Not for the sport of it," Charley said.

"Lara told me you'd be hearing soon. This week."

"I'll be hearing soon."

In fact Charley Fletcher did hear the following day from the Office of the President that the first appointed Deputy Director of Newspaper Censorship had become ill and Charley was asked to replace him.

"Graced," as Aunt Sad had said. "Graced from birth."

"We're going to Washington," Charley told Lara that night. "I decided today."

Her face softened. She kissed his hair. "I'm so glad, Charley. I'm so glad." She sat down beside him on the couch. "We're very lucky, aren't we?"

"Yes, we are," he said.

That night, lying in January darkness, chilled by the cold wind which slid through the window cracks, Lara had touched him, and he had frozen.

It was not the first time the life had fallen out of him like that. For more than a year, he had had long periods of impotence, sometimes weeks on end, enough to wonder about Sam's conception, but this night he went dead at the center of his being as if he had made a single leap to old age. He blamed it on the war.

He mentioned his flat feet only to his mother.

"Who had flat feet?" he asked. "They remarked on my feet when I took the physical for the army."

"Your father," she said. "Your father and his brother and

probably their father as well. Which is why your father got so tired on his feet. I have very good arches still at my age. Astonishing arches. I could have made a lovely dancer."

Charley had seen Tom Elliot once more in February of 1942 when Tom on his way to Europe spent a night in Washington and stayed with him in the rooming house. All night, Charley kept waking up, roused by unfamiliar rage. He left early in the morning before Tom was up.

"Goodbye," he called. "Good luck."

"You bet," Tom called back. "You bet your bottom dollar. And to you too."

At the farm that night, the Fletchers lingered after dinner wordless, lost in their own thoughts. Kate seemed anxious and distracted. She couldn't eat.

"Perhaps you're coming down with something," Lara said.

"I am," Kate said. "I feel terrible." She asked to be excused early and went to bed.

Kate had decided to leave home. That afternoon just as the bell rang for recess, Pole Trickett had taken her behind a forsythia bush, put his huge bad-smelling hand over her mouth and pushed her head down towards his exposed erection. She could not call out but she had bitten the palm of his hand hard enough to make it bleed.

"Rabies, rabies," he screamed, stuffing his penis back into his corduroys, rushing from behind the bush with his hand extended. "Kate Bergmann has bitten me."

"What did Pole Trickett do to you?" the principal asked her later.

"He behaved badly," Kate said.

"Tell me," the principal said.

"I can't," Kate said. "You should ask him."

"I did ask him," the principal said. "He said he was trying to kiss you," the principal said. "In America, we don't consider it an offense to try to kiss a girl. Perhaps things are different in Denmark."

"I have been in America already a long time," Kate said. She got up. "I'm going home."

"No," the principal said. "You are going to math with the rest of your class."

He walked with her to math class.

"I will have Pole apologize to you," the principal said.

"Sorry, sorry, sorry for trying to kiss you, Kate Bergmann," Pole said to her at lunch.

She did not bother to respond.

During afternoon classes, she planned her departure for Milan to live with her father, although she knew it was impossible to go to Europe now. She would tell her mother in the morning after she was packed.

"Just a few months to visit Papa," she would say.

Perhaps, Kate thought, she should tell her mother what had happened. She wondered whether Lara would understand or would she believe that Kate had brought about her own humiliation. She wondered whether people ever, even mothers, knew each other's lives. And gradually the sound of her mother's voice calling good night to Charley overtook her own thoughts and she fell asleep.

Charley stayed in the kitchen after Lara had gone upstairs to bed. He was too restless to sleep. He listened in the room above the kitchen to Lara's preparations for bed, softly back and forth across the room. Just the thought of her waiting for him lovely and expectant against the white pillow made him restless.

He would go out back.

He looked around the kitchen for a reason—a jar of preserves, fresh eggs, a catalogue of livestock—and found in the refrigerator an excuse. There were two six-packs of black beer from Lara's cousins in Leesburg.

• • •

Just after supper and dark, since the days were shortening, Aida had come over to Moses' cottage, her eyes blazing as they did whether she was angry or not and tonight she was angry.

"So, I've been fired at three o'clock this afternoon from Mrs. Cash for no good reason just when I was in the middle of ironing the shirts of Mr. Cash which have to be heavy-starched so the old raccoon can look like rigor mortis has set in."

She flung herself on the couch and asked Moses for a beer.

"There had to be a reason, Aida," Miracle said. "You are the best ironer in Vienna and Mrs. Cash won't find anyone to hold a candle to you."

"She's hiring Mary Pollard. Mary Pollard, she said to me in her snotty uptown voice, doesn't drink on the job and uses underarm deodorant," Aida said.

"So you were drinking on the job," Moses said.

"Don't go holy on me, Moses," Aida said. "I've seen you pee in the fireplace on Christmas Day from too much drink."

"So what'd you do, Aida Sue? Have a nip from Mr. Cash's stash of whiskey while you were doing up his shirts?"

"One sip," she held out her little finger. "That much bourbon. Not enough to make a mouse drunk." She lit a cigarette. "So she caught me and said she'd a mind to fire me and I said if she had a mind, she ought to do it and she could finish up the other sleeve of Mr. Cash's shirt although I'm sure she's never had an iron in her lily-white hand."

She got herself another beer.

"Don't get yourself so upset you lose all your jobs from drinking too much," Miracle said.

"I don't drink too much," Aida pouted. "And when I drink at all, it's to cool down the burning because Guy Bellows can't do it for nothing lately."

"Shut up, Aida," Moses said. "I don't want personal conversations in this house."

It was at that point that Charley Fletcher knocked on the door of the Bellows cottage with two six-packs of beer.

Moses straightened his shoulders as he had a habit of doing and cocked his head. "Can I help you?" he asked Charley without friendship.

Charley, still dressed for work, carried a large brown bag.

"I brought this beer down for you." He handed Moses the bag. "I thought you'd like to try it."

"Why, beer is just the subject of conversation," Aida said, standing a little at an angle, holding on to the couch. "I would very much like to try a bottle of that beer." She reached in and took a bottle. "Thank you, Mr. Fletcher."

"Please call me Charley," he said.

"Charley." Aida smiled.

"Sometimes, Aida Sue Bellows," Moses said, narrowing his eyes, "I think you should be locked up in one of those institutions for the mentally insane."

"Aren't you going to tell Charley Fletcher what happened to me this afternoon?" Aida pouted.

"That is not a subject of interest to Mr. Fletcher," Moses said.

"Aida's been fired from Mrs. Cash today where she's done beautiful ironing Tuesdays for eleven and a half years," Miracle said loyally.

"For drinking," Aida said. "I could iron a shirt better than God could, drunk as a lord." She slid down on the couch.

"I think you better go home, Aida," Moses said.

"Well I'm not going home. I'm going to sit right here and talk to Mr. Charley Fletcher like a civilized human being," Aida said. "You sit down, Charley, and we can have a conversation."

Moses took Aida by the arm, and willingly, because she was finally too drunk to resist, she went with him, out the kitchen door to her own cottage, where he put her to bed on the living-room couch and covered her with a lumber jacket.

Miracle concentrated on her knitting.

"Moses can be in a bad humor," she said.

"He seems perfectly pleasant," Charley said. "A little put out with Aida."

Miracle looked up.

"He's in a bad humor," she said.

She was indicating that Charley should leave, as he told Lara later. She had a note in her voice that suggested trouble. He put up the collar of his coat.

"Tell him I hope he likes the beer. It's heavier than ordinary beer," Charley said and left by the front just as he heard Moses open the back door.

Upstairs Lara's light was out and the wind from the open window billowed the sheets. He undressed and climbed into bed next to her, sensing her breathing was too strong for sleep.

"I took the Bellowses some of your cousin's beer," he said.

"Mmm." Lara slid her head under his chin.

"I don't think they particularly liked me coming over," he said.

He could not sleep. Hours after Lara's breathing had fallen shallow, he still sat propped up in the dark bedroom, wide awake.

When Moses came back, Charley Fletcher had gone and Miracle sat in the big blue flowered chair in the living room knitting a sweater for Prudential's baby, soon to be her own baby with Moses.

Moses picked up the bag of beer and looked at the labels. "Black beer," he said. "What man could drink beer the color of death?"

One by one, he threw the bottles against the living-room wall, where they broke spilling dark mud streams down the white walls, even dripping on the frame which held the picture of Jesus, the Savior, which he got after his parents died.

Miracle did not look up. She finished the back of the sweater without a word. When she got up, Moses was sitting in a straightback chair staring into the dark kitchen.

"I'm going to bed now," she said.

"My temper was for Charley Fletcher, not Aida, whom I love, dumb as she is," Moses said.

"I know," Miracle replied.

"Aren't you going to ask me to clean up the glass on the floor?" he asked.

"Suit yourself," she said.

October Eleventh, 1942

Early the morning of October 11, on her way to Vruels' market for cleaning supplies, Miracle saw John Spencer. Just the back of him in faded blue pants hung low on his skinny hips and a pale yellow sweater. His leg was bad. She could tell by the tilt of his shoulders and the way he slipped into the woods. She was a quarter of a mile from Skunk Farm—now called Skunk Farm "officially," as Charley Fletcher said—though Moses told Mr. Fletcher to his face that it struck him as wildly stupid to have such a name as Skunk Farm stick as it would surely do. And generations down the years, people would wonder *why* a name like that for good land and a fine house came to be, and by the name itself, the place could run downhill. But Charley Fletcher was a stubborn man and he was the one in charge.

Miracle had decided to walk off her bad temper at Moses that morning instead of letting him drive her to Vruels' like he did most mornings. And maybe by walking two miles back and forth in the clear starched autumn morning she could cool down enough to have a sensible conversation when he came home for lunch. So she was walking along the side of the road making plans. First off, she'd get salami and hot mustard, and that would certainly please him. And she'd keep her voice quiet so it swung over him like soft cloth, take hold of his wrist and rub her thumb along the underside like you do to calm the temper of an angry dog.

"Moses darling," she would sing to him. "You got to be the wiser man with Charley Fletcher because he's innocent as lambs." She couldn't say "He means well," although that's what she believed. Because Moses would say what difference does it make to mean well if you cause trouble by the well meaning. You might just as well mean ill for all the good it does. And he'd be right of course in principle. Moses was always right in principle.

Miracle was walking down Route 7, which was narrow with plenty of traffic in the morning, so she walked close to the edge where the high grasses brushed her legs and reviewed the events of the night before. She had an orderly mind with a strong and exact memory and could recall in detail not only the conversations of a past event but the physical surroundings as well. So when she was thinking, her mind blew up into a stage set with three-dimensional characters. She thought in color. Aida said that was the cat's meow. And she was lost in reverie when John Spencer crossed the road, probably a hundred yards ahead. The color of him crossing caught her peripheral vision like a bird flying overhead, a shadow just out of focus. She stopped in her tracks and her heart fell to her feet.

The man who had caught her attention was on the other side of the road and moving quickly. She kept him in sight for less than a minute but in that time and even with the great distance she was so certain of his identity that she sat down on the side of the road until her heart stopped beating too fast and she could catch her breath.

She walked slowly. She was weak-kneed, fearful of a man who comes back from the dead. As she passed the place where John Spencer had disappeared into the woods, she kept her eyes hard on the road ahead of her so as not to seem curious in case he was there watching. And she could feel him there watching, feel his eyes boring into the side of her, through her temple into her brain as if he was lying in wait to kill her. That's what it felt like as she pulled one lead-pipe leg after the other along the road. It felt like someone was watching her with intentions.

She wanted to get to Vruels' and get her cleaning supplies and call Moses and tell him she'd had a spell on the road to Damascus and could he come get her. But she couldn't help herself from thinking. If that was John Spencer, then Moses hadn't killed him. And she had been so sure. Why else would a man who had told her he'd see her at supper and to buy lamb chops—as John Spencer had told her that day—disappear unless he had been killed? Or maybe Moses had just half killed him and he'd come back from hell to get Miracle for letting him be in the position to be killed by Moses. Or Moses had simply threatened him, and with a threat from Moses Bellows, you might as well be dead.

She had grieved for John Spencer. She had grieved for the sense of herself he had given her. But from time to time—and she admitted this to herself forthrightly—she had also been pleased to think that her round body meant enough to Moses Bellows to kill a man for taking it from him. After they had all moved to the main house, she'd lie in bed next to Moses and think to herself: "Why Miracle Bellows, you must be something else."

Mr. Vruels called Moses for Miracle. By the time she got to the market, her head was so light on her shoulders she thought it might fall off, so she sat in the hardback chair next to the cash register and held Mr. Vruels' corncob cat on her lap for sympathy.

"So, I hear things are going different at Elm Grove since the Fletchers came," Mr. Vruels said.

"Different from the way they were going before the Fletchers came," Miracle said.

"Moses tells me Mr. Fletcher is a very friendly man," Doc Vruels said.

Miracle never answered unless she wanted to and she

didn't want to answer now. She liked Doc Vruels when he gave out information about lambing or horsefeed or recipes his wife had for chicken. But she didn't like gossip, and Doc Vruels was the distribution center for gossip in Vienna. He particularly liked bad news.

"Too friendly," Doc Vruels said. "That's what it sounded like Moses meant to say about Mr. Fletcher, but Moses is a man who keeps his counsel and I'm never exactly sure what he thinks."

He got Miracle's cleaning supplies off the shelves and bagged them.

"Wouldn't you say that's true about Moses?"

Miracle thanked him for bagging the groceries.

"Mrs. Fletcher is beautiful, though," he said. "I'd lock her in a cabinet for safekeeping if she were my wife."

When the call came for Moses to pick up Miracle at Vruels', Lara got the phone. She was in the kitchen feeding Sam, and Moses, who had come through the back door in a stone-cold temper, had one foot up on a kitchen stool and was lacing his boots. Doc Vruels said Miracle had taken a fainting spell.

"Is she all right?" Lara asked.

"You can't tell with the colored," Doc Vruels said. "They're one color sick or well."

Lara gave the phone to Moses.

She didn't know what to make of Moses Bellows. He had troubled her from the start, and lately, even in the same room, going about her chores, or reading or sewing curtains for their bedroom, she was unsettled by his presence.

"If Miracle isn't feeling well, I don't want her to work," Moses said combatively.

"Of course," Lara said.

He stood at the door with the screen open and looked at her directly.

"I used to live in this house," he said matter-of-factly.

"I know," she said. "Charley told me."

"We lived here for seven years," he said and left.

Lara watched him out the window. He walked down the path, picked two dead blooms off the golden mums and lifted one of the barn cats sunning on the hood of his truck. The truck was old with a stubborn accelerator, so Moses had to stand in the cab straight as a board slipped in under the steering wheel and pump the accelerator with his right foot until the engine turned over. The truck flooded. He got out, walked around the front, lifted the hood and looked inside. Then he tried again. She was mesmerized watching him.

In less than an hour, Charley would call from his office at Censorship. Weekdays, between the hour when Charley left for work and when he called her promptly at nine-forty the minute he arrived at his office, before taking off his jacket or getting coffee or looking at the newspapers, Lara was alone. It was the only hour in the day since they had moved to Washington that she was actually out of touch with him.

In that hour she had a ritual. She would feed Sam and put him down and then she'd go to her bedroom, painted white now, with a white bedspread and starched white curtains. Nothing extraneous. There was a simple dresser she had refinished, pale instead of dark mahogany, a round table with a cornflower-blue cloth on which she had a picture of her parents when they were young and loved each other deeply. Her books were stacked on the floor beside a wicker chaise—hundreds of books, in English and Danish and French. She read anything, even technical books, but lately she liked to simply look at books as she had when she was a child for the color in the pictures, not even the pictures themselves. At about nine every morning, she would escape into this room she had made for herself, take off her clothes, put on a thin cotton robe, made by her grandmother for her mother's trousseau, sit on the wicker chaise with her legs crossed and the robe open just so, and daydream. The daydream was always the same.

She was a young woman imprisoned by the Nazis in 1940 and had eventually been kept in solitary confinement, because she was beautiful and therefore dangerous, the Gestapo had told her. When she first arrived, however, before the confinement, she had met Tom Elliot, a young American photographer who had been captured; they had fallen in love but because of the circumstances their love affair was never consummated.

The dream opened in late summer. The war was over. The young woman had been released and returned to Denmark. And the man, badly treated, malnourished and ill, had been released from a hospital in Germany where he was recovering and had come to see her. She was sitting on her chaise in her flat in Copenhagen reading when there was a knock on the door. She put the book facedown on her stomach.

"Is that you, darling?" she called. "Come in."

Tom Elliot came in, still fragile from his imprisonment but handsome as she remembered him.

"Sit down," she said.

He sat beside her.

"Tell me everything," she said.

She was aware of a broad scar from his left eye across his cheek.

"Burned," he says. "It was one of their favorite games. To burn faces."

Sometimes it was a film she was doing, sometimes a play, but she preferred the play because it was more personal and true than film.

She reached out to touch the scar, and as she did, as she ran her fingers across it, it disappeared.

He reached up, felt his own smooth face.

"Magic," he said. "You are magical." He took the book from her stomach, put it on the floor, and dropped the sides of her robe.

In the first years of their great love affair, Charley would come home at midday, pressing his lunch hour because it was the only hour he could be alone with Lara when Kate was at school. "Hello, hello," he'd call from the front door. "I'm looking everywhere for the heroine of my great love affair."

90

And Lara would slip out of the kitchen in a long robe or naked under one of Charley's oxford-cloth shirts with the sleeves below her hands or once dressed in a long black velvet skirt and stockings and high heels with nothing above the waist except an amethyst necklace of her mother's which hung on a long chain.

"Hello," she said. "I have made you lunch."

"I don't want lunch," he said.

But she put her fingers across his lips.

"Just hot tea until you've warmed up."

He took hold of her.

"Wait," she said, turning her head away.

"I won't."

She went into the kitchen and came out with a cup of tea for each of them.

"There now." She sat down in the large wing chair in the living room. "Sit down on the couch."

He drank his tea in a single swallow and kissed her with his hot sweet lips.

"Now," he whispered in her hair.

Lara did not know when the mischief and romance between them had faded, when the lovemaking had changed. First there were long lapses as if their marriage had become familiar and ordinary and then the kind of awkwardness of characters in a comedy of manners and then after Sam was on the way, the romance was gone altogether.

The phone interrupted her reverie, and she leapt from the chaise to get it—nine thirty-five—but it was Moses, not Charley, calling from Vruels' market to say that Miracle would not be working and that he planned to plow the center field that afternoon. She waited for Charley's call. Sam woke up whimpering in his bassinet and she picked him up, sat by the telephone and fed him. By ten-fifteen Charley had still not called.

She went downstairs with Sam to the kitchen.

She would make supper, Lara thought. She took a chicken out of the icebox. When she was young, she used to cook with her mother side by side in the kitchen. They seldom talked except business. "You do the tomatoes, Lara," her mother would say. "Very thin, just so." And like a bird mama, she'd stick a small bite of everything she was cooking in Lara's mouth. Lara especially liked to bake with her mother. They sat on stools, their arms and shoulders touching, and kneaded the dough for brown bread until Lara's fingers hurt. Then when the bread had cooled they'd eat the ends—one for each slathered in butter.

By noon, Charley had still not called.

She had never known him not to call, she thought. Even in Minneapolis when their lives were rooted together. She took broccoli out and made a cream sauce with sharp cheese. She took out flour and sugar. She'd make pastry— perhaps fruit if there was any fresh at Vruels'. She got a cookbook in Danish, sat in a rocking chair back and forth, reading recipes for comfort in her native tongue.

The telephone rang and she flew to it but it was only Doc Vruels asking could he substitute five pounds of sugar for two pounds.

As a small child, she had lost her mother at a gift shop in downtown Copenhagen. The shop was tiny—one room with a glass counter down the center and shelves along the sides, a dressing room with a curtain because the shop sold a few handwoven clothes. Her mother was looking for a present—a piece of jewelry. She had several on the counter lined up and she even lifted Lara up to show her. Lara selected an amethyst pin with seed pearls around the oval center, but her mother, a slow methodical shopper, not easily bored, considered. What Lara remembered next was sliding behind the paisley cloth curtain and looking at herself in the mirror of the dressing room. She remembered as well, because it was daring with strangers on the other side of the curttain, lifting her white linen dress so she could see the flesh of her belly soft and peach against her pantaloons. Then she peered from behind the curtain into the shop and her mother was gone.

She could not move. She pressed her plump face into the soft cloth and peered intently at the place where her mother had been, where the jewels for Aunt Eva had been

92

set out—and no one was there that she could see but the shopkeeper.

A sound she had not intended came from her throat and rang through the small shop.

"MAMAMAMAMA."

The shopkeeper looked over at her.

"What is it?" she asked sternly.

Centuries later, it seemed forever, her mother swooped down from the corner just beyond Lara's peripheral vision and picked her up.

Lara could not speak at all, not in the shop or on the walk to the sweet and tea shop, but once they were seated, side by side in the hard iron chairs with a biscuit and chocolate on the table in front of her, she finally said:

"I thought you had left me."

"But I have never left you," her mother said. "There is no reason to be afraid I will leave you if you have no memory of it happening, darling."

"But I have a memory," Lara had said.

"The memory is not real."

Lara shook her head. She didn't know what to say to her mother.

"But I have the memory anyway," she replied.

She told her mother about looking at herself in the mirror but she did not mention that she had lifted her dress to see her flesh reflected in the shadowed room.

She went upstairs with Sam and sat in the window seat with the telephone under her hand.

On the morning of October 11, Charley parked his car in the lot at 9th and Constitution Avenue, walked into the Federal Trade Commission building, where the Office of Censorship was located, went up the one flight of steps to his office, said good morning to his secretary, to Jim Billings, his assistant, hungover as usual, and to the cleaning lady doing his office. He sat down at his desk and was just lifting the telephone to call Lara, which he did every morning first off before he did anything else as if he suspected she might evaporate or leave in his brief absence, when he noticed the United Press teletype which said in the first paragraph that Tom Elliot, photographer from Minneapolis, had been in an air crash October 8 after a mission over northeast Germany near Bonn and was dead.

He read the print over and over until the name Tom Elliot faded from familiarity and became a name he had never seen before. Then he put the teletype aside and went through the papers on his desk methodically, answering letters, telephone calls, memos from his immediate superior. He read the daily newspapers and listened intermittently to the news on the radio.

"So, Tom Elliot is dead" went through his mind in just those words, spoken aloud in his own voice. "Tom Elliot is dead."

He could not believe Tom Elliot's mortality.

He went to the outer office for a cup of coffee, took a call from the War Department and read a speech of Churchill's reprinted for his office. He had not called Lara. What could he say to her?

In the few hours since he had read the news item, Tom Elliot had assumed power. Charley Fletcher suspected everything. The news of his death would break Lara's heart.

"Lara." What timbre should his voice have? What modulation? "Tom Elliot is dead."

At noon, shaken by the news, Charley left Censorship to get lunch, he told his secretary, but lunch was not what he had in mind.

He walked. Constitution Avenue was a blaze of yellow leaves in the sunlight and he walked into the noon light to the Capitol, and behind the Capitol—behind the white impenetrable Supreme Court, into the area called the shadow slums because it lay in the long shadow of the Capitol where unemployed Negroes lined the porches of row houses which had once been the grand residences of Congress, with wide bay windows, paned stained glass and heavy carved oak doors with wrought-iron banisters in ornate rosettes. Deep into the slums he walked, a stranger, the only white man on the streets where Negroes slumped against lampposts and porch railings and broken fences, unemployable men, working-class in a nonindustrial city, beaten by the length of empty days, too old for war, their eyes glazed over with drink or drugs or long-drawn-out defeat.

Charley Fletcher wanted a war zone.

Moses fixed snap beans and ham for lunch and Miracle sat in the kitchen with her feet up on one chair and looked out at the rope swing hanging from a large unblighted elm tree which the Bellowses had put up for children which had never come.

"My pressure's up," she said to Moses.

He cut up a sweet red tomato and fixed her a plate of ham and beans.

"You're too young a woman to have high blood pressure, darling." Moses sat down next to her. "Now you eat." He put his hand down on hers. "You're too tired is what you are. These people wear you out."

"They don't wear me out, Moses."

"They wear me out. Mr. Fletcher in particular wears me out."

"The spell I had wasn't from being worn out," she said. "It was from seeing a ghost."

But Moses was too preoccupied with his anger at Charley Fletcher to put his mind to ghosts.

"You know as well as I do there are no ghosts," he said. "Only wishful thinking."

If she had confessed to Moses, which she did not, that she had seen John Spencer walking down Route 7, he would have said either she had hallucinated John Spencer or else there he had been on Route 7 alive as any man. And Moses would have been right, she thought. If her mind was flying off on her at thirty-one years old and only slightly overweight, otherwise in good health except for her pressure, she'd better take precautions.

Moses washed up the dishes, kissed her softly, pressed

his hand against her back. "Now you rest up," he said. And he left to plow the main field.

Miracle watched him walk down the path, across the field. "He has good carriage, Moses Bellows," her mother always said about him. "I've never once seen him stoop, even when his papa died."

Prudential sat on her bed writing a two-year plan in the spiral ledger notebook Moses had got for her in town. On the front she had written THE GREAT PLANS OF PRUDENTIAL MAGNOLIA WELLFLEET. The last two names she had added recently, since the name Prudential Dargon didn't suit the size of the world she had it in mind to occupy. The plan was a list and included books she should read and clothes she should have and skills she would need in order to be ready to go to the fine city of New York in 1945 when she would be almost sixteen. That was her great plan.

Her room at the Bellowses' was immaculate, with juice glasses of wildflowers on the dresser and pictures, abstracts she had made herself on shelf paper and wrapped around the wall. But hanging from the window overlooking the back field and taking up too much light was a life-size doll, handmade with a pillowcase head and face painted on and long brown hair made of yarn and the sundress Prudential had gotten from the Sears catalogue. There were no legs or feet. And from top to bottom, hardly visible unless you looked closely, the legless white girl was stuck through with straight pins.

Since August when Kate Bergmann had moved to Skunk Farm, Kate and Prudential had stalked each other. They seldom spoke directly. Prudential would stand behind a dead black elm and wait for the school bus to let Kate off, watch her climb wearily up the hill with her bookbag and jump out at her when she passed.

"Pussyfoot," she'd call. "Pussyfoot girl."

And Kate would march out back past the Bellows cottage carrying a basket of barn kittens and singing Danish songs.

She'd sing in Danish at the top of her voice.

"You hear her show off, Uncle Guy," Prudential would

say to Guy Bellows, who was cooling down on the porch after a long day, his feet on the railing. "Speaking to me in a foreign language like she thinks I'm stupid."

"She doesn't think you're stupid, Prudential," Guy said, closing his eyes against the falling sun. "That's her way of talk."

"She can talk English good as me," Prudential said. "She's poking fun, I tell you."

Guy opened his eyes and glared at the back of Kate Bergmann walking with her kittens, sometimes her baby brother Sam, to the end of the property beyond out back.

"You're sure of that, Prudential?"

"Dead sure," Prudential would say.

"I told you the night we moved out back that it was dangerous to provoke Guy Bellows," Moses told her once, overhearing that kind of conversation.

"She ridicules me," Prudential said.

"You ridicule her," Moses replied.

So Prudential made a stuffed Kate Bergmann and stuck her full of pins.

"I made a statue of you for my bedroom and stuck you full of pins," she told Kate in the kitchen. "And soon you're going to feel the pins all over your body. That happened to my auntie when she cheated on her husband and she died of it."

"Of pins?" Kate asked.

"They found her on the toilet with two thousand and sixteen pins all over her body. My mama counted. And then they found her sorrowful husband sitting in his bedroom with a voodoo doll of Auntie which he was sticking full of pins."

"That's a very unpleasant story," Kate said.

"It's true is what it is," Prudential said.

"We hate each other," Kate told her mother calmly. "She's the first person I have ever hated in my life." She was triumphant, as if the power to hate itself was wondrous.

Miracle sat down on the fat stuffed chair from Mama Bellows' house and put her feet up on the end of Prudential's bed.

"Working?" she asked.

"Making a list for the future," Prudential said. "Beginning after the baby."

"I got a letter from your mama this morning."

"Uh huh."

"You can read it. She says your papa and Holiday are feuding."

"She does?"

"That's all she wrote about except to say General Lafayette's been better and your papa changed filling stations."

"Papa drinks."

"I know that."

"And he used to bother me some when I was home, so I suppose he's bothering Holiday in my absence." She closed her notebook. "You know I don't like Papa."

"I know you don't," Miracle said. "Don't worry yourself about it. We can't like everybody."

The calico cat jumped on Miracle's lap, and she held him like a baby and played with his long whiskers and paws.

"I hope this is going to be a fine baby for you, Aunt Miracle," Prudential said. "That it comes out with all its fingers and some brains."

"It'll be a fine baby."

"I hope it will be sweet-looking like you."

And they went on like that for a while with the sun moving over past noon behind the Kate Bergmann doll, shedding light blankets across their faces until the spirit of confidence was alive in the room like fragrance and Miracle confessed to Prudential she'd either had a spell on the road that morning or seen John Spencer in the flesh and not under any circumstances to tell Moses.

"I'd like to determine for myself whether that man is dead and visiting my brain without invitation or if he was never dead at all," she said. "So you open your eyes, darling, and take some walks all around here. If he's around and not a vision from heaven, you'll find him."

She took a ragged picture from her apron pocket, worn from handling. "That's him in the year he disappeared. I found it in his desk."

"How come you bothered to keep a picture of him?" Prudential asked.

"I worked for him, darling," Miracle said. "You come to know the people you work for as well as your own."

"And why do you want me to find him?"

"I don't necessarily want you to find him," Miracle said. "I want to find out myself if I'm going crazy."

"I'll look," Prudential said, pleased with the secret and the opportunity for trouble. "I'll look all around on foot as far as Vruels'."

Prudential took a bath. She sat in the large claw tub and let the hot water beat down on a cake of Ivory soap and make white bubbles in a circle around her brown belly. She was big as a house according to Guy and he laughed out loud to see her walk with her stick legs wide apart as if they were set on the edge of her hipbone and hung from there. She was almost seven months and the baby was a mover, making foot circles on the inside of her tummy, changing the shape of her. Sometimes she was even curious to see if what came out was possible for her to love in spite of its daddy—her baby, after all, whoever the daddy. But those times were few and mostly she thought about time in slow motion and she hoped she'd live long enough to be free of that bastard baby clinging to the inside of her for dear life.

"Turn off the water, Prudential," Miracle called from her bedroom next door. "There won't be any left for Moses when he gets home."

She turned off the water and lay back in the tub so her belly was covered and the bubbles floated under her chin and she could pretend she was a sassy little chicken soup who Moses longed to have for his very own forever and ever, amen. And then ashamed of these thoughts, loving

Miracle as she did and Moses being nearly as old as her own hateful daddy, she flopped on her belly facedown and blew bubbles into the water, coming up for air close to drowning, so she told herself.

Miracle had made a baby room at the end of her bedroom. She had a bassinet she had painted white and laced through with wide blue satin ribbon and white roses she had made by hand and a blue-squared quilt and white pillow and white cotton bear for the end of the bed. Sometimes she'd just sit and look at the baby's place full of melancholy. Prudential would come in, sit down beside her and lay her hand on top of Miracle's.

"So what're you thinking about?" Prudential would ask.

"Thinking that it's a strange thing to be taking my sister's baby's own baby to be my own."

"But the same blood."

"The same blood. And then I think I wish I knew who the daddy was so I'd have some ideas about how things might turn out, if you know what I mean."

"Look how I turned out. How was Mama to know I'd turn out to be this Prudential? And she knows my daddy better than she wishes she knew him."

"So you're not going to tell me."

"Never," Prudential said.

She got out of the tub, toweled off, stood on the toilet seat to look at her belly stretched tight as a drum.

"How come the skin doesn't tear?" she'd asked Miracle.

"It's elastic."

"Then why doesn't it get stretched out like my pajama bottoms?"

"It does. Look at your mama's empty pillowcase of skin lying against her legs between babies, waiting for a new one to fill it."

Prudential cocked her head. "Well, my pillowcase is going to be empty till I die, because this is the first and very last baby I ever plan to have, so help me God."

She dusted baby powder on her shoulders and arms, put on her best underpants with lace, her old lady's brassiere with a cup large as a funnel, went into her bedroom, took the sundress away from the stuffed Kate Bergmann, took the pins, and put it on. It was still hot enough to wear a sundress in autumn, and besides this sundress was the best dress she had ever owned except a pink lace one when she was little bought for her grandfather's funeral which she never wore again because it smelled geranium-sweet of death.

Lately, she had been thinking differently about the baby. Not with affection necessarily but with a certain pride that this baby making away in her belly, thickening like butter, was for Moses and she was Moses' wife and this would be the boy he had wanted from Miracle who couldn't give him a baby. But Prudential Life Insurance Dargon, which she had called herself until she settled on the fancy name of Wellfleet, could turn a baby out of her own body easy as pie and deliver it to Moses as a gift.

She called to Miracle.

"I would be pleased to borrow your churchgoing purple lipstick."

"For what occasion?" Miracle asked.

"For the occasion of hunting down ghosts."

Miracle laughed. "Go easy," she said.

She put on the purple lipstick, making her lips smaller, took a little purple for her squirrel cheeks, squirted apple-blossom scent on her hair and went downstairs.

"If John Spencer is alive I'll find him before Christmas," she said to Miracle, who followed her down. "And if he's dead, I think we should have a funeral and give him a marker since he didn't get a ceremony like folks who die before they disappear."

She dipped a cup into the pot of vegetable soup and slurped it down.

"Will it make a difference in our happiness if he's alive?" Prudential asked.

Miracle closed her eyes and leaned back in her chair.

"It will make a difference," she said.

Miracle's face was too pale and her body looked old, just the sight of it spread out on the wooden rocker looked too old for the body of a woman who hadn't even started on

101

the main chapter of her life yet. Prudential put her face against Miracle's face.

"Are you sick, Aunt Miracle?"

"My head's flown off my neck," she said. "I don't feel good."

"Is that because you saw John Spencer?"

"Maybe. Maybe that's why."

"And was he a dangerous man?"

"All men are dangerous, Prudential. You've known that since you were a child."

"Except Moses."

"Sometimes even Moses."

Prudential rinsed out her cup, dried it, put it in the cupboard and left by the back door to find Moses in the field and kill the time until Kate Bergmann got home from school.

Aida Bellows was coming down the path from her cottage —swinging in fact from side to side of it, in her striped scarlet skirt and white peasant blouse which had been ripped straight down the center so on one arm she had a sleeve and bodice and the other arm was bare and half the blouse hung like an apron over her skirt.

"Hello, darling, hello," she called to Prudential, acting as if it was perfectly normal to be traveling outside with one breast hanging free and uncovered. "We seem to be strolling the same path this afternoon, maybe because it's the only path between us and anywhere."

Aida was drunk. Prudential could smell the sweet sick scent of whiskey coming off her body like perspiration.

"What's happened to you, Aida?"

"Why nothing whatsoever has happened to me," Aida said. "I got up, had coffee and an apple and did ironing for the Lewises until twelve."

"Your blouse is what I'm talking about," Prudential said.

"Darling, my eyes go out and not in. It isn't possible to look at myself." She took Prudential's arm for steadiness. "Today is October eleventh and sometime this day I will

102

be thirty years old. Nobody including Guy Bellows seems to remember unless they got a big surprise party planned this evening with presents and bourbon and fried chicken."

Prudential supported Aida's weight, which was slight, but the walking with her was awkward.

"Then happy birthday, Aida. I had no idea."

"Why thank you very much, darling. You are sweet to remember."

"And now I'd like to know why your blouse is ripped."

"My blouse?" Aida looked down. "Why, you're quite right, darling. There is my brown bosom plain as a rose for anyone to pick." She lifted the blouse and covered her breast. "I certainly wouldn't want Guy Bellows who's on the top field with Moses at this very moment to see me naked or he might get ideas."

Prudential walked Aida to the house and set her down on the front porch and brought her a work shirt of Guy's to cover up with. Then she went to Moses' garden and picked the last of the zinnias and mums and dahlias and put them in a pot beside Aida's chair.

"Happy birthday again, Aunt Aida," she said and kissed the top of her small head.

Miracle was still sitting in the kitchen rocker.

"Did you know it was Aida's birthday?" Prudential asked her. "She said everybody forgot."

"Is that what she said?" Miracle said.

"October eleventh. She told me she was born sometime October eleventh thirty years ago."

Miracle shook her head. "Aida's birthday is July fourth and has been since I met her. We always have fried chicken and bourbon and shoot off firecrackers."

"Well," Prudential said. "She's sitting on the front porch right now with the flowers I gave her for her birthday and I'm going to talk to her."

Miracle was just about to follow Prudential when out of the corner of her eye she saw Lara Fletcher in a yellow dress, the color of wheat, flying behind her run across the main field towards Moses.

"Now I wonder what she's up to," Miracle said out loud

to the calico barn cat she allowed to drink milk from a bowl on the kitchen floor. "That's what I wonder."

Miracle knew that from the first time he saw her Lara Fletcher danced through Moses' mind. And why not, lovely as she was and sweet-tempered. But it gave Miracle a start to see Lara running, which was not a thing for a white woman to do on her own farmland unless there was an emergency.

There was no emergency.

Lara had put Sam down for an afternoon nap and was sitting in the window seat still waiting for Charley's call, watching Moses gathering the cut wheat, tying it in bundles, and suddenly she was overcome with a girlish desire. She ran down the back stairs, through the kitchen door, across the patio, her skirt flying, running to him as if he had called her.

"Hello," she said, out of breath.

"Hello."

Moses did not look up.

"I saw you working," she said shyly, "and wanted to help you."

"Tie wheat?" He was perplexed. "What about the baby?"

"The baby's sleeping."

He wrapped the thin wire around the bundle and stacked it.

"It's not work for a woman." He meant a white woman but he didn't say that.

She laughed lightly. "In Denmark, there is no difference."

She knelt down in the fallen wheat, thick with the musty smell of dampness, sweet with vegetation.

"Watch me," she said. She gathered the wheat, armful after armful, flushed with unexpected pleasure.

Moses folded his arms and watched her. She could tell there was just the shadow of amusement in that magnificent face. And pleasure. She was sure of it.

"There." She stood. "Now give me some wire." She took the wire from his hand.

He cocked his head.

"You have to stack it tighter," he said. "There's too much air."

"Show me," she said.

He pressed down hard on the wheat. "It takes strength."

She pressed down with him. Their shoulders touching, their heads together on the large square of wheat.

"I have plenty of strength," she said, laughing. "See? Now give me the wire."

Her arms were not long enough to go around the large stack but she wrapped the wire halfway and Moses leaned across to wrap around the other half until there was a square as neat as those which he had stacked.

She sat down in the piles of wheat, warm in the sun, eased by the effort of her work, light-headed in the presence of Moses.

"You ought to go back now," he said.

"I could help you with more."

"No," he said. "Guy's coming and I need to check on Miracle now. You go home."

She lifted a pile of wheat in the air, let it fall on her lap, in her hair.

"Goodbye then," she said and in a single graceful move was off the ground and running back to the main house.

Charley Fletcher was almost thirty blocks northeast of the Capitol on streets so quiet he could hear the body noises of drunks propped against the walls of row houses—occasionally the voice of a cat. There had been no event. No one on the streets of the shadow slums seemed interested in his presence there. It was as if he were moving through a realistic painting in which the figures despite their verisimilitude were still-life, permanently inattentive.

He thought of himself as a reasonable man whose deep passions, even anger, were held in check. Always, since he could remember, he kept the matters of his mind and heart in slender trays with dividers like the drawers in which dentists keep their sterilized tools. Nothing interfered. Until lately, this fear, more like a nightmare terror

—something amounting to a revolution of the heart about Lara.

He could not get Tom Elliot out of his mind. He saw him dead. His eyes were closed, his golden-red hair matted from the pilot helmet he would have been wearing. Charley saw a fellow soldier hoist the body on his shoulder with Tom's head hanging down his back. Something about the imagining enraged him and he wanted to fight.

He did not even see the young boy until he had passed him at 30th and A. He was a body length beyond him when the unregistered memory of what he had seen caused him to turn back and there on the steps of one of the houses was a boy about five, with his hands folded in his lap, his head forward, fixed as in a stroke, and his spindly legs and feet resting on the back of a man, notable for the length of him, stretched out facedown on the sidewalk.

"I won't talk," the boy said before Charley had spoken to him.

Charley knelt down and the boy spread his small legs so one was at the shoulder blade and the other at the buttocks, possessing the man.

"I won't tell you nothing," the boy said.

Charley heard a door open and looked up to see a woman the color of purple grapes, her head tied in a turban, a bright red shirt and skirt and red lipstick painted on.

"Git," she said to Charley.

"Who is this man?" Charley asked.

"You heard me." The woman came down the steps so she stood behind the boy.

"He is my father," the boy said.

"Don't fib," the woman said.

"My father." The boy moved down the steps and sat in the middle of the man's back.

"He is not your father," the woman said. "Nor no man we've ever seen before in our lives but a stranger dead on the street in front of our home."

The boy was crying.

The woman walked down the stairs, stepped broadly over the legs of the dead man, took Charley by the arm.

106

"You must be lost," she said without a measure of hostility.

"I'm certainly not lost," he said.

"I said you must be lost." She tried to move him along the empty street, back towards the Capitol, and when he would not budge, quick as a flash and subtly, so the boy who squatted in the middle of the dead man's back would not observe, she took a switchblade knife from the pocket of her skirt, held it just under his rib cage with her finger on the button to release the knife.

"Git," she said.

He knew better than to test her patience.

He walked two short straight city blocks before he looked back and when he did an old Sealtest milk truck painted blue had been driven up on the sidewalk and the dead man was flung over the shoulders of a large man and put inside the truck. He saw the flash of red dress disappear inside the house, the truck pull off. The boy, a small dot in the middle of a sunny morning, not even recognizable as a boy, stood on the sidewalk.

He knew exactly what he ought to do and walked back a short space. The boy looked at him with sightless eyes.

"I know you told the truth," Charley said to the boy.

The boy opened his mouth.

"MA MA MAAAAAA," he called out.

Upstairs the window was flung open and the woman leaned out, still in her turban, but bare to the waist.

"You must be a crazy man," she said to him. "And soon enough you're going to get yourself killed."

An unfamiliar sickness slid over him as he walked towards the Capitol conscious that the woman was still hanging out of the window watching him, watching him, but when he finally turned around, she was gone.

The police would do nothing. On the way back to Censorship, he went to the police station southwest of the Capitol. They took down the information without interest.

"It happens all the time with niggers," the officer said. "We stay out of their business if it's personal."

Charley told them about the switchblade.

"I don't think he died of an overdose of drugs," Charley said. "I think she killed him."

"It could have been an overdose of drugs or she could have killed him," the officer said. "We'll check into it this afternoon and be in touch."

"You won't do it," Charley said coldly. "Whether there's a child involved or not. You won't do anything because they're colored."

"We're officers of the law, mister," the policeman said. "We do our duty."

"You don't," Charley said, this temper overtaking. "You do what you please."

"I said I'd call you if I find something out, mister."

"You bet," Charley said and headed out the door before he actually hit the young policeman. At the door, he turned. "What is your name?" he asked.

"Officer Williams," the young man said. "Badge thirty. You can turn me in to the chief, if that's what you had in mind," he said. "I do what I'm told."

"I know that," Charley said.

Back in the office, he did call the chief of police, who told him, "We do our best, Mr. Fletcher," and Charley knew the case was closed.

Prudential saw Kate come over the hill along Route 7, two hours at least before the bus was supposed to deliver her to Skunk Farm. There she was, the pussyfoot girl, in her fine blue-flowered dress walking merrily along in the sunshine as if she hadn't a care in the world.

"Don't make trouble," Miracle warned Prudential, sensing her temper. "There's enough trouble in the world already."

Kate had left school at noon, just after the lunch bell when the playground had filled with children and no one was likely to notice a young girl slip down the bank behind the school and head south.

The morning had been uneventful until eleven. In English they were doing grammar, and fractions in math and American democracy in social studies. She was very bored with school but had learned early on when she first moved to America to appear attentive while she wrote plays in her head. During the teaching of the subordinate clause, she was writing a serious play about the murder of a young Swedish princess by her boyfriend who was Russian and bad-tempered when a note came from the principal that she was to come to his office.

He was grave-faced when she walked in.

"I received a call from Pole Trickett's mother this morning." He walked around the desk and sat directly in front of Kate. "You broke the skin on his hand when you bit him and he had to have a tetanus shot."

"Yes."

"The Tricketts were very upset."

Kate hesitated. She did not want to tell the truth about Pole Trickett to this terrible man.

"I am sorry he had to have a tetanus shot," she said although she was to the contrary very pleased and hoped it would be painful for a long time.

"We're going to have to call your parents."

"For what reason?"

"To let them know you have bitten another child. It is an offense."

"I didn't bite Pole Trickett because he kissed me," she said in spite of herself.

"Oh?" The principal rested against the desk and swung his leg back and forth in front of her. "Why did you bite him, then?"

"I bit him because he had his hand over my mouth so I couldn't scream when he took his sticking-out penis from his pants and tried to put my face on it."

There was a long pause. Kate looked at the principal directly in spite of her embarrassment. He was flushed.

"Did you say 'penis'?" he asked.

"I did," she said.

"We do not use bad words in a Quaker school," the principal said in a fallen voice. He marched her into the bathroom, locked her arms behind her and washed her mouth out with a bar of Ivory soap. Then he sent her to lunch.

"Watch your language in the future," he said.

She went to the girls' room and washed the rest of the bitter taste of Ivory soap away, went through the corridor, out the side door to the playing fields, and seeing in the distance a route of escape between two enormous elm trees, crossed the playground and slipped away.

Prudential, standing on the front porch of Miracle's cottage, saw Kate walk down the hill and up the driveway to Skunk Farm.

"Why are you looking at me with your fiery eyes?" Kate asked as they met at the top of the drive. "Hoping I'll drop dead?"

"If I wanted you to die, I'd put a bullet in your heart, not pins," Prudential said.

Prudential looked larger than she was and vivid with her purple lipstick and chocolate skin.

Kate stopped beside her.

"At least I quit school today," Kate said.

"Quit?"

"Quit."

"Forever?"

"Probably forever," Kate said.

She had no thought to tell Prudential what had happened, no plan to tell anyone, even her mother, certainly not Prudential, but the news of Pole Trickett and the principal of Langley Friends flew out before she had a chance to clip it.

She sat down next to Prudential in the high grass between the road and the main house, hidden by the tall yellow stalks. They were extremely quiet. Their bodies touched along the arms and thighs, their bony knees aligned as if such order in presentation were intentional. The day was hot as summer and too bright to see without squinting, so objects slid through an envelope of space between their eyelids. They did not look at one another, but the field was alive with secrets like the airborne feathers of dandelions.

"So now you know everything," Kate said.

Her trouble with Pole Trickett had sealed their friendship.

"I had no idea that kind of misfortune could happen to a white girl." Prudential was subdued.

"Then you don't know much," Kate said matter-of-factly. "Misfortunes happen to everyone. Even in America."

On the drive home from Censorship that afternoon, longer than usual because of an accident on Chain Bridge Road, an uninvited story came to Charley Fletcher from the dark side of his imagination.

It was winter in Minneapolis, early in 1941. Lara was despondent. Her work as an actress had been put aside as the country seemed more and more likely to be caught up in the war, and they could not make a baby. In all probability she was not pregnant because of him, but they did not discuss it. In January she met Tom Elliot for the first time.

In the slow-moving traffic across Chain Bridge, Charley actually could see Lara in the lavender wool dress he loved to see her wear with a loose skirt that fell over her hips and moved gracefully when she walked.

"You have enchanted me," Tom Elliot said to her when she leaned over his chair at the party to tell him goodnight. "Enchanted" was the kind of word Tom Elliot would use. An Eastern word.

He called Lara at home and asked her would she like to go to a Danish restaurant he knew about in St. Paul for lunch.

"I called at lunch," Charley said that night. "Where were you?"

"Marketing," she replied. "And then I stopped by to see Louisa's new baby and took her a present."

She planned to see Tom Elliot every Wednesday.

"I'm going to be taking dance at the university on Wednesdays," she lied to Charley. "I want to be ready to act again."

The last scene of his imagined story was January 1942. Tom took her to a Danish restaurant again before he left for the war. They spoke of Charley.

"I find it odd he doesn't want to go overseas," Tom said.

Lara shook her head.

"He was turned down by the army."

"You're sure?" Tom asked.

"Quite sure."

"He told you?"

"I know him very well," she said.

Nights he lay awake with Lara sleeping next to him and rehearsed from memory their last two years, trying to name the moment they had lost each other.

The year before Sam was conceived, his mother had come for Christmas. The problem between them had started then, he thought—perhaps three days into her visit. One night, Charley had turned cold with Lara—not simply impotent but cold with unfamiliar anger.

"You expect too much," he had said to Lara the following morning.

"What do you mean?" she asked, bewildered.

"Just that. You want more from me than I have to give."

"I'm sorry." she said. "I did not know I was asking."

Chagrined, he had sent her flowers that day, carnations —with a note: "Forgive the stupid behavior of a mule who passed through your life this morning. Charley."

But that was the beginning and gradually they became foreign visitors to one another's lives. Weeks would go by and he could not make love. He'd lie on his side, his back to her, and listen to her secret weeping.

In January she met Tom Elliot, and by late February she no longer reached out for him. In fact she seemed curiously happy for a woman whose life was diminished. She wanted a baby.

"What if we can't?" he had asked, full of anxiety.

"Then we can't. But try, darling. Let's try."

They did. Through the spring and into the summer, he had made love to her three times, perhaps, no more.

At first when she told him she was pregnant, he could not believe his good fortune. And then of course he began to wonder whose child it was she carried, since certainly the chance the child was his seemed unlikely. Possible, he persuaded himself, but unlikely. That was the summer before Pearl Harbor—before the news from the army finished him like the blight of a fast-growing tumor cutting off his blood supply.

He could not stand to let her out of his sight. He called her from the office, from public telephones all over Minneapolis, several times a day. He was outraged if she didn't answer.

One evening in late January, just before he left for Washington, he came home to find her dressed as she used to dress for dinner with the table set in the window.

"What is happening, Charley? It is as if we have caught a disease."

"I don't know." He did not tell her he had been turned down by the army, but he had been thinking, night after night unable to sleep, about his mother's visit and why their lives had changed then.

"I remember your mother talked about your father and how he'd been a failure from the start, not even a satisfactory miner, she said—always sick from it—and how you were born with a great gift."

"Yes, I suppose she did. She always talked that way about my father and also about me."

"Well, I would have hated that responsibility," Lara said. "Nothing was expected of me whatsoever. Except to be polite and perhaps a mother."

He had been thinking what a familiar burden his mother's hopes for him had been. It struck him that especially in America where hopes run loose, mothers, disappointed by the failures of their husbands, fix their own futures on their sons, blow them into giants.

"Some giant," he had said to Lara after he told her what he had been thinking.

She ran her fingers through his hair. "Not to worry," she said sweetly. "We'll fix this."

When Charley arrived at Skunk Farm, Moses was plowing the main field. Upstairs, Prudential helped Kate unpack the clothes she had packed for Denmark as if they had been easy with one another, the best of friends, for years.

"I was planning to go to Italy this morning," Kate said. "But I've changed my mind."

"I'm going to Italy too," Prudential said. "After New York."

Very late, after the children were put to bed, Lara and Charley ate. They sat across from each other on kitchen stools at the counter where Miracle worked.

"Miracle had a fainting spell, that's why I cooked," Lara said at last. "I wish I could cook more often."

"You can cook whenever you wish."

"It's not cooking, of course." She brushed her hair out of her face, pulled it behind her ears. Exhausted as she was now, her gestures were childlike—the way she rubbed her eyes and held her small chin in her hands. He found her unbearably beautiful.

"Why didn't you call today?" she asked. "I was very worried."

He got himself a second bourbon, a strong one without ice. He had given no thought to this conversation, although certainly he knew he would have to tell her, straight out, simply, and attend to her reaction.

"Tom Elliot is dead," he would say, and she would reveal herself.

"Tell me what Kate was doing home in the middle of the day," he asked instead.

"Something happened at school. She won't tell me." She brushed her hand across the top of his. "Something unpleasant or she would have told me. Now tell me why you didn't call."

"I got to the office at the usual time." He lit a cigarette. "Generally in the morning the wire service pages are on my desk, and often when I sit down to call you I glance at the top page, which I did this morning. The first item at the top of the page was a report that Tom Elliot had been killed when the plane in which he was traveling crashed over Bonn."

He finished the bourbon and felt it spinning in his hands and legs.

114

"Yes?"

She had not heard him correctly.

"Tom Elliot is dead." He got up and poured himself another drink and as quickly poured it out. He should not lose his senses tonight. He did not trust his anger. It seemed complete, systemic, like blood poisoning.

"I didn't call you this morning because as soon as I picked up the phone I read on the UP wire that Tom Elliot had been killed."

She did not respond at all.

"I called his mother and spoke with his brother, with whom I went to college, and my mother, frankly so she wouldn't hear about it and call you before I had a chance to tell you myself. I have arranged to have his body sent home by the army quickly. Then I called his mother again because he is eligible to be buried in Arlington Cemetery to ask her did she want him buried there and she said yes." He was shouting. "I did everything I could do."

"You're shouting." She got up, put away the leftover chicken, wiped off the table, turned off the overhead light. "I am too tired."

Upstairs she checked on Sam and Kate. It was only nine, but she was too tired even to read. Out back the small cottages sparkled with lights and she could just make out the figure of Prudential hurrying down the lace path home. The lights in her bedroom were out. She undressed in the dark and slid into her side of the bed, glad for the coolness of the sheets, for the lightness of the summer cotton blanket skimming her body, for the merciful darkness.

She had not imagined Tom Elliot's death as she used to see Charley's at night before she slept in the weeks before he decided to go to Censorship instead of the war. Somehow Tom had always seemed too privileged for death.

"Lara?" Charley came into the bedroom.

"Please don't turn on the light, darling," she said.

"I'm sorry about Tom."

He undressed, dropped his clothes on the white wicker chaise and climbed naked into bed.

"Of course." Her voice was crisp and English. "But it isn't personal."

She lay very still on her side of the bed, and he waited for her to reach over and touch him as she did, almost always and sweetly, in spite of their estrangement.

"When I read about Tom, I left the office and went behind the Capitol into the slums."

He reached over and touched her eyes, which were dry.

"The only thing of interest was a child sitting beside his father who had been killed either by his wife or an overdose of drugs."

She turned on her side to face him.

"The police did nothing. I spoke to them."

He lifted his head to look at her.

"I'm thinking of going to war," he said.

She was still awake. Her breath had not sunk to the deep accidental breath of sleep.

"Lara?"

But she would not acknowledge him.

He waited for sleep but his mind turned too quickly, and finally, agitated and angry, he got out of bed, went into the room where Sam was sleeping and turned on the light.

Sam slept on his stomach, his small plump arms flat at his side, and Charley lifted him, put him on his back, pulled the bed over next to the light. He realized he had never actually looked at his son—examined him, that is, considering his features one at a time. Now he noted the broad long forehead, the nose still too formless to make out its eventual shape, the way the eyebrows formed straight and thick above the eyes. The eyes caught his attention. They were small and close together—"the funny little eyes of an aristocrat," Lara had said when Sam was born. And Charley looked at him now with the clear memory of Tom Elliot's fine-boned handsome and aristocratic face in mind.

Sam whimpered, and Charley rocked him until he settled, put him in the crib on his belly and patted his tiny back. A furious plan came over him. He would hide the baby. In the morning when Lara went to the room to nurse him, he'd be gone. He didn't wish the baby harm exactly. Although his feelings for him were locked in cold storage, available only as a memory of emotion. He simply wanted Lara to pay for his losses.

In New Philadelphia before high school, he had played football. What he'd loved about the season, especially when he was younger, was the release of furies when his body was hammered to the ground by the tackles. He needed contact now.

Downstairs, he drank another bourbon, lit a cigarette and went out back.

Moses lay on the outside of the bed, fully dressed, next to Miracle, who read him the letter her sister had written.

" 'I am having a time with Holiday who's taken a dislike to her father and threatens to run off to Prudential,' " she read.

"Uh huh," Moses said.

"Maybe she can come up for Christmas."

"That'll be fine," Moses said. "Just fine."

"She could sleep in Prudential's room," Miracle said.

"We'll invite her," Moses said.

He could not get Lara Fletcher out of mind. He saw her in parts—her small face that afternoon—her delicate bird hand when she touched him quickly, and the color of her eyes, which were intensely blue. He had always thought of blue as a cool color for eyes, a white woman's insipid color; but her eyes were not cool.

"You listening to me, Moses?" Miracle asked. "Or wandering?"

"I'm not wandering."

"Then listen and don't go wishing for things you cannot have."

He pulled her over, kissed her wetly on the lips. Somehow Miracle's moral axioms, straight out of the Southern oral Bible, always went straight to the heart.

"I'm wishing for you," he sang in her ear. She pushed him away.

"So what are we going to name this baby if it's a girl?"

"It's going to be a boy. I can feel it. And we'll call him Simon Peter Bellows unless he's too colored for the name Simon."

"What's too colored?"

"I'll tell you when I see him."

"The color of me?" Miracle was testy.

"No, Miracle. The color of trouble."

Miracle sat up. "You hear what I hear?"

"I hear knocking."

"I hear a fight and Guy's voice."

Aida started the fight. The night was cool and clear, and she sat with Guy on the porch of their cottage and agitated.

"Our lives have gone straight downhill since we moved out back again," she said. "You drink too much. I drink too much. I haven't changed the sheets in our bedroom for a month, and today is the first time I can remember bringing flowers in the living room and that's because Prudential brought them for my birthday."

"What birthday?"

"What birthday do you think? My birthday today."

"It's not your birthday today," Guy said.

"I'm losing jobs. Soon I won't be able to iron for anybody but you."

"Then you better get hold of yourself, Aida."

"Once your balloon is blown up and sailing, you can't shoot it down and expect it to fly again." She reached over and took hold of Guy. "Besides, you don't do it anymore. You're too tired on the weekdays and too drunk on Saturdays."

"Mind your own business."

"That is my business," she said. "It's my very own business."

She saw Charley Fletcher before Guy did. He was coming down the path in the dark without a flashlight.

"Evening, Charley," she called out in her sassy voice. "Good evening to you."

"What Charley?" Guy stared.

"What Charley do you think would be walking around the farm tonight?"

"Mr. Fletcher." Guy took her by the wrist. "You call him Mr. Fletcher and mind where you're familiar."

"Don't touch me," she screamed.

And then she went after him like a fevered cat, biting

him on the wrist where he held her, pulling his hair, beating his chest. Charley rushed up on the porch and took hold of Guy. Whimpering, Aida slipped into the blueberry bush by the side of the house. Charley reached out to help her.

"She can help herself," Guy said. He straightened and brushed off his pants. "Get up, Aida, and go inside."

"I'm very sorry," Charley said, recognizing that he had intruded. "I just came out back to see Moses." He stepped off the porch. "Good night."

"John Spencer never came out back," Guy said. "Not in all the years he owned this house."

Charley wiped the end of his nose, which was bleeding from where Aida's arm had flown against him.

"John Spencer is dead," Charley said and headed towards the main house.

Moses had gone as far as his front porch and seen that the scuffle with Guy wasn't serious. Then he went in, got a beer from the icebox and went back upstairs.

"Mr. Fletcher again," Moses said to Miracle when he went back into the bedroom. "Messing with a fight between Aida and Guy."

He lay back down next to Miracle.

"He must want World War II right here on the farm," he said, reaching for her. "And he's probably going to have it."

"He's a peaceable man, Moses, and you know it. He tries hard."

"He's the kind of peaceable man interested in war," Moses said. "Now go to sleep or you'll have another spell on the road to Damascus." He took Miracle's hand and kissed the fingers.

There was a full yellow moon just over the main house and the night was perfectly still.

Charley Fletcher turned off the kitchen light and felt his way through the corridor, up the steps, past Sam's room and Kate's. Lara was awake. He could tell when he walked in, but she didn't speak until he lifted the covers and climbed in beside her.

"Charley?"

"Yes."

"What was he doing when he died?"

Charley turned on his side away from her.

"The newspaper account said he was on a mission, so I assume he was taking pictures. Why?"

She reached over and pulled him towards her.

"Why is it you don't believe I love you?" she asked into his shoulder.

"What does that have to do with the death of Tom Elliot?" he asked.

"Everything," Lara said simply.

Through the still autumn night, they slept together fitfully, doomed like the soldiers in Europe, scrambling for a dream of safety, camouflaging their losses.

BOOK THREE

The Birth of the Blues

December Twenty-Fifth, 1942

The snow started Christmas Eve and fell in soft sheets through the night. By morning, the farm was hushed by a goose-down comforter stretched to the horizon—isolated from the sounds of the ordinary world.

The road was gone. The driveway. The path out back. The thick wet snow bent the limbs of trees, the large azaleas and boxwoods, dipped the telephone and electric wires and locked the rope swing outside the kitchen window in place. By Christmas morning, there were no signs of its diminishing.

In the middle of the night Prudential started pains. They were long and dull and did not seem like the sick pain her mother had described as labor. She was hot with fever. For hours, she lay in her bed and waited for something to happen.

Something was supposed to happen, the doctor at Fairfax Hospital had told her. Intermittent pains closer to as time passed, he'd said to her, talking as if he spoke a foreign language because she was Negro and thirteen besides, so she told Miracle later.

"You don't know anything about conditions," she told him one day when he was explaining labor to her.

"I know about pregnancy," he said.

"But you don't know anything about conditions of lives," she said.

He told her not to be impudent or he wouldn't take care of her; she said that was fine with her. But Lara insisted the baby be born in a hospital; Prudential was so young to give birth.

At dawn, quivering as if a swarm of maggots rioted just under the skin of her belly, she finally called Miracle.

"Something isn't right," she said.

"We'll make it right." Miracle put a cold wet cloth on her head and soaked a towel in the bathtub for her legs.

"Don't fuss, darling," she said, fluffing the pillow where Prudential lay. "Sometimes you get fever with a baby. I read about that once in a magazine."

Miracle knew about fever with a baby. Not from a magazine either, she didn't read magazines, but because her own sister Gayla had died and so had her baby of just that thing. No one, not even the hospital, could have saved them, according to Miracle's mother. As it was, Gayla never got to the hospital. The baby was born in her living room in Leesburg and didn't even whimper—born and died in a single moment. Gayla herself slid away slowly, first crazy in the head for days and then silent all one Tuesday until her breathing stopped.

"So you tell me exactly how you feel and I'll go up to the main house and call the doctor in Fairfax," Miracle said.

"I feel like a truck is parked on my belly." Prudential put her hands slowly over her stomach. "And the baby's still." She sat up on her elbow.

"What time is it, Aunt Miracle?"

"Just beginning to come up day."

"It feels so quiet."

"It snowed last night." Miracle went to the window. "It's still too dusty out for me to tell how much."

"It feels like we've been snowed out of civilization," Prudential said. "Maybe you should get Moses."

• • •

124

"She has the same thing that happened to Gayla," Miracle whispered in Moses' ear. "I can tell. She's burning up."

Moses got up quickly, dressed and opened the curtains in their bedroom. The morning light had just begun to turn the corner and the snow was deep, far up the elm trunks, deeper than any snow he had seen.

"I'll get the truck," he said to Miracle. "But it's not going to be easy with this weather."

She stood next to the window.

"You think the roads aren't passable," Miracle said. "That's what you think, isn't it?"

"Likely the roads aren't passable."

"You can telephone from the main house. Even if we can't get to the hospital, the doctor can tell us what to do."

"That's right. You give me the number and I'll call. And Miracle." Moses took her by the shoulders. "We don't know what happened to Gayla."

"We know she died of having a baby."

"We don't know how it happened."

Miracle sat down on the end of the bed.

"Is your pressure up?" he asked.

"No," she lied, although the pulse was beating hard in her temples, the blood coursing like it did.

"Then what are you thinking?"

"I'm thinking that I want this moment of our baby coming to go smooth and natural and perfect like the birth of the blues."

Aida woke up early before the light and took a bath. She lay in the tub with the water up to her chin and watched the sun rise out of the window on a snow the likes of which she had never seen before.

"What are you taking a bath in the dark for, Aida Sue?" Guy called from his bed. "You know I hate the sound of dripping water when I'm trying to sleep."

"I'm taking a bath to get clean on Christmas morning and start this day of the birth of our Lord Jesus Christ out well."

Guy was silent.

"Did you hear me, Guy?"

"All I can hear is dripping water."

She got out of the tub, toweled off and looked at herself in the mirror over the sink. She was acceptable for thirty, she thought. A nice high rear end, snappy-looking. Long legs, and her bosoms stuck out without hanging full as they were. Her face was going under from drinking, however, and that was the truth. It had occurred to her on Christmas Eve when Moses said he was disappointed in her for falling to pieces just because she had moved out back again that she should take hold and act sensible like Miracle did and not wish for things that couldn't be.

She wrapped a towel around her and climbed into bed with Guy.

"So Merry Christmas, Guy Bellows. I got you a present wrapped downstairs in the kitchen just waiting."

Guy opened his eyes. "You did?"

"I did. I got it last week when I was in town working for Mrs. Burns and you're going to be very pleased. Did you forget?"

"Forget what?"

"Christmas." She sat up on her elbow and looked at him.

"I didn't forget Christmas," Guy said quietly.

"But you did forget a present."

He was silent.

Aida lay back on her pillow. "I guess it was only Miracle who reminded you to get a present anyway," she said.

"Once. Miracle only had to remind me once," Guy said sadly.

Aida was almost asleep again, wrapped in a towel, Guy lying with his back to her, when they heard the loud banging of Miracle on the front door.

Aida pulled herself out of bed.

"It's Prudential's time and she's not doing well," Miracle called from downstairs.

Aida put on a skirt and sweater and her high rubber boots and went after Miracle along the path Moses had made.

"The roads are probably closed straight through," Miracle said. "So we can't get her to the doctors."

"How can you tell she's doing poorly?" Aida asked, scrambling on the porch after Miracle.

"You'll see."

The house was silent when they went inside and Miracle put her fingers to her lips.

"We have to keep our wits, Aida."

"I'll keep my wits," Aida replied.

The telephone at the main house was out, and the electricity. Charley tried to make a fire in the living room but the wood was too wet to catch.

"It's quiet as death," he said when he came inside with wood to dry by the stove in the kitchen. He kicked the snow off his boots and sat down at the table with Kate. Lara stood at the window.

"I just saw Moses coming towards the house and the snow is up to his thighs." She wiped the fog off the cold window glass. "Now, see him? He's brushing the snow off his truck."

They watched him get into the driver's seat and start the engine.

"Even if he can get the truck started, the snow's too high to move in this storm," Charley said.

But the truck wouldn't start anyway. Moses tried several times. Then he made his way through the snow to the back door.

"My truck won't start," he said. "I need to use your phone to make a call."

"The phone is out," Charley said. "And the electricity."

"Out?"

"Weighing down the lines, I guess," Charley said.

"Maybe there's one working across the road."

"I doubt it. Besides, it'd be too hard to even get across the road. Sit down," he said to Moses. "Have a cup of coffee."

"I can't," Moses said. "I've come because Prudential's in a bad way."

Kate looked up from her cereal. "What do you mean, a bad way?"

"She's burning up. And her eyes have the curtain drawn like they get when you're in a bad way." Moses took a cup of coffee standing.

"My grandfather's eyes were glassy when he was dead. I saw them."

Charley Fletcher put his jacket on and wool cap.

"We'll come," he said. "We'll all come out back."

Moses hesitated.

Lara put her hand on his arm. "Let me dress Sammy and put on a coat," she said.

"I'll just get Prudential's Christmas present and bring it with me," Kate said.

On one of the days they had had enough gasoline to go to Washington, Kate had bought Prudential a dress with the money she had gotten for her birthday. It was soft pink with long sleeves, a square neck and pleats around the waist. There was a rose belt and an actual dark plum rose buckle which fastened at the front. Prudential would like the rose buckle in particular.

"I'll save this for parties in New York," she'd say.

"But darling," Lara said. "What will Prudential do with such a dress?"

"Wear it to church," Kate said.

"She doesn't go to church."

Kate shrugged. "She didn't used to but she's thinking of starting again."

"I see," Lara said. "And all this money."

"The money is mine."

"I thought you might buy something for yourself."

Kate counted out her money for the saleslady. "I already have everything I want."

Kate had kept the present under the bed, hidden from Prudential, who spent afternoons in her room. At night she'd take the dress out of the box, hold it up to the front of her and walk back and forth before the long mirror in the bathroom. Then Christmas Eve after the presents with her family, always exchanged the night before Christmas, she wrapped Prudential's present in silver paper and made a card. "To Prudential Magnolia Wellington, my only true friend in the world forever till I die. Kate." She considered scratching out "till I die" since its inclusion might be portentous but she did not want to damage the perfect card so she drew a tiny rose at the bottom, put on her mother's red lipstick and kissed the corner of the card beside her name.

"It's like we were born together, halved out of the same eggshell," Prudential said to Kate, "and just last month we hated each other to death. Moses says it's very slippery to be alive and he's right."

Their friendship was deep. She was particularly careful not to let Moses know that the love she felt for Kate Bergmann was powerful as it was because he might disapprove of her loving a white girl. But that's what it was—so powerful she woke up in the morning on wings.

After the incident with Pole Trickett, Kate did not go back to Langley Friends School. First she had bronchitis and then the stomach flu and that took two weeks. Twice she hid in the barn on Monday morning until the bus had come and gone and then it was Thanksgiving. It didn't seem sensible to Lara to force her to go to school between Thanksgiving and Christmas. So Kate and Prudential had long days together.

In the morning they had school in the dining room of the main house. They did most of the courses for seventh grade at Langley Friends School during the month of November. They did Danish and some French and piano. They had lunch together in the kitchen of the main house and talked to Miracle about babies, or they sat side by side leaning against the wall behind Kate's bed and told secrets.

By December, Kate had told all of her secrets. She had even invented a few because Prudential had so many more and dangerous ones.

"But you haven't told me everything," Kate said to her one afternoon.

"I can't," Prudential said.

"But I'll never meet him," Kate said. "You make me feel as if we're not complete friends."

"We're complete friends," Prudential said. "But if I told you who he is, you'd know too much."

And there was no changing her mind.

In the afternoons, they looked for John Spencer.

Miracle had had two more spells since October. The day Guy butchered pigs for the winter, she had gone to Vruels' with Moses to get shells for Guy and borax. On her way out of the store, she saw John Spencer standing about fifty yards away near the Hamishes' mailbox. She was struck later by how long his hair was and dark his skin, but she kept her composure. She got into the car without a word to Moses about her nerves or blood pressure and watched his face as he drove by John Spencer without a flicker of acknowledgment.

The second time, she was in her own kitchen doing supper and she thanked the Lord that Moses was in Washington, D.C., collecting Charley Fletcher, whose car had broken down, because when she saw John Spencer this time, she screamed out loud.

It was dusk. She was sitting at the kitchen table peeling potatoes and there was John Spencer just to the right of Moses' garden with his back to her.

Prudential ran downstairs.

"What's wrong?" she called.

"There he is," Miracle said in a voice she hoped was butter-smooth and strong. "Mr. John Spencer in our garden." She got up and stirred a pot of navy beans. "You look for yourself."

Prudential looked.

"I don't see him, Aunt Miracle," she said.

"Look to the right," Miracle said.

"There's no one in the garden now that I can see."

Miracle stood beside her. "Why, he was there," she said. "I could have sworn he was right there just a minute ago." But he was certainly gone now.

Kate put on heavy boots, a coat of Charley's, a wool hat, stuffed the present under her coat and followed Moses out back.

The path cleared by Moses earlier had formed a snow

wall which remained intact but the sky was dark gray and the snow still fell steadily. The walk out back was slow and difficult.

Charley followed close on Moses' heels, warmed by the larger man's body, wonderfully secure.

Through the weeks after Tom Elliot died, Lara had become exquisitely polite, and formal. She would inquire at dinner after events at work, elicit information and listen attentively. She was only interested in details.

"You are driving me crazy," he said to her.

She would not have personal conversations.

"Maybe we should divorce," she said. "If I am driving you crazy, we should."

"We won't divorce," he replied.

Once he threw a casserole of macaroni and cheese at her which struck and covered her dress with noodles and thick yellow cheese sauce. Coolly she had unzipped the zipper of her dress, stepped out of it and walked upstairs in her slip.

In early December, he had slapped her while they sat at dinner. At the time they had been discussing the invasion of North Africa, when out of the blue he said, "What happened between you and Tom Elliot?"

He had not planned to say anything about Tom Elliot. But he couldn't help himself.

"What happened, Lara?"

She had reached for the blue crockery water pitcher. "Would you care for more water, darling?" she asked. He had slapped her then.

They had eaten in silence and read that night in separate rooms. After midnight, he went in to apologize and she was sitting up in bed with the light off.

"You have frozen me out, Lara." He sat beside her.

"In self-defense," she said. "I am not a frozen woman."

"No," he said sadly. "You're not."

"I wish you would see a doctor, Charley. Our lovely lives are getting ruined."

He turned on a small light and hung up his clothes.

"I will see a doctor," he said.

• • •

He had not. He couldn't imagine what he would say to a doctor. Besides he came from a family, from a part of the country, where crazy people are locked in attics and ordinary people wrap their crippled souls in private and grimly keep their secrets to themselves.

They had to move carefully through the snow. Occasionally Charley did not stop in time to keep from falling against the back of Moses. Moses would straighten so Charley could get his balance. And Charley was struck by an unfamiliar longing that contact awakened, not sexual at all but rather a longing for a father twice his own size, strong enough to elude him.

At birth, he had overtaken his own father, and much as he liked to invent a man of equal proportions, facts were facts and his father had been a diminished man. He was suddenly flooded with a kind of happiness when the magic of some unspecific possibility explodes unexpectedly. He saw the lot of them—Moses, then Charley, then Lara and the baby and Kate—between the snow wall thrown up on a movie screen in black and white, a story of the social history of America for Fox Movietone News played on a Saturday in theaters all over America—Milwaukee, even New Philadelphia. After the war he'd write a book, he decided, third-person but his own story: "In 1942, Charley Fletcher and his wife Lara moved to a farm in Vienna, Virginia, and began a life in equal community with a family of colored people called Bellows."

His mind swung to another picture, concealed even from his daydreams for months, since before Sam got started. He saw himself take Lara wearing her lavender wool dress and make love to her under the canopy of their four-poster bed. Now, he stopped on the path and kissed her snow-frosted lips.

At Guy's cottage, Moses stopped and called.

"I know about Prudential." Guy came to the door. "Aida's gone on over."

"We're on our way," Moses said.

"I'll be there soon as I put on my trousers," Guy said. But he had another plan in mind.

In the kitchen, Guy saw the present Aida had for him wrapped in red poinsettia paper and white ribbon done into a huge bow. "To my man, Guy," the card said.

In the main house, in the fine bedroom where he and Aida had lived those seven years of John Spencer's disappearance, before the people in Vienna had decided he was dead, there was a mirror on the door of the closet, tall as Guy was, in a thin gold frame with colored daisies in the corners for decoration. The first morning after they moved to the main house, Aida had stood in front of that mirror in a long silk blue slip, the color of a robin's egg, rich against her brown skin, and said to Guy in a voice which had the song of wonder to it, "In this mirror, I'm a pretty woman, Guy Bellows. And I never in all my life been a pretty woman before."

He put on his trousers, his heavy work jacket and his papa's hat pulled down to his eyebrows and headed through the snow wall towards the main house. It was his first time since he'd moved out back.

"I won't go," he had told Miracle. "Never again until it's mine."

"It won't ever be yours again and you know it, so don't be mule-eared and thank the Lord you had a day on earth when the sky rained pennies," Miracle said.

"I don't have a mind to be thankful," Guy said. "I was born unthankful."

He went in the back door through the kitchen. There was a different look to the living room and some of the furniture belonged to the Fletchers but the place still smelled the same as it always had when Guy came home from work in the evening, went in the front door, took off his boots so as not to dirty the rugs and took his chair by the fireplace in the living room blazing with sufficient warmth for an army platoon.

He went up the back stairs. He and Aida always went up the back stairs because their bedroom was just to the left. It made them feel particularly rich to have their own staircase. The room at the top had not been changed at all since they had moved out back but it didn't seem to Guy like their room any longer. After the first night in the main house, they had moved the beds together and put rose chintz pillows from the couch under the window on the bed.

"So it looks like we're sleeping in a flower garden," Aida had said.

There was the spot on the hooked rug where Aida had spilled her pink nail polish when she was doing her toes one evening.

"Mrs. Cash tells me the ladies in the movies are doing their toes now," she told Guy.

There was the broken plaster on the wall as evidence of the only fight they had had in all the years in the main house and that over a simple matter of whether Aida had run the colors in Guy's new work shirt.

The mirror was still screwed to the closet door, and Guy unscrewed it. Then he walked to the back of the house. The master bedroom where Moses and Miracle had slept had been made all white now by the lady of the house but the dressing table was there. Miracle had never used it but from time to time Aida would sit in front of the mirror and try on lipsticks, doing her lips in stripes in all the colors of red. There was a basket with makeup on the dressing table. Guy took a tube of Cherry Red lipstick, put it in his pocket and went down the main staircase with the head-to-toe mirror under his arm.

In his own cottage, he set the mirror up on the wall at the bottom of the bed so Aida would see herself first off in the morning and when she went to sleep at night. With the tube of lipstick, he wrote: "To my pretty woman."

Downstairs in the kitchen of the Bellows cottage, sweet with the smell of turkey roasting, Miracle snapped the beans and cut the potatoes. Around the long table, the adults discussed what could be done with Prudential. It was almost noon and the storm continued with a surprising steadiness. Already the path to the main house was covered with inches of new soft snow. The snow wall had

134

softened and chipped. They were probably marooned, Charley Fletcher said.

Prudential was delirious.

"Bring me Papa on a platter," she sang wet against her pillow, her voice frail as a winter sparrow. "Let me carve him for the devil's Christmas supper."

Kate sat solemnly at the end of the bed.

"I am boiling," Prudential called out. "Set to fire and flying to hell on angel wings. You hear me?"

"I hear you," Kate said.

"Then do something to make the burning stop."

Kate took the cloth, hot on Prudential's forehead, and ran it under cold water again.

"Mama?" Prudential asked, eased by the coolness of the cloth.

"It's Kate." She took Prudential's hand.

"Kate." Prudential considered. Her eyes were closed and her face was drawn, her forehead folded in narrow lines of pain, and with her free hand she pushed hard at the belly of baby stuck on the top of her child's body as if it were in her way and she wanted to throw it on the floor.

Her eyes fluttered open. "I think the baby's dead and rotting in my belly," she said. "Get it out of me." She squeezed Kate's hand too tight. "Tell Moses to come get it out of me."

Moses would not go upstairs. Miracle, Aida and Lara ran up to the small bedroom and found Prudential half out of bed.

All they knew to do was fuss over her and so they did, patting her, combing her hair, washing her face, changing her gown.

"The baby's dead," Prudential said. "I want you to get it out."

"Why do you think it's dead?" Lara asked.

"Because it's heavy as lead and still."

"Babies go still right before they come," Lara said.

"This is not normal," Prudential said. "I know this isn't normal."

Kate crawled between the women and sat down on the

bed next to Prudential. "Just lie down," she said. "Lie down and hush and it will be over soon."

Moses wanted the men to make their way out back to the road parallel to Route 7 where the Godfrys' farm, set low, might have been sheltered from the force of the storm and there they could find a telephone.

"We can't just set all day like we're waiting for death," he said.

"Prudential's too high and mighty for dying," Guy said. But he was worried and so was Moses, glad to have something to do besides lie on the couch in the living room with the fire spitting from the wetness of the logs.

Charley called upstairs to say they were leaving and would be back soon.

When the pains started in earnest, Miracle was in her room and Prudential screamed out with such a howl, as Aida said, you'd have thought a wolf had bitten off the bottom half of her.

Kate flew to Miracle's room pale-faced.

"Something horrible is happening," she said.

Aida threw up the bedroom window and called to the men just as they left the cottage.

"The baby's coming," she said. It was too gray to see them.

"Guy? You hear me?"

"We hear," Moses called back.

He stopped on the front porch and took off his wool cap.

He reached in his pocket and handed the telephone number of the doctor at Fairfax Hospital to Guy. "Tell the doctor about the fever and ask him what we should do."

"Aren't you going to come with us?" Charley asked.

Moses shook his head. "I think I should be here," he said.

He took off his boots in the front hall, hung up his cap and jacket, took a swallow from the bottle of bourbon he'd laid in for Christmas dinner to lighten his mind in case this birth turned to more trouble.

He had never thought to have a child. That had been Miracle's idea from the start and he'd always believed that the absence in her womb had made her susceptible to John Spencer. He had never wanted a baby, certainly not his own flesh and blood repeated down the years to live out back of Elm Grove one more generation. He was perplexed to see Miracle every night fitting out their room for life, knitting sweaters and hats in all the colors of the rainbow. She'd bought a pink plastic rattle and a soft bear with the little money she kept stashed beneath her underwear. And he was moved by her mysterious attention to their future as if this baby would fix in place their wandering desires.

She stood at the head of the stairs with her hands on her hips.

"How is she?" Moses asked. "I sent Guy on over to the Godfrys' farm in case their telephone still works."

"Good." Miracle shook her head. "But Prudential's not good."

"Do you know what you're doing?" he asked.

"I know to cut and tie the cord," she said. "Is there more to know?"

"I only know hogs and cows," Moses said.

He went into the bathroom and washed his hands. When he came out, Miracle was standing off guard at the door to Prudential's room with a sweet expression on her face he recognized, familiar from their childhoods together when she had been safe kept for a Negro girl growing up in the South by a mama whose mind didn't bend to conditions. As a child, Miracle had been full of expectation, untrammeled by history, and he had been struck then by a girl with such simple hope. There was that hope now glossing her pretty face; he kissed her light as petals on the back of her neck.

Out back the land dipped unevenly. There was no path but low bushes unattended and places where the tree roots had broken through the ground, so the travel was difficult under the best of circumstances. Guy, built long with stilt legs and a small torso, unevenly balanced, kept falling, tripping on a root of low bush, slipping on the wet ground, his face pressed into the snow. The back of his neck was damp and under his hat and in his boots. He was bad-tempered and humiliated to fall on land where he'd grown up and should know by heart every impediment. The snow seemed to thicken and sting their faces as they walked against it. The day was darker than it had been at dawn. By the time they got to the bottom of the hill, Guy was already too tired to imagine making it back to the cottage. The baby had probably popped out fine as a fettle already, Guy thought. So what was the use of this trip after all, he thought, not pleased with Moses for staying back and making him travel with Charley Fletcher. Not that he hated Charley Fletcher the way Moses did, though he agreed Mr. Fletcher was a man who didn't know his place and had to be watched. But he was certainly a man who took an interest, and as far as Guy could tell from his thirty years on earth, hardly a man he knew took an interest in a thing outside himself.

"So?" he said finally, stopping at the bottom of the hill. "This is no way to spend Christmas."

They pushed on. The path became flat. The pines were thick and sharp-smelling and cut the strength of the wind. They stopped at a glen at the end of the pine forest, now lost in snow, and looked ahead to the place where the Godfrys' farm should be and was although no more than a shadow on the horizon.

"We should turn back."

Charley shook his head.

"We should go on and hope the telephone works." He wrapped his muffler so it covered his mouth and started off.

"The phone is out," Guy said. "I feel it in my bones."

Guy was right. The phone was out but Mrs. Godfry had remedies. She gave them three bottles of pills—"One should do, and they won't hurt anyway"—one for uremic poisoning which Mr. Godfry had gotten from a rusty nail, one for a urinary-tract infection and one for another part of the insides, she'd forgotten. "Just take them all," she said. Mr. Godfry gave them whiskey to heat them up which they were glad to have and told them a pornographic joke about the Baby Jesus before they started back.

It was almost three when they got to the pine forest. The storm had let up. Far into the heavens, the sun spread a thin yellow line which filtered through the pines and gave the woods a sense of movement. The walk back was easier because the path had been made and they moved in silence.

The hill to the cottage was too slick and steep with snow to make the travel possible alone. Charley grabbed hold of the young saplings, pulled himself up a little at a time, wrapped his leg around a small tree to steady himself, took Guy's hand for support. They continued up the hill slowly that way, both of them thinking it was a long hard trip for nothing.

"How far?" Guy asked from time to time.

"Far enough," Charley said.

Once Charley slipped and fell backwards down the hill and would have gone all the way down if a tree hadn't broken his fall. Guy backed down and pulled him up again.

At some point during the long climb after he had fallen, Charley became uneasy. There was nothing specific—nothing was said and the feeling came and went without a clue to its origin—but he had a sudden sense of incipient danger and looked for signs of anger in Guy Bellows' face, which was absent of any expression.

"On Christmas Day 1942," Charley began in his head when they crested the hill, "Guy Bellows and Charley Fletcher went off in a bad storm to find a doctor for Prudential." His mind rushed to possibilities.

The birth began subterranean, deep in the bowels. And before any one of the women locked in place around the bed could adjust, the baby boy was out, lying on the sheet, between the long bony legs of Prudential Life Insurance, covered with blood thick as plum jelly and arched for combat.

Later, Kate lay next to Prudential, still hot with fever and half sleeping. The house smelled of Christmas, of turkey and pine needles and burning candles. Downstairs she could hear her mother singing Christmas songs in Danish and Aida laughing, and in the room across the hall she heard the deep melodic voices of Moses and Miracle talking and talking to the baby.

It was early evening, just after five. The baby boy was two hours old, swaddled, fed sugar water, since Prudential refused to suckle the child herself. She had looked down at her puffed breasts, large and lined as muskmelons, her rose-tipped nipples, and put her hand up when Miracle brought the baby to her.

"I'm too sick," she said.

She would not look at him.

"It burns like fire when I pee," she said to Miracle. "I could be sick enough to kill the baby."

"You don't have to feed him," Miracle had said. "But you're not that sick anymore."

"Then why do I burn?"

"Mrs. Fletcher thinks you have an infection in the bladder and Guy brought these pills from Mrs. Godfry."

Prudential took one of each pill from Mrs. Godfry, promised Miracle she'd feed the baby later and slept.

"I've been thinking," Prudential said when she opened her eyes. "Maybe I should go to New York now when my stomach flattens out and not go home."

"Or stay here."

"I can't stay here." Prudential said.

Kate bent down and reached under the bed for the Christmas present. "I got you a present to take to New York."

"I don't get presents for Christmas. Only the same lilac talcum from my mama." She sat up on her elbow and opened the present. "I don't want to tear the paper. All these poinsettias." She took off the top of the box. "I've never seen such a dress," she said, suddenly quiet. "This is the kind of dress from fashion magazines." She rubbed the thin cloth through her fingers and along her cheek. She pulled off her nightgown over her head. "I want to put it on."

Kate stood on the bed and pulled the dress over Prudential's head, helped her put the arms through the sleeves.

"There," she said.

"Now get me the looking glass from the bureau," Prudential said. "And stand with it at the end of the bed so I can see myself."

Kate stood at the end of the bed.

"Maybe I need some lipstick and color on my cheeks too. And my hair. Do you think you could do something about my hair?" She pulled the dress down to her hips.

She got lipstick from Miracle and a brush and plaited Prudential's hair.

"See the belt?" Kate said.

"I see," Prudential said and kissed the middle of the rose. "I never have seen such a belt in my life even in the movie magazines. So you think I look presentable?"

"You look beautiful," Kate said. "You look beautiful as a movie star."

"Now get Moses to come see how I look for Christmas dinner," Prudential said.

Miracle couldn't take her eyes off the baby, who for all the world looked to Moses like any Negro baby he'd ever seen, only there was something a little strange about his face, familiar, something he'd seen before and could not identify.

"So you think he looks right for the name Simon Peter?" Miracle asked.

"I do," Moses said.

The snow had stopped but the day had passed through without light; it was evening again and the room was thick with the sadness of winter. Moses was disturbed. He was too clear-minded a man to be easily depressed, but a certain loneliness had overtaken him since morning and he felt inconsolable.

"Look at his hands, Moses. His papa must have been big

—big as barns, big as you." She unwound the tight fist and stretched his fingers against her own. She unwrapped him, looked at his fat thighs, his taut belly where she'd cut and tied the cord, neat as a pin. Then she wrapped him up again in the blue knit blanket she had knitted for him and put him on his side in the bassinet.

"He is lovely, isn't he, Moses." She sat down on the bed beside him. "Only he doesn't cry." She had noticed that from the start. He had cried, bellowed, when she got the mucus out of his throat, but not since and that was two hours. Too much silence for a baby, she thought.

"You should be pleased he doesn't cry," Moses said.

Miracle shook her head. "He ought to have something to say in protest to coming into this world."

Kate looked at Prudential with fascination. She could not believe she had witnessed the birth of a baby out of the fragile body of a child her own age, her most dear friend. She touched Prudential's belly lightly.

"What are you looking at me for?" Prudential asked, her eyes tight shut.

"To see if you're the same as you were," Kate said.

"The same," Prudential said. "The same today, tomorrow and the next day." She opened her eyes. "Except for the burning when I pee. Did the blood make you sick?"

"I didn't look," Kate said.

"Did you look at the baby?"

"I held him. You saw. He's sweet-looking."

"I couldn't look at him in case the face of his papa would be shining up at me."

The singing from the kitchen filled the small cottage. A table long enough for everyone had been set with a lace cloth and silver from John Spencer's and the table stretched from one end of the living room to the kitchen. Guy carried Prudential in her new dress and put her at the head of the table and they all sat—Kate next to Prudential, then Moses and Lara and Charley and Miracle and Guy and Aida—in a room lit only by candles so their faces in shadow were all dark and similar, familiar faces—warmed by the bourbon, by the rich smell of baking apples, by the melodies of their own voices.

Late in the evening, Lara did the Christmas story.

"After all," she said. "We have a baby."

They moved the furniture and Miracle put the bassinet with the silent baby next to the fireplace.

"You be Mary," Lara said to Miracle.

"But Prudential's the mama," Miracle said, nevertheless taking her place in the chair Lara had brought for her.

"You are the mama now and forever, Aunt Miracle," Prudential said. "I am a girl again and an angel in this play."

"And you be Joseph," Lara said to Moses. "You just stand there next to Miracle."

"I can't stand," Moses said. "I'll have to sit down for Joseph." And they all laughed, merry with drink.

"Guy and I will be shepherds," Charley said.

"And I'll be a wise man," Aida said.

"You could be an angel," Prudential said.

"And you be a shepherd boy," Lara said to Kate.

"Who's going to watch the play?" Kate asked.

"We are the play and the audience both," Charley said.

Lara placed them all around the fireplace and then sat down herself with Sam in her arms and began:

"And there were in the same country shepherds abiding in the field, keeping watch over their flock by night."

In the small flickering room of Moses Bellows' cottage, a friendship, even a trust, settled in the air light and temporary as snow.

January,
1943

At the beginning of January, the weather suddenly warmed with long days of bright sun and the snow was gone. Overnight, Skunk Farm turned to a soft sponge of red clay and there was no memory in view of the storm which for a single night had set their lives in order.

Kate returned to Langley Friends School and was put in a different class from Pole Trickett. Mornings, Miracle took the baby with her while she worked at the main house, took him with her everyplace, even to the market, where Mr. Vruels said Simon Peter looked kin to Moses but then he could never tell with the colored. Lara was warmed by Miracle's presence with the baby in the house and found herself taking residence in whatever room Miracle was working. Their conversation was domestic, reminding her of the feeling in their flat in Copenhagen when she was a child, and she grew softly melancholic. Aida got her job back with Mrs. Cash, since Mary Pollard couldn't iron, and every morning she sat up in bed, looked in the mirror Guy'd taken for her, still bearing this message, "To my pretty woman," and said to herself, "Be careful, Aida Sue Bellows, and mind your pretty face."

In the first week of January, Charley Fletcher had to spend several nights in town because as the war escalated he was working late and the Fletchers were low on gas rationing. Often Moses stopped by the main house at noon when Miracle had taken the baby back to feed and Lara was in the kitchen with Sam in a high chair. He came in, took off his boots thick with red mud at the mat and usually stood in stocking feet, somehow shyly, as if exposed without shoes. He had grown different since Christmas.

"More friendly," Charley said, pleased with himself, holding himself responsible since the tempers at the farm had calmed. The Fletchers and Bellowses were easier with each other, even informal. Soon, he imagined, by the year's end, they would begin to live as family.

"Moses is more pensive," Lara said to him. "Not necessarily friendlier."

But she found him accessible.

He would sit down at the kitchen table across from her, give Sam a Ritz cracker from his pocket, spread his arms across the table in a warm and expansive gesture and ask Lara about Denmark or acting or her childhood. One or two questions and then after ten minutes—he never stayed longer, as if he timed himself, she began to notice —he would leave for lunch which Miracle had fixed for him at the cottage.

Once he asked her about the baby and did it seem unusual to her that the baby didn't cry. Perhaps, she said, but then she hadn't noticed until he mentioned it so it couldn't be too unusual and likely he was simply a very good baby.

"Have you held him?" Moses asked another time.

"I have."

"And did you notice the expression on his face?"

She had held him several times and certainly she had noticed his expression, which was peculiar especially in the eyes somehow, but she assumed it had to do with being a Negro baby and therefore his features were unfamiliar to her.

"Maybe I noticed," she said. "I'm not sure."

He had gotten up to leave and at the door, he said more to himself than to her, "Miracle loves that baby. I have never seen her so happy."

After Tom Elliot died in October, Lara had stopped her morning ritual in which he came to her. She did not think of him often or even miss him. The loss had been a loss to her imagination. But after Christmas, the story came back to her in an altered form.

A young Danish woman meets a colored American soldier during the war and offers him sanctuary in her apartment. She did not know what it was with Moses, whether the absences with Charley had damaged her perspective, but her heart flew up when he came to the house at noon, sometimes after work or in the morning to bring milk and eggs or simply news from town.

This morning the news he brought was about Prudential.

"So," he said when he came in the back door. "Prudential's in a mood to color the ceilings black."

"I noticed," Miracle said. She was making sausage when he came in from the top field where a lamb had died during the night. He was concerned about an illness going through the sheep which the Godfrys' sheep had got the year before. He called the veterinarian, who promised to come that afternoon, gave Sam a Ritz cracker from his pocket and leaned over the buggy where Simon Peter was sleeping.

"We take him in for his first appointment with the doctor today," Miracle said to Lara. "Moses is concerned."

"He just seems still for a baby," Moses said.

He arranged to pick Miracle up for the doctor's appointment and later Lara to take to Washington in the evening because she had been invited to a party with Charley at the White House.

After Moses left, Miracle picked the baby up, held him to her and kissed his black curls.

"You're a fine boy, Simon Peter," she whispered to him. "And don't let Moses Bellows' suspicious mind get to your heart."

She worried. Nights she lay awake listening to his breathing to be sure it didn't stop and she had noticed there was a slowness in the movements of his hands and the silence. Even now, three weeks on earth, he had not claimed his space.

After breakfast, Prudential sat on her bed looking out the window at nothing, bad-humored and agitated as she'd been since days after the baby came, in fact, since she felt well enough to feel bad. And this morning she was tired, troubled as she'd been all night by dreams of Moses coming after her, blue-black angry for letting him down.

The night before—late, after midnight, everybody in the house asleep—Prudential got up from her bed, put on her pink dress with the rose buckle which fit around her waist now she'd flattened out, did her hair in pink ribbons Holiday had sent her in an envelope for Christmas with a letter which said: DEAR PRU, MERRY CHRISTMAS TO YOU, TO YOU. PINK IS MY FAVORITE COLOR. I HOPE THAT BABY COMES FAST AND YOU GET HOME TO HELP ME WITH PAPA BEFORE I DIE OR KILL MYSELF OF THIS BUSINESS AND YOU KNOW WHAT I MEAN AND I BEING ONLY 12 YEARS OLD. YOUR SISTER, HOLIDAY DARGON. She put on lipstick and shoes from Mrs. Fletcher and walked back and forth in her room rehearsing for New York.

There was a quiet knock at her door. At first she didn't hear it, then Moses called Prudential softly and she opened the door.

"What are you doing, girl?" he asked when he saw her dressed up and after midnight.

"Practicing," she said simply.

"Practicing?"

"For New York."

"Well, I couldn't sleep and I heard you up." He sat down on the bed. "I've been wondering tonight."

"What have you been wondering?"

"I've been wondering did your papa ever bother you."

"How come you ask?"

"I just asked."

"I don't like Papa. I didn't since I was nine. On my ninth birthday I quit and I've never liked him since."

"I know that. And I know from Miracle that lately he's been bothering Holiday and I wondered whether he ever bothered you."

She stood and went to the window, pulled up the shade, leaned her head against the cold glass.

"No," she said. "Not in the way you're thinking."

Moses didn't like his brother-in-law and never had. Ulysses Dargon was his name, after the Civil War general, and people were afraid of him. He was a large angry man with a withered leg from a car accident, mad about being part crippled, and strong—so strong he had a reputation in southern South Carolina for it. But what struck everyone in Okrakan about Ulysses was the clear fact that he would do anything. He had no rules, and when he drank, which was plenty, he beat his wife.

"Move in with Mama," Miracle said to her.

"I can't," Lila replied.

And whenever Miracle would press, Lila's face went stone cold, her eyes narrowed to slits. "You heard me say I can't. That's what I mean." And she was a sweet-tempered woman with a pretty face and capabilities although her body had gone to fat from so many babies.

On the night Moses went to Prudential's room, he had been lying with Miracle and the baby between them, Miracle's face so warmed you'd have thought a band of angels had taken residence.

She touched the baby—his short broad nose, his eyes set close together, his small bow mouth. He was plump-faced with a very long forehead and a certain flatness or plane to his face.

"He doesn't look like Prudential, does he?" Miracle asked.

"She's small and her eyes are in the corner of her head," he said. "Maybe he looks like Lila."

"No." She looked up and narrowed her eyes at him. "I know who you're thinking."

Moses started to contend.

"And you're wrong," she said.

He brushed his hand across her forehead. "He's a beautiful baby, darling," he said. "We have us a beautiful baby."

When Prudential came down to the kitchen late in the morning Moses was there, back from burying the lamb. He had already been to the main house and stopped by the cottage for coffee before he headed over to the O'Learys'.

"Good morning," he said and poured a cup of coffee for her. "Are you doing better?"

She took an orange from the bowl in the window and sat down at the table to peel it.

"I said good morning."

She looked up at him blankly.

"Is this about last night?" he asked. "Is what I asked you last night worrying you?"

She shook her head.

"I'm going home," she said.

"Soon?"

"Tomorrow. If someone could call Willoughby's country store and get a message to Mama I'll be taking the morning bus to Charleston tomorrow."

"Why don't you stay the winter?"

"No."

"Mr. Fletcher spoke to me about your going to school with Kate."

"Are you crazy?" She turned the orange half inside out and ate the pulp. "There're no colored allowed in Kate's school."

"Mr. Fletcher says yes because her school is private and Quaker and they'll take anyone, even colored."

"I don't want to go," Prudential said.

"What about New York, baby? You've always had ideas."

"I want to go home," Prudential said. She put on her galoshes and jacket, tied a scarf around her head.

"I'm going out," she said and left by the back door.

• • •

At the main house, she looked in the window of the kitchen. Miracle was there, sitting in a wicker rocker by the fireplace with Simon Peter on her lap, and it made Prudential's teeth lock in her jaw to see her aunt so blissful with that damaged baby she'd whipped up out of bad sperm in her belly. She opened the kitchen door and shut it behind her.

"I have got ten eighty-three, which is not enough to get a ticket to Okrakan," she said to Miracle.

"What do you need a ticket to Okrakan for right now?"

"I need it for tomorrow."

"I was hoping you'd stay around for spring," Miracle said.

"Well, I won't," Prudential said.

Miracle was patient. She thought Prudential's temper had to do with being a child too young to have a baby boy and then give him away for good and go back home as if not a thing had happened but a long visit with relations. And she was right but only right in part.

"Do what you wish," Miracle said. "There's nineteen dollars in ones in my jacket pocket for the doctor today. Take what you need."

"The doctor?" Prudential reached into her jacket pocket.

"Simon goes to the doctor today for the first time."

"I forgot about that." She stuffed ten dollars into her pocket. "I'll have ten dollars and send you a money order when I get home. Now I'm going to Vruels' to put a call in for Mama and buy a bus ticket."

"Are you sure this is what you want to do?"

"Yes, I'm sure."

"Kate is certainly going to be sorrowful about this news," Miracle said.

Prudential's black eyes snapped. "Nothing sticks," she said. "Kate Bergmann may as well learn that now."

She walked down the hill to Route 7 and turned right towards Vruels'.

At Vruels' she put in a call to Willoughby's in Okrakan to say she'd be in at six o'clock on Tuesday evening. Then she bought a ticket, two packages of Life Savers, a Clark bar, a fashion magazine and a bottle of Clorox. The Clorox on the shelf caught her eye when she was looking for lye. The word WHITENS under "Clorox" was what she noticed and she was pleased to remember that Clorox also burned although not as badly as lye.

"So now you've given your baby to Miracle and Moses, you're going home?" Mr. Vruels asked in his cheerful voice.

Prudential didn't reply.

"Speak up. I'm not going to bite you," Mr. Vruels said.

She counted out the money for the ticket, the candy, the Clorox, the magazine and the telephone call and turned to leave.

"I hear you're the one who changed the name of Elm Grove," he said. "The chief of police told me. I wasn't there watching at the time."

"Yes I did," Prudential said politely.

The walk to Langley Friends School was three and a half miles and she walked quickly, half in the road, hoping to get there before lunch. It was gray and though not cold, damp to chill the bones. She ate the Life Savers one after the other without sucking and then the Clark bar before she even got to the one-mile mark, so there were no more prizes to spur her on her way. She did not think about the things really on her mind, about the baby or Kate or New York or even her room at home and what it would be like to sleep there after so long, years and years since July. She thought about candy and how she wished she'd bought a Milky Way as well as silk stockings because the wool itched her legs when she walked and whether when she was sixteen she could wear her hair unplaited in a wire-bush circle around her head, whether she would be beautiful to men and they would swarm to her like bees and she could shoot them down with flyswatters. She thought of herself in her pink dress walking along Fifth Avenue in high-heeled shoes.

She did not think at all about Pole Trickett until she got to the foot of the hill where the sign for Langley Friends School was and started up the long gravel drive, deep in red mud, scattered with the wet black branches of oaks and shaded gray.

When she had gotten up that morning and known for

certain she would have to leave Skunk Farm, she knew as well she'd have to settle the score with Pole Trickett before she left.

The school itself was an old clapboard farmhouse, spread out in wings and surrounded by fields of flat land dipping to a woods, where at the time Prudential crested the hill, children were playing. Next to the driveway where she stood two teachers were talking back and forth, one with a whistle in his mouth.

Prudential walked up to the younger of the teachers, who stood with his collar up against the cold, his neck like a turtle hunched in his jacket.

"I am looking for Pole Trickett," she said.

"Pole Trickett?" The teacher looked around. "He was here just a minute ago. He's got on a red jacket." He pointed to a small thick black-haired boy leaning against the front porch with a basketball under one arm.

"There," the teacher said.

"Thanks," she said and memorized Pole Trickett in a glance. He was actually smaller than she was and broad with a thick face and neck.

"Can I help you?" the teacher with the whistle asked.

"No sir," she said. "I have a message for Pole from my mama who does ironing for the Tricketts," Prudential said with exaggerated humility. She walked across the field to the steps where Pole Trickett was standing. The teacher with the whistle blew it as she went and the children ran to line up. Out of the corner of her eye, she saw Kate, way off in the field, walking with another girl. She'd have to hurry. She reached into the paper bag with the Clorox and uncapped the top.

"You Pole Trickett?" she asked, walking up the steps.

"What's it to you?" he asked.

She looked around quickly, assessing the situation. All of the children on the playground were lined up or on their way there. No one else was on the steps with Pole. No one even seemed aware of a colored girl on their territory, standing face to face but one step below.

"My name is Prudential Life Insurance," she said to him. "And I have a message for you."

Quick as a flash, she splashed the bottle of Clorox in his face. "This is to turn you white, nigger boy," she shouted and jumped over the banister and down the hill. She heard Kate call out, and by all rights she thought Pole Trickett should be after her, should be faster than she was, but she was running down the hill alone, unpursued, into the woods behind Langley Friends School. When she turned back, no one was left on the field, no one in sight, only the white farmhouse and some trees stood between her and the horizon. She sat down on the ground and leaned against a tree out of breath. She was especially glad Kate had seen her—and probably, although she was not entirely sure, glad she had not been caught.

For a small moment, she was triumphant. If Kate was home when she arrived, they could go upstairs to Kate's room, shut the doors and talk about what had happened—about the long walk to Langley Friends and Pole Trickett and how surprised he'd been when Prudential sailed right up to him and called him a nigger and poured Clorox on him—and how he'd tripped when he tried to run after her, which was probably the case, and fallen facedown in the red mud with Clorox burning his cheeks. They would have told the story over and over, sitting knee to knee on Kate's bed, until it took on the sound of magic and Prudential, capable of miracles, grew wings in her heart.

But Kate would not be home when Prudential arrived at Skunk Farm. Only Miracle with the baby come back from the doctor's drum-tight with bad news. And today after school when Kate did come home, it would be too late, because Prudential had another matter to which to attend.

Miracle was in her bedroom when Prudential arrived bone-tired from her long walk.

"Prudential?" she called. "That you?"

"Coming," Prudential said.

She was rocking Simon Peter in his bassinet.

"Mrs. Fletcher said there was a call from Kate's school." Her voice was weary but not cross.

"I suppose there was," Prudential said.

"That you poured Clorox on that poor boy who got his hand bit by Kate."

"I did. I had reasons."

"And what were your reasons?" Miracle asked.

"I did it for Kate since she couldn't very well stay at that school if she poured Clorox on Pole Trickett, now could she, so I did it for her."

"It might have been just as well if nobody did it for anybody." She rubbed her hand back and forth across the baby's back. "You have to go there tomorrow morning and speak to the principal and the boy's parents. The Clorox burned him."

"Bad?"

"Not bad but he's not in an accommodating humor." Miracle put a sweater on. "Moses is taking Mrs. Fletcher to a party in town to meet Mr. Fletcher and I'm going to stay with Sam and Kate. So I'd be pleased if you'd take care of Simon here at the cottage until I get home."

"You're not mad at me, are you?" Prudential asked.

"I'm . . ." She considered. "I suppose what I am is over-tired, sweetheart."

Prudential reached down awkwardly and patted the back of her baby boy. "Did the doctor have good news?" she asked.

Miracle stood aside so Prudential could leave the room first, then shut the door.

"Listen carefully for his crying while I'm gone," she said.

"He doesn't cry," Prudential said. "Did the doctor tell you why?"

Miracle went down the steps, put on her overcoat and boots to go to the main house.

"The doctor says he's fine." She went into the kitchen, took a piece of bread and ate it plain. She poured a glass of milk and checked the pot of beans for supper. "About the crying," Miracle said slowly. "The doctor said he might have something flat out missing in his brain. 'Re-tarded' is the word he used but he said it's too soon to tell." She wrapped a scarf around her head. "I didn't like the doctor. He is a snake-cold man."

154

Lara was resting on the canopy bed when Kate came home from school. She walked upstairs and stood in the door to her mother's room.

"Hello, darling." Lara sat up.

"Have you seen Prudential?"

"I had a call this afternoon from your principal," Lara began.

"That's why I want to see Prudential."

Lara patted the bed beside her.

"Tell me, darling."

"You won't understand," Kate said.

"If you'll tell me, I'll understand."

It was four. Shortly she would be going with Moses to Washington and she did not want Kate to learn of Prudential's plans to leave for South Carolina while she was away.

"I have to go down to the cottages," Kate said. "I need to tell Prudential something."

"Later, darling," Lara said. "Prudential is taking care of Simon and Miracle will be here soon to give dinner to you and Sam while I'm in the city. Here. Sit."

Kate sat.

"Take off your coat, love."

"I suppose the principal told you that Prudential arrived out of nowhere and threw Clorox on a boy called Pole Trickett," Kate said.

"He did. But I was certain she did it for cause. Prudential is a very principled girl."

"It was for cause," Kate said.

And as she had planned on the bus home from school she told her mother the story of Pole Trickett inexactly.

"Why didn't you tell me at the time, Kate?" Lara sat up.

"I told Prudential."

"But a grown-up would have been able to do something."

"No," Kate said matter-of-factly. "A grown-up would have made a catastrophe. If I had told you and you had spoken to the principal and Pole Trickett's parents, he would have done worse to me the next time."

She lay down next to her mother.

"Now Pole Trickett will never bother me again," she said in a voice thick with emotion.

They lay together quietly, warmed by a gentle shaft of sun from the window.

"Tomorrow," Kate said, and rolled on her side and put her head against her mother's shoulder, "I'd like to stay home and spend the day with Prudential."

"Perhaps, darling," Lara said. "We'll talk about it in the morning."

When she got up to dress for the evening, Kate had fallen into a deep sleep on her pillow.

In a small room on the second floor of the FTC, overlooking Constitution Avenue, Charley Fletcher made decisions, sometimes in the company of assistants, mostly alone. On Monday, the news of the Allied Powers ANFRA Conference in Casablanca where Roosevelt and Churchill were meeting following the success of the invasion of North Africa came through to Censorship. At the final press conference in Casablanca, Roosevelt set forth the doctrine of unconditional surrender of the Germans and Japanese. At nine-thirty, an unidentified caller phoned naming two government employees in Censorship as agents for the Communist party. Before ten that morning, Charley had spoken to the Secretary of War about the conference in Casablanca and the highly classified report he had received that since June 1942 there had been secret talks concerning the development of an atomic bomb. At eleven, he spoke with a few of the members of the President's cabinet informally on censoring the news, and at one, he spoke formally to a group of wire service reporters about the principles of censorship pertaining particularly to the safety and well-being of the country. He met with the Director of Censorship after lunch about spies in Censorship and the two men mentioned in the morning phone call in particular, although his mind wandered as it often did in recent weeks to Lara or the book he was writing about Skunk Farm.

At two he had a call from Lara to say that Prudential had thrown Clorox on a boy called Pole Trickett and should she wear her lavender dress to the White House even though it was out of fashion.

"Wear the lavender dress," he said to Lara. "You are so lovely in it."

Alone in his office for the first time that day, Charley Fletcher fell into a brown study.

That morning a speech of Churchill's reprinted in the London *Times* caught his eye. "Impotence," Churchill had said, "is a lack of power or ability. The Allied Forces lack neither the power nor the ability in this war but rather the recognition of their great strength."

Lately he had become fixed on the word "impotence" itself. In print, the word flew off the page as if it were as familiar as his proper name; he'd find himself reading and rereading the paragraph where he'd seen it in search of a secret between the letters.

"Impotence is not an uncommon affliction in the American male." That he had read in a medical journal in the dentist's office just last week. "And may in part be a result of the high expectation for performance in this country."

"Poor Prince Hamlet," Lara once said to him.

"Hamlet's problem is not mine," Charley had replied crossly. "To avenge my father's death would be a piece of cake."

He had dreams of Lara drowning, slipping out of reach. She was in a black river, naked, with her arms over her head, and he was lying on a fallen tree extended into the water reaching for her each time her head and arms bobbed up. Sometimes he woke up believing he had missed her intentionally.

"We are a country of isolation and impotence." These lines were from a history of the South which Lara had marked with a pencil on the page. "The isolation is geographic. Impotence, however, is more insidious and results in part from our nation's betrayal of democracy with slavery."

He had wondered when he read the lines whether Lara too was obsessed with the word "impotence" or simply had been interested in the reference to the Negroes.

At four, he left for the White House, where the President was expected to arrive soon from Morocco.

As soon as he was out the door of the FTC, on Constitution Avenue, walking briskly because of the cold and quick-flooding darkness, his father was with him in a business suit appropriate for the occasion. His father had never owned a suit except the one his mother bought him to be buried in—twenty-two dollars of the money she'd been saving for singing lessons from the choir director and that she'd mentioned often since after his death she gave up on singing lessons.

"You'll have a chance to meet the President," Charley said. "And I bet you'll like him better than you think."

His father looked quite well and youthful and proud in his dark gray suit and Charley was pleased to have imagined him walking along Constitution Avenue.

"It is a fine moment for me, Charles. I never in my dreams believed I would see a President of the United States."

His father had not liked President Roosevelt, on whom he blamed the daily miseries of his life. Had John Fletcher lived, he would not even have come to Washington to visit his son. He only left New Philadelphia once to go to Cleveland to see his sister. He would never have gone to the White House.

"You do your job and do it well," he would have said. "But don't unsettle your stomach by hopes larger than your brain and don't waste your time wishing for famous company to be a mirror for your own face."

He wondered what his father would have made of Moses Bellows. Whether they could have been friends.

At the South Gate, his father vanished and Charley showed his invitation to the guard, walked across the lawn and up the steps to the White House. It was five o'clock. In an hour, Lara would arrive.

• • •

Lara sat in the front seat next to Moses. The car was warm and smelled lightly of hyacinth from Lara's perfume and the strong earthy odor of Moses Bellows. Outside the darkness had fallen early with the weather, and driving through the country there were no lights, no stars, no moonlight, only the long skeleton fingers of winter trees. They did not speak.

The drive from the farm was along a country road to Chain Bridge, which separated Virginia from Washington over the most turbulent and rocky section of the Potomac River, and as they crossed the river, the sound of it rushing downstream over the rocks, just the sound of it and the empty darkness, set the silent occupants of the car free of their ordinary lives.

"What time do you have to be there?" Moses asked.

"Six," Lara said. "I'm meeting Charley by the South Gate."

"Then we are in plenty of time."

Moses drove with the seat pulled all the way back and his hands on the bottom of the steering wheel, his arms resting on his lap. Lara was pleased to watch him. He was a large man in every sense, she thought, entirely competent. That pleased her particularly. Although they were not touching, she felt the strength of his arm against her own.

And as they drove through the darkness, she thought Moses was going to stop the car and kiss her. Her mind rushed forward to possibilities—how she would behave.

This Charley had not considered when he boxed her in the soft tissue of the country for protection from his own failures. That a Negro, who understood his place in history and did not take exception, fired by passion so submerged, so subtle, could be capable of conflagration, could ravish Charley Fletcher's wife. Just the rich sound of "ravish" in her brain stirred Lara's senses.

She leaned against the front door. Moses did not look over at her, but she could feel the heat of him.

"Would you like a cigarette?" she asked finally.

"No thank you," he replied.

"I don't smoke either," she said. "I just carry them in case."

"I smoke," Moses said, "but I don't want a cigarette now."

She waited. She wanted him to touch her but the smallest gesture on her part seemed inappropriate.

They fell silent, but the silence was comforting as it is between children. Lara settled softly, sleepily into the corner of the front seat. Moses drove down the Canal Road to Georgetown out M Street to Pennsylvania Avenue, stopped the car at the South Gate, got out and opened Lara's door.

"Have a good evening," he said as if nothing personal had happened between them.

She leaned over just slightly and put her cheek against his shoulder. "Thank you for driving me," she said.

By the time she reached the place where Charley was waiting, she was out of breath.

The President was late. The guests mingled in the Blue Room in postures of studied formality. It was not a group that Charley Fletcher knew, although the party was for journalists, mainly publishers. Secretary Ickes was there, burly and high-tempered, calling him Fletcher so it sounded like a swear word. Jane Ickes, a woman with a sharp tongue and a certain chill about her, talked warmly with Lara, who had not been to the White House before. Charley had come on several occasions but they were business to meet with the President and this was the first time he had come as a guest. It was entirely different, satisfactory, to be invited to the party. He allowed himself the rush of pleasure of belonging for a night to a circle of people who would call him by name—Fletcher, as Secretary Ickes had said. He was a long way from the back porch of New Philadelphia shelling beans, from the fields behind his house having footraces with his brother, from the dark kitchen, heavy with the smell of stew, where the large Fletcher family bowed their heads resisting gratitude for the food, for their lives, blessed from the end of the table in their father's tired voice.

The President arrived. He wheeled across the room, his

160

large powerful torso dominating the wheelchair, and Charley who had never seen him in movement, in fact only behind a desk, was struck by the enormous energy of a man who could not walk.

"Charley Fletcher," Roosevelt said loud enough for everyone nearby to hear. "You're just the one I want to see."

What he wanted to talk to Charley about was the statement he had made the previous night in Morocco but that was of no consequence in the light of those words "Charley Fletcher" in Charley Fletcher's ear.

"Lara." He grabbed her by the wrist. "I want you to meet the President of the United States."

Prudential sat on Miracle's bed and listened. The baby was making soft sounds, not crying exactly but groaning deep in his small throat. He lay quite still on his stomach in a yellow kimono covered with the blue knit blanket Miracle had made for him. For a long time or it seemed a long time, after six and completely dark outside, Prudential watched the steady rise and fall of his breathing. Then she got up, went to the bathroom, rinsed off her face, her hands. She was frightened but resolved. That she knew. She was absolutely resolved.

First she went downstairs to check. Miracle was at the Fletchers' fixing supper for Kate and Sam. Moses was in town taking Mrs. Fletcher to the White House, and she could see Aida and Guy through the window sitting at a table in their cottage. She turned out the kitchen light so Aida wouldn't notice it on and come over to be sociable. Then she went upstairs.

She didn't turn Simon over when she changed his diapers. She didn't want to look at him. But she wanted to change him so Miracle would know when she came home later that evening Prudential had been attentive. It was six-twenty by the clock on Moses' bureau. She turned on the light beside Miracle's side of the bed, turned off the overhead light, took Miracle's pillow from the bed and put it in the bassinet under the baby's face. Then she held

Simon's head facedown on the pillow and waited until the clock on the bureau read six-thirty. The baby did not struggle. When she finally took her hand off his head, lifted the pillow, turned his head to the side, his breathing had stopped.

She put the pillow back on Miracle's bed, straightened the blue knit blanket over the only child she intended ever to bring into this world and went downstairs shaken to the marrow of her bones.

Moses found Simon Peter.

He got to the cottage at seven, went in the back door, took off his boots and ladled a bowl of beans, which he ate standing. Prudential was in the living room, sitting on the edge of the couch staring at the fireplace, but when she heard him, she opened her fashion magazine and pretended to read although the colors on the page spilled before her eyes as if she were drunk.

"Moses?" she called out in a voice thin as blue milk.

"You in the living room?" he asked.

"Uh huh," she replied.

"Want supper?"

"I've eaten," she called back.

She listened to him stir about the kitchen; she was pinned to his movements, getting more soup, rinsing the bowl, putting it in the cupboard.

She heard him start upstairs.

What she had done, she had done for cause, she told herself fiercely as she waited and waited for Moses' battle cry. There was no other way, no one else to interfere with the baby's damaged life, no one with a right to it, but her, flesh and blood in whose womb he had grown crippled in the brain, and as he grew, the bad blood of his father was winning and winning.

"Prudential," Moses called out in the voice of God. "Come here."

She stumbled to her feet.

He stood at the top of the stairs with Simon in his arms.

She kept her head down and pulled herself up the steps, her legs amputated at the knees.

"Simon's dead," he said.

And finally, finally, she screamed out with the horror and fury caught for months in her windpipe cutting off the air.

Midnight in the Bellows cottage, and in her room, humming deep in her throat, Miracle made preparations. She was alone. In the next room, Prudential packed in a navy laundry bag her few clothes except for the Sears, Roebuck sundress, which she put in a paper bag and wrote in pencil, "For Kate, my first best dress for you. Forever, Prudential." Twenty yards from the cottage under the elm tree where the rope swing hung by the light of a flashlight pressed in a crevice of the tree, Moses and Guy were digging.

"Deep," Miracle had said.

The ground was soft clay, not easy to dig, and besides the roots of the elm scarcely allowed for the space Miracle had in mind.

"I'm putting him in the bassinet," she said to Moses.

He did not take exception.

On the table in the kitchen was a fifth of bourbon—Guy had had a swallow or two. Aida was tempted. Her eyes were pouring water like rain over the mounds of cheek flesh. She put the open bottle to her lips, pressed her lips into the neck of the bottle, but she did not allow herself to drink. Not tonight when all the troubles of the world had fallen on the sweet heart of Miracle Bellows. She turned out the kitchen light so she could see them digging and they worked in a temper blasting through the ground with their shovels.

Miracle was almost ready when Moses came in the house to say he was done. She wrapped Simon Peter in the blue knit blanket, put him in the bassinet and tucked into the corners all the tiny clothes she had made for him, the toys she'd bought him and his bottle full of milk pressed up beside.

"You don't want to get rid of all those pretty things you

made, darling," Moses said. "There might be a baby for us. Nobody's ever said there wouldn't be."

She was singing.

"Uh huh," she said between verses.

"There," she said to Moses when she had finished. "Now you get the Fletchers and have them down here for the funeral."

"We can't have the Fletchers, Miracle," Moses said. "It's after midnight."

She lifted the bassinet from its stand and set it on her bed.

"Get the Fletchers," Miracle said.

They stood in a circle around the deep red hole and waited for Miracle, who'd said she'd come alone and for them to be there waiting. They were touching, Aida with her arm through Lara Fletcher's, Charley pressed up next to Moses, who stood like a tree. Prudential did not speak. When Kate arrived at the cottage with the Fletchers, Prudential kept her seat in the living room next to Aida but turned her head away.

The night was soft for winter, overcast with a sliver of gauze-covered moon in the distance and no stars.

Miracle kept them waiting.

"What's that woman doing?" Guy asked, already drunk with more swallows of bourbon. And Aida hushed him.

When Miracle finally came, they heard the door of the cottage shut, they heard her footsteps pad across the ground so slowly each one of them tightened in anticipation, but they could not see her until her body heaving the weight of the bassinet covered with a lace tablecloth she had taken from the buffet in the dining room of John Spencer's house the night the Bellowses moved out back fell into the light circle and her face, chiaroscuro, seemed to those who watched her luminous as the face of an angel.

She was singing a supplication no one had heard before, not from the Church of God where she was raised although the melody was familiar but the words she put together as she went along were personal. No one had the courage to watch but fixed his eyes at a point in the darkness, leaned up against one another and wished for the night to end.

"Now Prudential Dargon, you say goodbye to your boy," Miracle said at last.

"Goodbye," Prudential said.

"Sweetly, sweetly. He never brought harm, he didn't even whimper. You lean down and touch his body and say goodbye, Simon Peter, and thank you."

Prudential leaned down.

"Goodbye, Simon Peter, and thank you," she said.

And then one after the other while Miracle stood at the head of the bassinet, Aida, then Guy and Charley and Lara and Kate and finally Moses.

"Goodbye, Simon Peter, and thank you."

Miracle and Moses put him in the ground. Miracle kneeling heaved the mound of dirt over the bassinet and then they all joined until the ground was level and there was no mound, no trace that the earth concealed a child.

At dawn, Prudential slipped out of the back door of the cottage and along the path to the main house, left the paper bag with her Sears, Roebuck sundress on the back step, stole eighty dollars from the cookie jar and headed towards Vruels', where she traded in her ticket for New York City.

BOOK FOUR

The Shadow of the Groundhog

February Second, 1943: Morning

Trouble settled over Skunk Farm after Simon Peter died, easing into the bone marrow like bad weather. The days were gray and heavy-footed. The nights had an edge as if somewhere in the cottages or the main house, someone was at risk. It rained. The firewood stacked outside the cottage was too sodden to burn. The furnace could not diminish the dampness which slipped everywhere, even into the bed linen. The families kept tenaciously to themselves.

On the night after—Miracle had not come to work that day, had sat instead in her own bedroom, covered over with wool blankets, and watched John Spencer in the flesh devil the corners of her room, sometimes double-exposed sitting on the wooden rocker where she'd rocked Simon Peter to sleep—on that night Charley Fletcher went out back and asked Moses for supper. Lara had cooked a Danish soup, he said to Moses standing in the door to the cottage, and they should all come up—Guy and Aida as well.

"No," Moses said. He made no effort to be polite. "We'll be eating here."

Kate would not go to school. She put on the sundress Prudential had given her, put the note under her pillow, climbed into bed and read stories in Danish.

"She'll be back, darling," Lara said, although they would not know for days that Prudential had gone to New York and not Okrakan and could be lost there, young as she was with a slick-magazine knowledge of the world.

"Don't lie to me," Kate said.

She could not be consoled.

Groundhog Day was a day so black there was no separating its beginnings from the night. No chance the groundhog's message was a promise of spring. That afternoon at two, Tom Elliot would be buried in Arlington National Cemetery and his living presence in Charley Fletcher's mind, strong as if he were sitting in their bedroom, had aggravated days already troubled.

The trouble came as if delivered in the mail or by carrier pigeon or a message from God by the angel Gabriel or from Mercury on winged feet but clear in every body in every bed on Skunk Farm.

"I do not like what's going on," Guy said to Aida even before he opened his eyes that morning.

"What is going on?" Aida asked.

"I can feel it."

Aida could feel it too, even hungover as she was from the bourbon she'd taken to drinking again in the bathroom, hiding in the cupboard behind the Lysol. Someday she'd mistake Lysol for the bourbon and burn out her throat if she let herself go downhill. But that's what she had been doing since the baby died. Flying downhill on a snow sled fast as she could.

"Don't get fired from Mrs. Cash again," Guy said.

Miracle woke up with the pulse beating in her temples after a night's sleep without dreams. It felt as if her blood was going to soar out of her body, and she pressed her face into Moses arm, licked him for comfort.

"Groundhog Day," she said.

"So much for spring," Moses said. "I can't see my fingers in the dark."

If she opened her eyes, John Spencer might be there. He had been in the main house when she went to work the day before, standing at the buffet in the dining room.

"The silver's gone, Miracle," he said.

"I know it's gone," she replied. "I took it because I thought you were dead."

"Well, I'm here," he said.

That night when she took a bath, she heard him on the steps and climbed out of the tub, dried quickly so he would not see her without her clothes.

"I have nerves," she said to Moses. She had not told him John Spencer was around so often. He might have her sent to her mother's until her mind fell together properly. But she couldn't help it. What she saw, she saw unless she went around with her eyes tight closed. John Spencer had come to live with her and she couldn't get him out.

Moses turned over, turned Miracle over on her back, bore down gently.

They had made love so often since the baby, sometimes with the desperation of war, sometimes soft enough he could not bear to let his body weight sink onto her. There was a sweetness between them but no coming together as though a board separated their faces and they could not see one another's eyes.

"I am in trouble," Miracle said when he rolled onto his back.

"I can tell."

She lay there looking up at the ceiling.

"I see a dead man in my room. I see him everywhere I go, even at work."

"You're a woman of powerful imagination," Moses said.

He got out of bed and pulled on his trousers. He turned on the light on his bureau and put on a shirt.

"You know who it is?" Miracle asked in whisper.

He put on his coat, pulled a wool hat down and kissed her.

"I'm going to tell Mrs. Fletcher you won't be at work for a while until your pressure's down and you are yourself again."

"It's John Spencer is who it is," Miracle said as Moses left the room. He started down the steps.

"Moses?" she called. "Is John Spencer dead or not?"

He didn't answer.

Outside he put his collar up against the dampness, waved to Guy, who stood in the window of his cottage, and headed towards the high field to check the lambs first and then the main house.

Moses had known about John Spencer from the start, from the first evening Miracle came home after work, fixed supper silent as night, sank her body into a deep warm bath. When he came upstairs, there she was propped up on the pillow in their room, removed from him.

"Miracle?" he'd said. "What is going on with you?"

"Not a thing but the same that always goes on with me," she'd said, her eyes closed, herself an island, a ten-mile stretch away from his arm reach.

He thought he would kill John Spencer then—go up to the main house and strangle him with his hands. He saw the scene exactly in his mind's eye but he did not act on it.

She had wanted a baby since she was seventeen.

"I don't understand it," her sister Lila said, holding her own baby-swollen belly in her hands. "You got your evenings to yourself with Moses and your complexion. Let well enough alone."

"Only one baby," Miracle said. "I don't have in mind to be a rabbit."

But the one baby didn't come. Year after year they had waited and gradually, the way those things happen, Moses saw the hope begin to spill out of her, darkening her eyes.

"I won't have what's going on," he said to her one evening sitting across from her at the kitchen table, watching her eyes float downstream away from him. "I'm going to stop it."

Moses opened the cattle gate and headed up the hill deep in mud and spread with clusters of feeding lambs.

. . .

172

Charley Fletcher woke up with a strong sense that something had happened. He checked the baby and Kate and went downstairs, where the only presence of life was embers in the fireplace burning golden red. Then he remembered that Tom Elliot's body was due to arrive at dawn at Andrews Air Force Base and just his return to the United States disturbed his peace of mind. It was five by the clock in the kitchen and he was wide awake.

Lara, still sleeping, moved closer for warmth when he climbed back in bed and to his surprise the soft, almost sweet smell of her and the stillness of her body brought a rush of feeling and he pulled her to him.

She opened her eyes.

"Charley?"

But the feeling fled as soon as her body was lined against his. There were only small traces of passion teasing like fragrance diffused in the air.

She turned on her back and when he looked over, her eyes were open to the ceiling.

"Sometimes I feel in danger."

"From Moses?"

"I don't know," Lara said. "I feel as if we broke a promise to the Bellowses when the baby died."

Lara was right. There was a feeling of actual danger, as if the lot of them, himself as well, wanted a catastrophe to express their grief.

In the shower, Charley had an imagined conversation with Moses. They were on the high field together with the lambs checking the lambs' feet for damp rot between the soft pads. On their way down the hill, early morning with a chill in the air but the promise of sun in a cool yellow circle beyond the Blue Ridge, Charley made his proposal.

"Since Prudential's baby died," he said, "we have been at war."

Moses nodded.

"At Christmas there seemed to be the possibility of friendship."

"The baby brought false hope and then he died," Moses said. "He shouldn't have lived anyway, damaged as he was."

Charley stepped out of the shower and toweled off.

"I'm going alone," he said.

She was taken aback.

"Eggs, I believe, and potatoes and toothpaste."

"The grocery money is gone from the jar."

"I know. I checked this morning."

"Prudential," he said without further explanation.

He was not unpleasant, but in the week since the baby died he did not come to the main house unless it was necessary; he was no longer personal and—this she noticed in particular, oddly sad about it—he did not take off his boots at the door and walk in stockinged feet.

This morning, cooking oatmeal in the dark, dank kitchen, she was weak with losses. The thought of the arrival of Tom Elliot's privileged body made her weep.

She didn't hear Moses along the path until he was there in the kitchen behind her, larger than life in his dark blue jeans and lumber jacket smelling of the earth-damp air. She turned.

"Moses," she said. "You surprised me."

He had seen her in the kitchen light standing by the stove when he came around the side of the barn and walked quickly across the grass, knowing exactly what he would do, fueled by desire and fury without regard to consequence.

He kissed her hard on the lips and when he let go of her, she fell backwards, over a kitchen chair, knocking it down.

Which was the crash Charley heard and ran downstairs.

Moses stood his place.

Lara on her back, her legs caught in the rungs of the chair, struggled to right herself.

"I fell over," she said lightly, reaching out her hand to Charley to help her up. "I stepped backwards and didn't know the chair was in the way."

"Are you all right?"

"Fine," she said.

She did not look at Moses.

Charley picked the chair up, said good morning to

"I'm going alone," he said.

She was taken aback.

"Eggs, I believe, and potatoes and toothpaste."

"The grocery money is gone from the jar."

"I know. I checked this morning."

"Prudential," he said without further explanation.

He was not unpleasant, but in the week since the baby died he did not come to the main house unless it was necessary; he was no longer personal and—this she noticed in particular, oddly sad about it—he did not take off his boots at the door and walk in stockinged feet.

This morning, cooking oatmeal in the dark, dank kitchen, she was weak with losses. The thought of the arrival of Tom Elliot's privileged body made her weep.

She didn't hear Moses along the path until he was there in the kitchen behind her, larger than life in his dark blue jeans and lumber jacket smelling of the earth-damp air. She turned.

"Moses," she said. "You surprised me."

He had seen her in the kitchen light standing by the stove when he came around the side of the barn and walked quickly across the grass, knowing exactly what he would do, fueled by desire and fury without regard to consequence.

He kissed her hard on the lips and when he let go of her, she fell backwards, over a kitchen chair, knocking it down.

Which was the crash Charley heard and ran downstairs.

Moses stood his place.

Lara on her back, her legs caught in the rungs of the chair, struggled to right herself.

"I fell over," she said lightly, reaching out her hand to Charley to help her up. "I stepped backwards and didn't know the chair was in the way."

"Are you all right?"

"Fine," she said.

She did not look at Moses.

Charley picked the chair up, said good morning to

Moses and poured himself a glass of orange juice. The air in the kitchen was charged, smoldering, and Charley felt as if he had just missed a conversation in which the subject was himself.

"I'd like to talk to you," he said to Moses.

At the stove, Lara stirred the oatmeal, her back to both of them, rubbing her hip, which had been bruised in the fall.

"I have to go to the O'Learys' now," Moses said.

"Fine," Charley said, taking his coat off the hook. "I'll walk with you to your truck."

The kitchen door shut and Lara watched them walk towards the truck together, Charley smaller by a head, animated—Moses erect, his head straight forward, squared off against the world.

She knew she had provoked Moses. She had turned her soft bewildering sex on him, and he had floundered in his resolve to keep a distance.

Moses was not forthcoming.

Charley spoke to him about the trouble on the farm since the baby's death, the way the families had pulled apart.

"We were never together," Moses said, taking the keys out of his pocket, getting in the truck.

"That's not the point," Charley said. "The point is that Miracle is not well. You've had a bad time of it and you don't have heat."

"I've lived without heat most of my life," Moses said.

Charley leaned against the truck and spoke through the open window.

"You are welcome to move to the main house for the rest of the winter," he said.

"No," Moses said. "We have a place to sleep already." He rolled the window halfway up and let the engine idle.

Charley wanted to hit him. He imagined opening the door, hitting Moses full in the jaw, watching his head snap, his body fold, watching him tumble out of the truck. And in the kitchen window, Lara would be contemplative.

"Move off the farm," he wanted to say. "Get a place of your own and a regular job with a salary. Get off my land." He took a pack of cigarettes and lit one.

"Another thing," he said to Moses. "If you feel the way you do, you shouldn't come to my kitchen for conversations with my wife."

"Yes, sir," Moses said, facing front.

"Don't yes sir me," Charley replied. "I'm younger than you are."

Lara was in the window as he had imagined when he headed down the path out back, still steaming angry at Moses Bellows. When he next saw him, he thought to himself, he'd tell him not to take off his shoes in the kitchen again.

Aida had a plan. It came to her that morning dressing for work at Mrs. Cash's so she dressed pretty with bright purple lipstick and the turquoise sweater Miracle had given her for Christmas just in case Guy was still in the kitchen with his coffee and could have his head turned.

"So good morning." She sauntered into the kitchen, ran her painted fingers through his hair.

"Good morning," Guy said.

She opened the refrigerator and took out a grapefruit, which she halved, put on a plate for him.

"So what are you up to this morning," he asked, "dressed like a peacock and so light-footed?"

"I'm up to nothing."

She sat down beside him with her grapefruit, took a sip of coffee from his cup.

"Mrs. Cash as usual and then Mrs. Fletcher, since Miracle is sick. I'll be home late."

"How late is that?"

"Seven o'clock."

"Seven o'clock? And what are you doing between Mrs. Fletcher and seven o'clock?" He reached over and rubbed the smudge of purple lipstick off her teeth.

"I'm doing a surprise for Miracle to put the yellow light back in her eyes."

She leaned over and kissed him, leaving a smudge of purple on his lips.

"Why that's very nice."

He dumped the finished grapefruit in the garbage can, rinsed the plates and set them in the drainer.

"The reason it feels like trouble here is because Miracle is heartbroken," Aida said.

"You may be right, and besides, Miracle is always doing for us," Guy said.

"What surprise do you have in mind?" He poured another cup of coffee.

"None of your business," Aida said. "You'll see soon enough."

They heard Charley Fletcher come up the steps of the cottage, heard his knock on the door and thought it was Moses, so Guy called out, "Come in," and Aida struck a sultry pose with her hip out and her bottom lip pouting like she did with Moses sometimes to stir his temper.

"Why Charley Fletcher," Aida sang when she saw him come through the living room, and she could feel Guy stiffen at her familiarity.

"We thought you were Moses," Guy said.

Charley stood beside the table where they sat. He asked Guy to do some errands and talked about the bad weather and the way the night seemed to go on all day. He told them about Tom Elliot's funeral and how a funeral at Arlington went with the flag on the coffin and the gun salute and taps. Then he brought up the plan he had mentioned to Moses for Skunk Farm.

"Ever since the baby died, we've been at civil war," he said to Guy.

"Have you spoken to Moses?"

"I spoke with him this morning."

"And he said no," Guy said.

"Moses might have said yes," Aida said. "The cottage is cold and Miracle's been ailing. You don't know for certain."

"Moses said he had a place to sleep."

Guy got up. "We had our chance to live in the main house for seven years, you know."

"I do know. That's why this thought occurred to me."

Charley drank down his coffee, rinsed the cup and turned to leave.

"Think about it," Charley Fletcher said. "We'd be happy to have you."

Guy waited until he heard Charley Fletcher's footsteps across the porch and down the steps and then he beat the wall beside the refrigerator until he broke the skin on his knuckle.

Upstairs, where Aida had gone when she felt her husband's temper, the radio was giving news from the European front. She made the bed, opened the curtains on the still dark day, dropped a tube of lipstick in her skirt pocket and went downstairs.

Guy had his coat on.

She took his hands, turned them over in her own and shook her head.

"We could have our old room back," she said to him.

Guy pulled his hands back and put them in his pocket.

"You be careful, Aida," Guy said when he dropped her off on Route 123 at the Cashes' house. "I feel trouble all around me this morning."

Guy arrived at Hawkins Lumber at eight o'clock and there was a note to see his supervisor.

"Laid off," his supervisor said. "Today is your last day."

"What did I do wrong?" Guy asked.

"Too slow," the supervisor said.

Guy put his lunch pail in his locker, took off his coat and went into the lumberyard for his assignment. He knew he was slow. He'd been told that a hundred times but he'd never missed a day of work or been late and he worked overtime without pay to finish what he'd been asked to do. He always worked carefully. He did not make mistakes.

At ten by the watch of the foreman working next to him, he went back to the building, got his lunch pail, told his supervisor he might as well leave since he was not coming back.

"You won't be paid for the whole day," the supervisor said but Guy did not turn around or say goodbye to the men with whom he had worked for three years and thirteen days. He got into his truck and drove to the Negro bar south of Leesburg, where he had two beers with William Oliver Johnson, whose place it was where the Negroes around Leesburg went to fraternize and drink.

William Oliver took exception. He told Guy to go back to Hawkins Lumber and ask for an explanation.

"No," Guy shook his head. "What's done is done."

But William Oliver persisted and called him a chicken and compared him for courage to Moses. Finally Guy, brave-winged with beer, agreed.

It was just after lunch when he arrived at the lumberyard. The owner sat in his damp cold office veiled by the smoke from his cigarette.

"Mr. Hawkins," he said. "I don't know whether you know me personal. I'm Guy Bellows."

Mr. Hawkins held up his hand for Guy to wait. He finished the computation he was doing on the ledger open on his desk, made two telephone calls, one to his wife, called "honeybun," and then looked up through the smoke at Guy.

"Yes."

"This morning the supervisor fired me for being slow and I have come here to take exception."

"I fired you for being slow," Mr. Hawkins said, entering two engagements on his February calendar.

"I do the job complete," Guy said.

"You're too slow."

"I'm never late and I never make mistakes."

Mr. Hawkins ground his cigarette into the ashtray on his desk.

"You have made a mistake right now," he said. "You have come here drunk and smelling like a nigger. Now get out."

It happened that fast.

Guy went.

He turned slowly, opened the door, walked across the drive to where his truck was parked, standing straight as a stick like he'd seen Moses do since they were boys. Feeling Moses in his own body, he kept his temper although the dike had been tested this morning and he knew the sea rush of feelings spilling in his brain.

When Lara went down to the road for mail, there were three letters from Prudential—one to Lara, which read:

Dear Mrs. Fletcher,
    As you can see I borrowed $80 from the grocery jar and will send it back soon when I get paid by the donut factory where I plan to work before I get a job on the radio which the man in the donut factory says I can have through his connections since he says I have a perfect voice.

Yours truly,
Prudential Dargon

There was a card of the Empire State Building for Kate:

Dear Kate,
    I live near this building and hope soon you can visit me only I can't give my address since I move around. It looks like I'm going to be on the radio. Here I pass for 18 years old. I wore the pink dress to a party last night with new high heels and met a boyfriend.

Forever,
Prudential

The last letter was for Miracle. Lara put on her coat, put Sam in his snowsuit and headed out back with a jar of plum jam and yellow begonias for Miracle.
    She heard Moses' truck as soon as she left the house and assumed it was Moses although it was early for him to be home for lunch. But she did not turn around even when she heard him call.
    What had passed between them that morning had separated their lives. She did not know how to conduct herself.

Miracle was busy in the kitchen peeling potatoes. Pots of soup and beans simmered on the stove, the house was warm and pungent with the smell of cloves. She was singing for John Spencer, whom she imagined sitting at the kitchen table in a heavy sweater against the cold and waiting for the vegetable soup to be done.

"I bought you flowers and a letter from Prudential." Lara did not even notice Miracle's distraction, so distracted was she by the events of the morning.

"Prudential." Miracle clucked. "That child. My sister is beside herself with worry."

She sat at the kitchen table and opened the letter.

> Dear Aunt Miracle,
>
> I am sorry to leave without saying goodbye but I know if I stayed around Skunk Farm to witness your broken heart, I would die of it.
>
> Someday I will be back and you'll be proud to know me and forgive me my trespasses.
>
> Love,
> Prudential Dargon

"She won't last," Miracle said, folding the letter and putting it back in the envelope. "Not in New York at thirteen years old."

"She's very tough." Lara said.

Miracle shrugged.

"You have to have a cold heart to be very tough."

"Well, I hope she'll be fine," Lara said vacantly. She wished to detain Miracle until Moses got to the cottage so she would not have to meet him on the path alone. They chatted about Miracle's health and the weather and how Kate was surviving Prudential's departure. She had a cup of coffee.

"Are you expecting Moses home for lunch today?" Lara asked finally.

"Not today," Miracle said. "Today he's working on the O'Learys' barn."

182

"You're sure?" Lara said. "I thought I heard his truck."

"That's what he told me," Miracle replied.

So Lara wrapped her scarf back around her neck, zipped Sam's snowsuit and said goodbye.

Maybe, she thought to herself, he had already gone back to the O'Learys'. But the truck was in the driveway when she came into the clearing, so she braced herself and went into the house.

He was not in the kitchen.

She took off Sam's snowsuit and her coat and hung them in the mudroom. Then she stopped to listen but there were no sounds in the house. She made Sam a bottle of apple juice and got a piece of zwieback for him and one for herself which she scraped across the top of the butter, still in the churn, unsalted and warm.

Then she went upstairs to dress for Tom Elliot's funeral. She expected Moses in the corridor or the sitting room. She listened by the bathroom, where he had been fixing the pipes during the weekend. In her bedroom, she called, "Moses," loud enough to be heard if he was upstairs.

Once after a performance of A *Doll's House* in Copenhagen when she had just started to act, Wilhelm Ader, who played the role of Torvald Helmer, flew into the back room where she was dressing, shut the door and took hold of her. She had not provoked him, she thought at the time, but later, ill-tempered and rebuffed, Wilhelm had said her hands were too soft and she should keep them off the backs of men's necks or she'd have trouble all her life. She didn't even remember putting her hand on the back of his neck but she must have done so—perhaps she had touched him in sympathy after the first act when he had muffed his closing lines. But with Moses, it was clear. She had wanted him.

She changed quickly into a navy-blue suit, stopping to listen, but there was no sound, only the warbling of water in the radiators and the sense of another presence in the house. Perhaps he was in the barn, but when she looked out the window, there was no one in sight. Then she heard his footsteps on the front stairs ascending in heavy boots without a rush and she was frozen in place.

After Moses saw Lara go down the path out back, he walked around the main house to the front door, which was unlocked, sat down on the couch placed at an angle to the fireplace, took the newspaper from the table where Charley Fletcher had left it, put his feet up on the ottoman as he used to do when the house was his and waited.

He was a predictable man who did not surprise himself, and he had surprised himself this morning. The sense of balance had shifted and he was not certain where to place his feet; there was a promise of natural disaster, visceral, in the blood.

His mother used to speak to him of boundaries. She was a sensible woman and lived a life of dignity in spite of her situation, which was poor and colored with one bad leg and a heart condition which killed her at forty-four. No one, white or colored, spoke badly to her ever. She saw to that. She used to talk to Moses about rules, how it was important to know the rules and play by them. Freedom if it comes to a colored man at all, she'd say, comes by minding the boundaries and keeping your eyes open.

He thought about her now as she used to sit in the rocker in the kitchen, out of breath, fanning herself with her apron, even in cold weather because the heart condition made her all the time hot.

"Don't run away with your head," she'd say, and then her eyes would roll back in her head and she'd sing out, "Watch your p's and q's."

He had heard Lara come back in the house, her footsteps on the stairs, across the second floor into her bedroom, where she would be dressing for the funeral to which he was expected to drive her shortly. Aida would soon be back to take care of the baby.

He went upstairs, down the corridor, through the sitting room, and knocked on the woodwork by her door, which was open. He could see her just to the left of the mirror above the dressing table.

She saw him. In an instant, she saw the scene as it might happen. Moses would take hold of her, rip off her navy jacket, and while he held her arms behind her, he would unbutton the white blouse, tear down the straps of her slip. With one hand, he could easily cover her mouth.

"Mrs. Fletcher?"

"What do you want?" she asked in a paper-thin voice.

"I will not be driving you into town today."

He would have left immediately if Aida, fired with temper, had not come in the back door and headed upstairs calling for him.

"I suppose you know already," she said.

He took her arm and led her down the stairs to the kitchen.

"What's happened?"

"Guy Bellows was fired this morning at eight o'clock from Hawkins Lumber. Plain eliminated like that." She sat down. "and now he's drunk."

"You should be sympathetic."

"Sympathetic to his drinking?" She blew her breath in Moses' face. "I haven't had a thing to drink but coffee. Smell?"

Moses turned his head away.

"Where is Guy?"

"You tell me, please," she said. "Gone to the cottage to get his gun I imagine. He picked me up at Mrs. Cash's just a while ago."

"For what has he been fired?"

"For slowness and a sweet nature." She headed back up the stairs. In the middle of the landing she turned to Moses. "I meant it about the gun."

Moses went out back. Behind him he heard Lara Fletcher leave the house. He heard her try to start the car, again and again. She had flooded the engine.

He listened, stopped and listened, until the engine caught and she drove down the driveway to the road.

Guy was on the front porch in the rocker with his feet up on the banister. He and Aida sat there on fine days. His eyes were fixed on the field beyond the cottage. His gun was under the chair.

Moses came up the steps, sat down in the chair beside him, put his feet up on the banister, crossed them as Guy's were crossed.

"He said I smelled like a nigger," Guy said.

"Who said?"

"Mr. Fielding Hawkins said that. I suppose Aida caught up with you and told you the news, loving bad news like she does."

"She told me," Moses said. "She was reasonable about it. But she didn't say you were fired for smelling like a nigger. Is that what you were told?"

"That's not the reason they gave. But it's the reason that's true."

"If it's true, then you shouldn't be working at a place to make you mad."

"I'm not mad," Guy said.

"Uh huh," Moses said. "You must just seem mad."

He sat with his brother until it was too cold to sit still any longer. But Guy would not move. He seemed drunk but Moses could not tell how drunk. What Moses did know was Guy's anger from childhood was in charge of this February afternoon.

"I'm going to see how Miracle's doing," Moses said. "Come on over."

"I might."

Moses kicked the gun gently. "There aren't any rabbits in the winter."

"I'm not interested in rabbits," Guy said.

The day had grown heavy as a tumor in Moses' heart and he had the sense his mother used to talk about during her long dying. "I wish the sun would get back over the mountain," she'd say, "and rise again."

When he went into the house, Miracle was in the kitchen talking.

"Who's there?" he asked crossly, knowing very well it was Miracle chatting up her spooks again.

"No one, darling," she called from the kitchen. "Just the cat."

She was at the stove with her back to him—looking old for a young woman, too plump, her hair uncombed, heavy on her feet. It angered him to see her letting herself go like that.

"You were talking to John Spencer is what you were doing, Miracle," he said. "And I want to tell you about John Spencer like you asked me this morning."

She picked up the cat curled in the rocker and sat down with him in her lap.

"I changed my mind," she said.

She had been talking to John Spencer. She had been telling him about Simon Peter and how he'd died soon as he found out he was retarded so as not to be much trouble to them.

Miracle was sane. She knew perfectly well that she was sane and that somehow she grew John Spencer in her living room like a tomato plant so she would seem troubled and wouldn't have to go back in the world until she was ready. Not that she didn't see him. She did and he talked to her and she believed it at the time. But deep down she knew her own powers and need had put him there. If she let go of him, he'd be gone and she would be Miracle Bellows earthbound once again, as people knew her to be. Except Moses, who had married her for her powers to dream, and now he'd come into the kitchen in a bad humor to make alterations.

Moses thought she had slipped off center, that he was in danger of losing her altogether. He thought she believed John Spencer was with her day after day, and she was going to end up certified crazy, he decided, if he didn't do something right now on this day falling to the devil for the Bellowses one and all—Guy fired, Aida on a rampage and he full of rage, kissing a white woman with her husband upstairs putting on his trousers.

"I killed John Spencer," he said.

"No," Miracle replied.

"So he's dead and not in the room with you, you understand." Moses reached forward and took her hand.

Miracle looked him straight in the eye with a hard edge, pulled her hand away.

"You mind your own business, Moses Bellows, you hear?"

February Second, 1943: Afternoon

The car wouldn't start. Twice, three times, Lara pressed the accelerator to the floor and it would not catch. She saw Moses walk down the path. Surely he heard the stubborn engine making its small insufficient roar. Then finally—he was still in sight, just beyond the barn—it caught. She turned the radio to news, turned on the heat and drove Route 7 to 123 to town.

It was only one o'clock but the sky was the color of squirrels, too dark to see without headlights. The road was almost empty and she drove on half listening to the news from Europe. Her head, usually filled with stories, was empty, even of details.

At the light on Old Dominion Drive, a man in a lizard-green car motioned her to unroll the window, which she did. He asked directions to Arlington, which she gave.

"I'm going there myself," she said.

As he leaned in her car window he was smoking a pipe and only after she closed her window trapping some of the smoke inside did she recognize the familiar smell of her father's English tobacco.

She had not smelled that tobacco for years. Now it

brought not the actual loss of her father but the shock of finding him sitting up on his own couch, his head dangling like the head of a marionette.

She could not pay attention to the road.

She crossed Chain Bridge and headed towards George-town but as she drove, she felt the onslaught of stomach flu triumphing, of feelings concealed in the attic of memory unleashed. She could not contain herself.

At Arizona Avenue, she waved the man in the green Ford on and she turned left, pulled the car to a stop on a cul-de-sac and wept.

The sounds she made were strange, primeval, from the deep caverns of her body as if some sort of revolution of the heart had turned her inside out and she was dying of exposure.

Once she had witnessed a man struck by a car in Odessa, and his body had shaken as hers was shaking, out of control as if the bones were gone. Then the shaking stopped abruptly and he was dead.

She did now know what grief had overtaken her.

Afterwards, her body weak with exertion, her mind smooth as a clean-pressed sheet, she turned the car around, turned left at the light and drove quickly—she was late now—to Arlington Cemetery, perplexed by what had happened, at ease, as if the bile of her bad dreams was spent. Surely it had not been her father's death which struck her with the smell of his tobacco—or Tom Elliot, whose face was vague as a living face.

As she drove across the wide Memorial Bridge towards the high hill of Arlington Cemetery, the yellow mansion of General Robert E. Lee, crossing the horizon, she knew that it was Moses called out of his dwelling place in her body. And her weeping had to do with shame.

Charley was standing next to the entrance to the cemetery when she drove up. He was talking to a guard, so he did not see her car pull in and park in the near-empty lot overlooking the river. She got out, put up the collar of her trench coat, opened her umbrella against the steady drizzle and walked across the lot. She could tell, just by his posture, the way his arms were folded across his chest, the way he stood in the weather defying the rain, that he was angry.

His anger had always roused her interest—but in years past it had been impersonal and gave him the attraction of accidental danger. Now it had to do with her.

"Hello." She leaned forward to kiss him.

"You drove yourself?"

"Yes, I did," she said.

"You're very late," he said.

"I know," she said. "I'm sorry. At the last minute, Moses couldn't drive."

He took her elbow and they walked up the sidewalk.

"It's a long walk," he said. "They will have started."

They had started. As Lara and Charley crested the hill, she saw a small gathering of civilians just in view, three men in uniform and a priest. There was Tom Elliot's mother in a black coat and hat, her hands tucked in a fur muff, and his father, extremely tall as Tom had been, elegant, silvery gray, and his brother, whom she had met, and his brother's wife and baby.

As they crossed the grass to the place where Tom Elliot's gunmetal casket squarely covered with the American flag matched the dark day of his interment, Charley looked at her.

"I want you to tell me," he said in her ear, "if Tom is Sam's father."

Had she heard him correctly?

She stepped across a mud pocket in the wet grass and stood next to Tom's sister-in-law and the baby, the heat of Charley's anger heavy at her side.

The Episcopal priest was saying his final prayer when she arrived. The gun volley sounded hard against the trees and then the clear mournful bugle sound of taps strung across the horizon.

They had eaten lunch already, the Elliots said. They would not have tea or drinks, they said. They were grateful to the Fletchers for taking time. They shook hands all around. Then the Elliots walked away from the gravesite, maintaining the demeanor of their Eastern upbringing with its windchill factor, fixed together like the pieces of a jigsaw puzzle, only the eyes of the baby turned out on the world.

"That was very odd," Lara said when they were out of earshot.

"Tell me." Charley had her arm in a tight grip as they followed down the hill.

"You're hurting me," she said.

He grabbed her shoulders. "Answer me," he said.

Charley Fletcher had imagined Lara's betrayal in the years of their marriage but never specifically until the silver-cold winter of early 1941 when she met Tom Elliot. In those months when Charley's sex had frozen, it was as if the other man had a lien against his fortune. He could not act.

One night, he remembered lying on his back in a cold and living anger and Lara laid her arm across his chest, ran her finger softly over his forearm in a gesture which seemed cruel to him, a tease.

"Please don't," he said.

But she leaned over to kiss him good night anyway and his mind saw, in the darkness, her perfect lips black with Tom Elliot's kisses.

Now, on the day of Tom Elliot's burial, the possible truth which had tormented his slumber for months woke him in a nightmare. Charley pulled her off the path.

"Please, Charley."

They wound through the lines of narrow white markers on the hill above Tom Elliot's slender grave.

"Can't we get in the car and talk?"

He pulled her behind a tree so the Elliots should they turn around could not see them.

"Now tell me what happened," he said, his breath hot on her face.

"There is nothing to tell."

"What about Tom Elliot?"

"Nothing."

He put his hands against the tree on either side of her head.

"And Sam?"

"What you are thinking is crazy," she said.

He dropped his arms, slipped his hands in the pocket of his raincoat.

"I don't believe you," he said.

"I am telling the truth."

She turned away, walked down the path ahead of him, following the dot of Elliots ahead. At the parking lot, she did not wait but walked across, nodding to the Elliots gathered around the priest's car. She knew Charley was behind her. She got in the car and waited for him to knock on her window but instead he walked beyond to the next line of cars, got in his own and drove too fast through the parking lot and away.

In February 1941—the beginning of February she remembered—the weather was colder than she had ever known, with nights which began in the afternoon in absolute darkness—she lost Charley Fletcher. That is how it seemed. He was in the house, all right—and in her bed, although late, sometimes one or two in the morning after finishing a story—but gone to her, a cadaver of a man.

In those months, Tom Elliot slipped into her imagination. She only saw him at large dinners with too many people. She never saw him alone. But they developed a friendship by telephone. He called daily and their conversations fell almost at once to the breathless immediacy of a love affair that began before she became pregnant with Sam and lasted until he left for Europe.

He said he loved her but he never suggested they meet in person, that he stop over or have lunch. She might have been agreeable, bereft as she was with the loss of Charley. Instead, he grew in her imagination and she thought of him as a man in a dream as women saved by paper lovers denied exit from the closet of their own lives will do. She knew she did not love Tom Elliot. Not ever. He was only a substitute for Charley Fletcher, who had died.

What Aida had in mind was a soft yellow gown with lace on it for Miracle. And then she'd do Miracle's hair and put some of her white gardenia perfume behind Miracle's ears and on her wrist to kill the heavy winter smell of soup in the kitchen, to fill the bedroom with uncommon sweetness. She had money saved in her bra for two weeks from Mrs. Cash, and Mrs. Fletcher would pay her well for the day. She put Sam down, gave Kate, bad-humored since Prudential's departure, supper. Just as she saw Lara Fletcher pull her car up by the main house, she took two swigs of bourbon from the bottle in the larder, rinsed her mouth, wiped her hands on her skirt and was in the kitchen cleaning up the dishes when Lara walked into the house.

Aida took the car. She seldom drove. She didn't have a license to drive a car and what she knew about driving was to steer straight and in a pinch put on the brake. But every time she put the clutch in the car leapt so she lurched to Seven Corners in the evening darkness and hoped to God she didn't meet another car head-on.

She was light-headed from the bourbon—stirred in the way whiskey will do to the body—someplace between sobriety and passing out. Otherwise she would not for a moment have brought a baby piglet home for Miracle instead of the yellow gown with lace she'd had in mind all day.

But there she was at Vruels', stopped to get some milk and loose tea and trade in the cans of bacon fat she'd been saving, and Mr. O'Leary pulled up in his truck with the back full of baby pigs.

"An early litter," he told Mr. Vruels, who was selling Aida her purchases as well as a bowl of paper-whites forced to early bloom.

Outside of Vruels', Aida peered between the slats of O'Leary's truck and by the spotlight overhead she could see the tiny piglets, pink as babies with their curled tails and stickpin legs, squealing up a storm, and she wanted one for Miracle.

194

By seven, she got the car back to the safety of Skunk Farm, stuck the piglet she'd bought for twenty-five dollars under her coat for warmth and headed out back to tie his neck in blue ribbon and take him over to Miracle's cottage, where everybody—she could see from the path—Miracle, Moses and Guy—sat around the kitchen table drinking beer.

Lara was lying down on Kate's bed in darkness when she heard Charley's car in the driveway. She didn't move.

"It's Charley," Kate said softly in Danish.

"I hear."

"You're fighting again, aren't you?"

"Not fighting. We seldom fight."

"It's as if you live in separate rooms," Kate said.

"Most people do," Lara said.

"For a while, Prudential and I knew each other completely."

They listened for Charley. He opened the front door and stopped in the hall, probably to read the mail as he usually did when he came home at night.

"Did you see my postcard from Prudential?"

"Yes," Lara said. "I got a note from her too about the money in the cookie jar."

"I tore it up," Kate said.

"You did?" Lara slipped her arm across Kate. "Why did you do that?"

"I didn't like what she said."

"What didn't you like?"

"She could have sent that postcard to anyone. It wasn't written to me."

"Prudential is still upset about the baby."

"Maybe. Who knows? I don't want to talk about her again."

Downstairs, Charley walked through the hall, the dining room, the kitchen. He did not call upstairs. Aida had left supper for him in the oven, and Lara could hear the clattering dishes. She also heard something else.

"Did you hear that?" she whispered to Kate.

"It sounded like a crack."

"Listen," Lara said.

They listened. The sound came once more—loud and flat against the night.

"Gunshot," Kate said.

"I think."

Almost immediately, they heard the shrill unremitting call of a wounded animal or perhaps a woman. Lara went to the window.

The outside lights had not been turned on and the back was in darkness. Out back, she could see the yellow dotted swiss of light in the cottages, and then through the clearing she saw someone running. Kate was up beside her mother.

"It's Aida," she said to Lara.

"I think you're right," Lara said.

"She must be hurt." Kate ran down the back stairs. "I'm sure she's hurt."

When Charley Fletcher opened the kitchen door, Aida fell against him.

"Help me. You have got to help me," she cried. "Guy Bellows is trying to kill me."

Kate stopped at the bottom of the back stairs.

"Mama," she called. "Please hurry."

For there was Aida Sue Bellows, clinging to Charley's shoulder, pouring blood from her head all over his white shirt.

February Second, 1943: Evening

Guy sat at the kitchen table rolling a near-empty can of beer between his palms, telling once again the story of his dismissal from Hawkins Lumber.

"We got that story memorized," Moses said. "We could tell it to the police in your very words case you'd like to have Mr. Fielding Hawkins put under arrest."

Miracle laid her hand on Moses'.

"Never mind. Let Guy talk, darling. It goes away in the telling," she said.

"I do mind."

Moses got up and opened the refrigerator. There were four beers left and a dish of beef stew, which he ate cold at the sink.

"I don't want to arrest Mr. Fielding Hawkins," Guy said without humor. "I want to kill him."

"Well now." Miracle got up, took her brother-in-law lightly by the shoulders. "Let me get you some chicken, Guy. I'll just heat it up in the oven."

"I don't want chicken," Guy said. "I want another beer."

"You had enough beer, Guy," Moses said.

197

"I want another beer because I'm thirsty. Don't tell me what to do, Moses. I've got my shotgun under the chair, see?" He kicked the barrel with his foot.

"I'm not classified blind," Moses said.

"So don't tell me I should be eating chicken. Where's Aida?"

Miracle took another can of beer out of the icebox and gave it to Guy. She took a plate of stewed chicken from Sunday supper.

"You said yourself Aida wouldn't be home until seven and it's just seven now," Miracle said. She put the chicken in a pot and set the kitchen table.

"I don't have an appetite."

"I'm giving everybody supper. You're not being singled out," Miracle said. She looked at Moses to let him know with her eyes that trouble was afoot and they'd better be attentive. But his black eyes were too hot for sight. He didn't even catch her expression. She laid her hand on his arm.

"Maybe I should make some biscuits," she said softly. "I'll just make some biscuits and we'll have chicken and I might even do a bread pudding. What do you think of that?" she said to no one in particular, but Guy answered once again.

"I don't have an appetite."

When Aida Sue walked in the door with the piglet under her coat, calling "Surprise, Surprise," the tempers in the Bellows cottage were burning.

She put the frightened piglet down on the floor, and it ran squealing through the kitchen.

"She's for you, Miracle, a baby to light up your eyes again."

"For chrissake." Moses picked the piglet up. "You bought this ugly thing to live here? Have you got brains, Aida Sue, or cream of wheat in your head?"

Miracle took the piglet from Moses.

"Why, it's a lovely pig, Aida. And you got it as a present?"

"And these flowers." Aida put the bowl of paper-whites

in the middle of the kitchen table. "It was an inspiration," she said. "I saw these pigs and I saw Miracle setting in the rocker in the kitchen rocking away with a piglet on her lap like we used to do when we were children. I couldn't help myself."

"You can help yourself a lot more than you've a mind to do," Guy said.

"I want you to take that pig right back where you got her before supper," Moses said. "Aida? You hear?"

"Don't touch my wife," Guy said.

"I'm not touching your wife," Moses said. "I'm talking to her if you'd listen."

"I will not take back the piglet. It's a present for Miracle and not you. If she wants me to take the piglet back, then I'll do it," Aida said. "So Miracle. You want me to take this pig back or not?"

"I think this is a very thoughtful gift," Miracle said softly. "She is a beautiful pig."

"A beautiful pig." Moses opened the refrigerator. "There is no such thing as a beautiful pig." He sat down next to Guy with another beer.

"I'm making supper," Miracle said but Moses interrupted her.

"I meant it about this pig, Aida. Get it out of here. We've had enough trouble this winter."

"I will not."

"Then go home."

"I'm not going home either," Aida said. "I'm eating Miracle's supper and then I'm packing my clothes and moving up to my old bedroom in the main house like Charley Fletcher asked us to do this morning as you very well know, Moses Bellows."

"You are doing what?" Guy stood up.

"You heard me perfectly clear." She marched across the room and got a glass of juice.

"Charley Fletcher asked us to move in. He said he'd love to have us. Those were his words and that is exactly what I am going to do."

"Over my dead body," Guy said.

And before anyone had a chance to stop him, he had taken his shotgun from under the chair.

"Now get out of the way," he shouted, waving the gun around, and he shot at the piglet, grazing the rear quarters.

"Don't kill him," Aida cried, going after Guy, her arms out to take hold of the gun or else restrain him. But Guy was gone to the world now and he hit Aida hard with the end of the gun. Almost at once, she was pouring blood from the top of her head. She ran out the door and across the path to the main house.

"Don't get close!" he shouted, pointing the gun at Moses.

The piglet spun around and around. Accustomed as Guy was to hunting, he was too drunk to track the frantic pig. He shot once more but this time missed completely and the piglet scrambled under the kitchen table.

"Sweet Jesus." Miracle sank into a chair.

"Don't anybody come near me, you hear?" Guy said. "I'm going after Aida."

"Don't hurt her, Guy," Miracle said. "She's a good woman. A very good woman and you love her. Remember you love her."

"If she goes in that house and asks Mr. Charley Fletcher to take care of her because I could hurt her, I will hurt her bad."

Guy went out the door and headed up the path.

"Don't go after him, Moses," Miracle said. "He could do anything."

Moses said nothing. He took a large terry-cloth towel from the shelf, picked up the injured pig, wrapped her, put her on Miracle's lap and went out the back door.

"Aida." Guy Bellows went towards the main house, not quickly because he kept hearing Moses behind him and stopped and turned around. "That you, Moses? It better not be you."

Moses was following, but far enough behind and carefully. He knew Guy in such a mood as he was in and did not wish to be the one who paid for his brother's humiliation.

"Aida," Guy called out. "Aida Sue Bellows. Come back home."

...

Inside the Fletchers' house, the lights were out and Charley had bolted the kitchen door with the only lock it had, which was an old brass one above the doorknob. He stood next to the door expecting Guy.

Aida sat in a kitchen chair holding an ice pack to her head and weeping.

Kate was under the kitchen table. Charley had turned out the lights and told her to go upstairs but she had ducked under the table instead, wrapped her arms around Aida's legs.

When Guy reached the back door, Lara was on the telephone with the chief of police.

"Send Aida out here," Guy shouted.

"I certainly will not," Charley called back. "She's hurt."

"She's my wife," Guy said. "Aida Sue? You get out here right now."

The sound of his voice made Aida weep louder.

"Open the door and let Aida out, Mr. Fletcher," Guy said in a cold reasonable voice.

"I won't," Charley replied. "Go home, Guy, and sober up."

The chief of police told Lara he would not send a car.

"This is a personal fight," he said. "I won't endanger my men in a family squabble with colored people who are always shooting off guns like they were popcorn."

"We're in danger," Lara said evenly.

"You're not in danger if you send Aida Bellows outside. Guy's not going to shoot you."

"What about *her*?" Lara's voice shook with anger.

"He's not going to shoot Aida either. And if he does, it's not your business or ours. It's a personal matter, like I said."

Lara put down the receiver.

In the darkness, silent except for Aida's weeping, she could see the outline of her husband and was just crossing the kitchen to tell him what the police had said when the window next to the kitchen table shattered and the shotgun went off twice in the black room.

Lara dropped to the ground when the first shot sounded

and crawled under the table with Kate, grabbing her daughter. Across the room where Charley had been standing guard against the kitchen door, there was a deep groan and he fell backwards against the wall and slid to the floor.

"You coming now, Aida?" Guy shouted through the open window.

"I'm coming." Aida shook her legs free of Kate's grip and struggled to her feet. "I'm coming." She made her way in darkness across the kitchen and tried to open the kitchen door.

"It's bolted," she called to Guy. "I can't."

"Unbolt it," Guy said, but he kicked the door instead and it flew open, just missing Aida.

"You're coming with me," Guy said as Moses ran up behind them.

"Who's shot?" Moses called. "Guy? Is that you?"

"It's me," Guy said in an even voice.

"What happened?" Moses was out of breath.

"I don't know," Guy said. "Something's happened. You take the gun." He handed the gun to his brother. "You take it for me. I've got to help Aida. I've got to take her back to the cottage."

When Moses went in the kitchen door, Charley Fletcher was lying on his back bleeding at the belly through his gray sweater.

"Wait here," Moses said to Guy.

Guy stood in the doorway.

"He wouldn't turn Aida out," Guy said. "He was keeping her."

Moses put the gun on the kitchen table and called the ambulance.

"Don't call the police, Moses," Charley Fletcher said. His voice was clear. "It wasn't Guy's fault."

Lara looked up at Moses.

"Don't," she said.

"We won't tell the police what happened," Charley said. "It's not their business. Lara?" He turned in the direction of where she sat.

"Don't talk," she whispered.

"I won't," he said. And he could not.

The moment of extreme clarity after the shock of the wound had passed and he was sinking quickly into unconsciousness.

They waited. Kate under the table, Lara beside Charley holding his hand, Moses standing by the kitchen door, Guy outside holding on to Aida.

"I'm hurt," Aida whimpered. "I want to go home."

"You're not bad hurt," Guy said.

"I want to go home now," Aida said.

"You shouldn't have come up here like you did," Guy said. "You made me angry."

"Let her go home, Guy," Moses said. "You stay."

Aida pulled her coat around her. The bleeding had stopped but she felt sick and weak-kneed.

"I'm sorry, Guy," she said to him, touching his arm. "I shouldn't have come up here."

When the ambulance came, Lara ran upstairs with Kate. Quickly she packed a suitcase, put Sam, who was sleeping, in a snowsuit and rushed back downstairs.

"Do you want to follow us in your car or come in the ambulance?" the driver asked her.

Moses touched her shoulder.

"I'll drive you," he said.

She shook her head and climbed into the back of the ambulance with Kate and Sam. The driver shut the door and the last she saw of Moses as the ambulance pulled out of Skunk Farm was his splendid face framed by the high window of the ambulance.

Kate pressed hard against her mother.

"It's all right," Lara whispered in Danish.

"Will we be back home tonight?" Kate asked, hiding her face in her mother's coat.

"We will never be back here," Lara replied.

She leaned her head against the window of the van and closed her eyes against the sight of her husband's dying.

Early Spring, 1943

The long wet days of early spring had no definition. They fell together undivided by names—except Tuesday when the laundry went out and Sunday when there was no traffic. It was as if the people in the pictures of familiar photographs were overexposed, had suffered a loss of short-term memory and did not recognize the bright white reproductions of themselves.

The day after Charley Fletcher was shot, Lara moved with her children into the Mayflower Hotel in downtown Washington. The hotel was large and elegant for wartime with two dining rooms and a genteel staff, a place of temporary safety in a country which had become a war zone for Lara Fletcher.

The Fletchers' rooms at the Mayflower were on the third floor with ample windows overlooking Connecticut Avenue, and signs of spring dotted the trees spread just beneath the window where Kate Bergmann sat by the hour staring at the scenes of the street waiting for change.

Mme. Porte, reed-thin, smelling of the high sweet perfume of funeral parlors, bad-humored from an early aging, came at eight to care for Sam just as room service arrived with the breakfast table covered with linen, steaming with silver-lidded plates, ice bowls with orange juice glasses, a pot of black coffee for Lara. They had become a family in an English novel, Kate thought, with servants and carefully organized days.

Lara spoke to Mme. Porte in French. Take the children out, perhaps to the park. Send out Sam's diapers. Pick up saltines and milk at the market. Take Kate to the library to exchange her books. Don't allow her to remain in the hotel room by herself.

"I would like to go back to school." Kate followed her mother to the bathroom, where she was dressing. "*When can I go back to school?*"

"Soon," Lara said. "When we're settled."

She did not mention Skunk Farm; they had not been back.

"We can't settle in a hotel," Kate said crossly.

"We have settled here," Lara replied.

There was a routine. By eight-thirty, Lara left for the day in her lavender dress—always the same dress with a different scarf or a small lace collar of beads. She wore makeup, deep blue on the eyelids and mascara. She had never worn makeup before except in films. She curled her hair in rollers at night and wore it fluffed around her face. The strangeness of her mother's new appearance silenced Kate.

At eight-thirty, she would walk with Lara to the elevator, kiss her solemnly, longing for a personal exchange. But her mother was rarely available and then only on the fly, so the old familiar intimacy between them could not be fixed in place.

All spring, in the heavy damask rooms of the Mayflower, locked in like an invalid, Kate wrote letters.

"Dear Prudential," she wrote in late February.

I suppose you have been writing and that your letters from New York are piled on the table in the hall waiting for me to read them.

I have not been back to the farm for quite a while.

In early February, we moved to the Mayflower Hotel in

Washington, D. C., which is a fancy place with velvet curtains which draw across the window and stiff upholstery on the couches and a radio on which I listen to soap operas during the day since I no longer go to school.

At the beginning of February, there was an argument at the farm and Guy Bellows shot Charley because of a misunderstanding. Aida was hurt by Guy as well but I don't think badly. Or so my mother says.

I spend my days reading books and listening to the radio. I order up room service, sometimes three Coca-Colas a day, and at night after the dreadful Mme. Porte who cares for Sam has left, Mama, Sam and I have supper in the dining room.

Since the argument my mother has changed the way she looks. She puffs her hair and paints her face a sort of peach color and looks quite a lot like the stars you see in movie magazines. You would not recognize her. Three nights a week after dinner, she dresses in a slinky black skirt and silver top and goes to a place called the USO where she sings and dances for American soldiers. She tells me the USO is her safety net in troubled times. I tell her I should be her safety net. And Sam. Why else have children? Sometimes I am afraid she will meet an American soldier and leave us here at the Mayflower Hotel for the rest of our lives. In which case I would begin by poisoning Mme. Porte.

I hope things are going well for you in New York. I am sending this to Okrakan and expect your mother will forward the letter to your new address. Please write to me c/o the Mayflower Hotel, Washington, D.C., since I will probably live here forever.

Love now and always,
Kate

P.S. Thank you for burning Pole Trickett for me. It was very thoughtful of you.

"Dear Papa," she wrote, although she knew he might not get the letter and certainly she couldn't go to Italy until the war was over.

You would be very surprised to see how we're living. Mama has moved us into a splendid hotel with room service. I have my own radio and have written three soap operas which I put on for Sam and Mme. Porte who have to listen because we cannot escape our rooms.

Mama thinks America is more dangerous than Europe in spite of the war there. I no longer go to school because of the danger and so I would very much like to come to Milan for a visit with you.

I forgot to tell you, we have four courses at dinner, always tomato juice and celery first which I hate, and Mama gives me some of her wine so I won't notice when she slips out to dance in practically nothing for the American soldiers.

I am hoping to get married early in order not to have to spend so much time alone. Trinket, who makes our beds every day with crisp sheets—can you imagine?—was married at fifteen.

As you see, it would be a very good idea for you to send for me.

Please write.
Love,
Kate

She had started several letters to Miracle.
"Dear Miracle," she had written on February 22.

Do you know we have moved to the Mayflower Hotel?

"Dear Miracle," she had written on March 1.

I am well. I hope you are too. And Moses. I had a dream about you and Moses on the porch of Guy's cottage. Moses was singing.

"Dear Miracle," she had written on March 15.

I suppose you don't know what has become of us.

"Dear Miracle," she had written the following day.

Perhaps you could call me at Decatur 3000 during the day. I am in room 312.

Once she called Skunk Farm and Miracle answered.

"The Fletchers' residence," she said. Kate waited listening for sounds of her house through the telephone wire, relieved that another family had not moved in in their absence.

"Hello," Miracle said in her familiar voice. "This is the Fletchers' residence." And when nobody spoke a second time, Miracle hung up. Kate didn't call again.

Prudential in her pink dress, her hair in ribbons although it was afternoon of a Tuesday in March—no cause
for celebration—was in the kitchen of her mama's house
when Holiday came home from school with the mail,
which included a bill from the hospital for Ulysses Dargon's drunken car accident, which by some twist of fortune
did not kill him but left him unable to work, only to devil
his daughters, now Holiday and Mercury, just nine. There
was a Sears, Roebuck catalogue and a letter from Kate
Bergmann.

"Read it to me," Holiday said.

"It's private," Prudential said.

"Like New York was private." Holiday flounced out of
the room. "Everything you do since your baby is private,
Prudential Dargon. It makes me sick."

"That's right," Prudential said. "You're just going to
have to be sick."

She opened the letter and read it. Then she put on her
jacket, told her mother, who was rocking the new baby,
called Audie Murphy at Prudential's suggestion, that she
was going to the market for milk of magnesia and would
be back soon.

"Did Aunt Miracle mention any trouble on the farm?" she asked.

"She says the weather's bad and it doesn't look like spring will come this year."

"Did she ask about me?"

"I told her you were doing just fine."

"You said I was still in New York, didn't you?"

Her mother shook her head. "I didn't say you weren't."

At the market, she bought yellow stationery with tulips, sat down on the floor next to the cash register and wrote a letter to Kate.

Dear Kate,

I was glad to get your letter which came today at the apartment where I am staying in New York.

I love New York. I worked for two weeks at the job at the donut factory and then I got discovered by the Radio and so I'm training to be on soap operas which you listen to now you don't go to school.

Please write to me about the argument at the farm. You did not say how Mr. Fletcher is and why you had to move to a hotel. Aunt Miracle hasn't mentioned an argument.

I broke up with my boyfriend since I started to be a radio personality. He said he couldn't keep up with me. Now I have different boyfriends and eat at restaurants. Here in New York, colored can go anyplace.

I still move around a lot so send my letters to Okrakan 'cause Mama can always find me.

Right now I'm living in a high thin house with a lady named Melody Pinky who is a magazine model. She lets me wear her makeup. But I'll be moving soon.

Love forever,
Prudential Dargon

She stamped the letter and mailed it. Then she read *Good Housekeeping* and *Vogue* cover to cover, bought a small bottle of milk of magnesia and walked home wondering, since her baby died, how she simply didn't know what was true and what she made up any longer. There were these lies like Melody Pinky sprouting dandelions in her mind.

The fact was Prudential had spent twenty-seven hours in New York from the time the bus arrived at 6:00 P.M. at Port Authority to the time she left at 9:00 P.M. the following evening for Charleston, South Carolina, and the local to Okrakan. On the bus, she had met a white man named Harry Fine who got on in Baltimore and said he had a doughnut factory and connections with radio. He bought her a Milky Way and a hot dog in Wilmington and offered to have her stay at his place at 40th and Seventh Avenue, which he said was an easy walk from the bus terminal. It was a very short walk to the mud-brick apartment building where he raped her with her coat on, then he spit on her feet, lit a cigarette and left her in the foyer of the apartment building, where she stayed until the gray light of morning shone through the glass door and she ran to Port Authority. At the bus station, she bought a postcard of the Empire State Building for Kate and note paper and wrote to Miracle and Mrs. Fletcher. She got a tuna-fish sandwich and a Coca-Cola and sat down on the brown bench close as she could without being too familiar to an elderly soft-looking colored woman with her granddaughter, counting the hours until she could leave the city of her dreams.

John Spencer was dead as a doornail. Miracle hadn't seen him once since the shooting. As winter wore on and on into late March when the sun ought to have lit their windows in the morning and was instead invisible from day to night she grew hard-edged and bad-tempered.

"Things should not have come to this," she said to Moses.

"And what is this but another opportunity to move into the main house and lay claim to our canopy bed, darling Miracle."

"You call me May, which is my rightful name."

"I will call you Miracle," he said.

They did not speak of Charley Fletcher except from time to time after work. Moses, sitting in the dark living room listening to Miracle cook away food enough for armies as if cooking kept her standing, would call out:

"Remember what my mama used to say about boundaries, May Bellows?"

She heard him but she didn't answer.

"Well, Charley Fletcher went out of bounds."

Guy saved the piglet. After the shooting, he went back to Moses' cottage with Aida and there was Miracle in the living room with the piglet laid out on the couch on a terrycloth towel.

Guy picked the piglet up, wrapped the towel around her, took her home, put her on the kitchen table with a bag over her head so she wouldn't react, sterilized Aida's tweezers with a match and took the shot out of the piglet's thigh. Then he dressed it with ointment his mother used to use for burns and cuts, wrapped the piglet's leg in gauze, and kept her in a pen in the kitchen until the leg was healed.

"You see?" Guy said to Aida one morning at breakfast. "I saved her life."

"I do see," Aida said, "and you were good to do it, Guy. It does make a difference she didn't die."

Aida was right. So much had gone wrong that winter at Skunk Farm, the fact of the pig's life did make a difference.

Mornings before he went to work at the O'Learys', Moses stopped by Vruels' and bought the *Post*. In the truck, he'd skip the front-page news from Europe and turn to the obituaries. Once or twice a week, he called the fourth floor of Doctors' Hospital and asked for a report on Charley Fletcher.

"Unchanged," the nurse said every time.

Charley Fletcher's room at Doctors' Hospital was kept dark, and usually, unless the cleaning woman had just left, it smelled too sweetly of disease as if he were in the process of rotting. Weeks went by. He did not get better and he did not die. There were signs of change—sometimes that the infection was almost under control, sometimes that the poisons would gallop through his body in a matter of hours and kill him. Either change seemed preferable to Lara to the endless repetition of days.

She would arrive at nine, speak to the nurses, who described the night he'd had, stand at the head of his bed while the doctor changed the dressing on his belly. Often they'd put a new tube in to drain the infection into a jar under the bed. He went in and out of consciousness. Sometimes he called her darling, sometimes Lara, once or twice Aunt Sad, but as the days wore on, the conscious moments made less sense and his eyes if they were open were clouded.

She read to him all day. Late in the day, she'd read plays in Danish, taking all the roles, moving about in her lavender dress filling the small hospital room with her strong voice, and the nurses would gather in the hall to watch.

"You keep him alive," they told her. "No one in our memory has gone on so long with an infection like this."

Mostly she read Trollope. She liked the sane, sensible, predictable world in Trollope where manners and reason and good sense prevailed. Besides there were so many Trollope novels to last the long weeks of his precarious life.

Aunt Sad would call almost every day and Lara would speak to her on the telephone at the nurses' station. His mother never called.

"He's more like his father than I had dreamed," his mother had said furiously when Lara told her the story of the shooting. "Imagine getting himself in trouble with the colored in the South when he has such great gifts."

"She's brokenhearted is what she is," Aunt Sad said. "You can't prize things too much, you know. Nobody's safe."

For Charley Fletcher, the days were not bad except for the pain, which was occasional. Perched on the edge of consciousness, like a drunk without the dizziness, he lived in a child's dream world. He saw himself in slow motion licking a regenerative chocolate ice cream cone or sleeping with a warm hamburger on the sheet or lying on a naked white-skinned woman with breasts the size of pillows. He knew Lara was there. He heard her voice. He knew the hyacinth smell of her. Sometimes his father visited, sitting at the end of the bed in his baseball cap. He would ask him about the book he was writing on Skunk Farm. Or had he finished the book? He couldn't recall.

He didn't remember what had happened. He knew someone had shot him and sometimes the face he saw holding the gun was Guy Bellows. Sometimes Moses. Once it was his mother.

It was late April—the 24th. All over the blue-and-white city, sheets of crocuses moved in the light wind and the starlings argued on the eaves of buildings. The day was cool and sunny and smelled of the earth. Lara was late to the hospital. She had overslept, from staying too long at the USO the night before, and now as she hurried down the corridor of the fourth floor of Doctors' Hospital, she knew in her bones there had been a change.

Her heart caught. She looked at the nurses at the nurses' station for an expression of sympathy but there was no sign.

"How is he?" She leaned over the counter and whispered to the head nurse.

"See for yourself," she said

Charley Fletcher was alone when the balance of his life shifted. It was three in the morning by the round black-rimmed clock over the nurses' station, which he could see through the open door from his bed. There were no nurses in the corridor, no sound of them. Likely they were resting between emergencies.

At first he thought he had been awakened by an emergency. He felt different. There was a clarity about the things around him, the IV bottle, the door, the end of the white iron bed, the clock itself above the nurses' station—not unfamiliar sights from the last months but revealed now whereas before he had seemed to live in a place vacated for the summer, with objects covered by sheets.

His mind was clear, and what woke him was a memory of being on his knees. He even felt the lingering discomfort of remaining too long in a kneeling position by his narrow bed in the house at New Philadelphia next to his mother also kneeling, smelling richly of bread dough, her voice in his ear too high-pitched and anxious. "Thank you dear Lord for my great gift which I will give to the world."

It made him laugh out loud—just the desperate sight of them in his mind's eye kneeling by the bed in a depressed Midwestern town made him laugh. Not even with sadness, although certainly it was sad for both of them, he supposed. But rather he was struck by the absurdity of the scene, for how could a boy with the burden of a great and unknown gift, the answer to his mother's prayers, his mother's secret spouse—how could such a boy careful of his moments for fear of failure or reprisal, handcuffed to his mother's dream for him—survive failing as he seemed to have survived it in a land where to succeed is holy, on the right hand of God?

A nurse came in.

"I heard you call, Mr. Fletcher." She took his wrist automatically.

"I had a comic nightmare and must have laughed," he said. "Do I have a pulse?"

She patted his wrist.

"Of course." She stuck a thermometer in his mouth.

"Taking my temperature in the middle of the night?"

"It seems to have broken. Can't you tell? You're lying in a stream of your own perspiration." She turned on the light beside his bed, and he closed his eyes against its brightness.

She left and brought another nurse with her and a tray with a tall glass of orange juice. They checked the thermometer.

"Normal," the second nurse said. "This is the first time your temperature has been normal since the infection set in."

"I'm better then," he said.

"It looks that way."

He took the juice and drank it down. They changed his bedclothes without moving him, although he said he was sure he could get up and walk to the chair. Then they turned out the light.

"Now you should go back to sleep," the first nurse said. "You're lucky. You've been very sick."

He closed his eyes and settled into the fresh sheets, at ease, in a kind of somnambulant peace he had never known, not even as a boy. What he felt was a certain joy that he had come through a long darkness to understand the gift his mother had him praying for in gratitude had been there all the time. Not for the world as his mother had imagined. But for himself.

When Lara Fletcher went into the room at the end of the fourth-floor corridor of Doctors' Hospital that morning in late April, there Charley was, sitting up against the back of his bed, his eyes on the world again.

BOOK FIVE

Independence
Day,
1943

Spring, 1943

Late April, when the hill dipping from the main house was a blanket of yellow daffodils, the willow bending over the drive sprinkled with tight buds, a FOR SALE sign went up at Skunk Farm. No longer Skunk Farm. The real estate agent had instructed Moses to put up the old sign, since no one in his right mind would buy a place with a name like Skunk Farm, so Moses turned the sign around. *Elm Grove, 1803* faced the road again.

"Get rid of the dead elms as well," the real estate agent said. "They give the place a bad reputation."

On a Saturday in a thin rain, Moses and Guy cut down the elms, chopped the wood, loaded it on the back of the pickup and took it to Vruels' to sell.

"I liked the Fletchers," Guy said to Moses.

"You should have thought about that earlier," Moses said, bad-tempered at the selling of the farm again.

"I was drunk when I shot the gun."

"You were angry. You would have done the same thing sober."

"Maybe." Guy was thoughtful. "I could have gone to prison, you know."

"You could have," Moses said. They stopped at Vruels' and unloaded the wood.

"I suppose you know what they do to niggers in prison."

"I wasn't born yesterday."

Mr. Vruels came out and said he'd heard Mr. Fletcher was doing better, back at work at his important job, and that the beautiful Mrs. Fletcher was going to Denmark to live with her daughter. He wondered about the baby boy.

"That's not the information we have," Moses said.

"What is your information?" Mr. Vruels asked.

"They have a house in Georgetown closer to his work."

"And you haven't heard anything about a divorce."

"It's not my business," Moses said.

"Well she certainly is lovely to look at and I'd hate to think of her unhappy, wouldn't you?"

Moses didn't reply.

Mr. Vruels paid them for the wood and stood outside to watch the Bellows brothers climb back into the cab of the pickup and head home.

"Have you ever wondered why Mr. Fletcher didn't have me arrested?" Guy asked.

"No," Moses said, although he had many times, lying awake at night next to Miracle. He wondered why a man, shocked into lucidity as Charley Fletcher had been right after he was shot, would protect from blame the man who shot him. He had even asked Miracle.

"He was ashamed," she had said.

"Of what?"

"Of causing trouble in our lives. Mr. Charley Fletcher is not a stupid man," Miracle said.

Moses turned the corner and the farm came into view. Along the horizon was the vast white house and lines of black stumps, two feet high with a rounded look.

"It looks like a plantation with broken-down Negro women working in the fields," Guy said.

"Well it's not a plantation," Moses said. "You need glasses, Guy. It's our home."

"I don't want to live here anymore unless the Fletchers come back," Guy said. "Anybody could buy it."

"Look what happened when the Fletchers were here," Moses said, turning up the drive.

"It wouldn't happen again."

"Who knows?" Moses shook his head.

No one even came to look at the house. All during May, Miracle kept the main house sparkling and the cottages as well just in case, but no one came and the first week in June the FOR SALE sign disappeared. It was gone one evening when Moses came home from work.

"The place isn't for sale any longer," the real estate agent said when Moses called him on the phone.

"Does that mean the Fletchers are coming back here to live?"

"That's my understanding," the real estate agent said.

That night, lying in bed in the dark, Miracle could feel Moses' unsettlement.

"You're worried," Miracle said.

"I suppose I am," Moses replied.

"Charley Fletcher is not going to come back here with ideas again," Miracle said, resting her head on his arm. "You know that."

"I know that."

"Then you're worried about her."

Moses' heart picked up. That was it, of course. There had been no reckoning of the day when he kissed Lara Fletcher and there would never be. What was there to be said between two people who have flown outside the force of gravity and disturbed the universe?

"You know what we are to white men, darling?" Moses said.

"What?" Miracle asked.

"We're the other side of the moon," he said.

"What we are to white men, Moses, is sex," Miracle said. "Sex and spirit. And they are the unsullied angels of God." She kissed him hard. "Now you come here."

There was a ballerina figurine in Lara's childhood home which her mother bought on her only visit to Paris. She was small and delicate with a pale pink skirt made of real lace, dipped to hold its form, incongruous in the Bergmanns' spare Scandinavian flat. The only time Lara could ever recall her mother losing her temper was when she was a child, perhaps five, and broke the dancer's head.

"She was perfect," her mother said, " and she'll never be perfect again."

Ever after, the head, reglued, tilted a little to the side.

Lara never touched the dancer until one morning when she was eleven, days after her mother had died, the dancer caught her eye and just the sight of it there with its fragile lace skirt, its imperfect head, angered her. She picked it up and tossed it against the wall of the living room, where it broke in many pieces.

"Why did you do that?" her father asked, weak with the loss of his wife.

"She had a broken head," Lara said.

He took the pieces of ballerina, wrapped them in newspaper and put them in Lara's top drawer.

"That was your mother's favorite," he said. "Someday you will be glad for the pieces."

"Never," Lara said. ""She was too fragile to keep."

In Georgetown, in the narrow three-story furnished house on 34th Street, just above the Potomac River, the Fletchers' lives seemed too fragile to keep.

Charley Fletcher was released from the hospital in early May and they moved from the Mayflower Hotel. Kate entered the public school. Charley returned part-time to work, but he was frail for conversation when he got home and spent hours sitting in an overstuffed chair in the living room, the unopened newspaper in his lap. He did not think or daydream or listen to the radio. He simply sat very still and recovered.

They were like an elderly couple long married with bones too brittle to risk falling.

Only once did they speak about Skunk Farm.

"Sell it," Lara had said. "I won't go back."

So Charley put it on the market without an argument.

But with June and the first week of warm weather something changed and suddenly, almost overnight, Charley Fletcher felt his life fill up like a cup.

Evenings, lying side by side in a rented bed, they began to talk of returning to the farm not as an actual possibility but as if the farm were a place to go for a holiday or an adventure. They spoke warmly of the Bellowses and laughed about their lives there. They spoke particularly of Moses.

"I think he was very taken with you," Charley said without an edge.

"He was," Lara replied simply.

Some deep alteration had taken place in Charley Fletcher. He had let go of his life as if by holding it so firmly in grip, by taking charge of every wind change, of his wife and her wandering thoughts, of his job and Tom Elliot and the Bellowses, he had no hold on a life at all.

Once, as a child, he had gone tubing with his older brother on a fast-moving creek off the Ohio River. In the white water, he had slipped through the wide black hole of the rubber inner tube and tried to drag himself out of the current, head against it, take control—his older brother calling from just ahead, "Don't fight the water, Charley. You'll lose."

So he sank into the rushing water on his belly, his eyes fixed on the extended tree branch where his brother was holding, and the water took him downstream, his head just above the white waves—into the tree trunk and his brother's arms.

"You have to test the current first or you'll drown," his brother said to him on the way home over the dry Ohio fields that afternoon.

One morning Kate looked into their bedroom and saw them sleeping on the same pillow, face to face breathing the other's air as animals will do in the cold. And she slipped back into her own room, playing happily on her bed with Sam eased by the recovery of her parents' lives.

"I want to move back to the farm," Charley said one

morning in the middle of June. "We have a chance to make a home there."

Lara did not argue. She did not agree to go with him but she did not argue.

Prudential was sitting on the back porch doing snap beans thinking about what she was going to say in her next letter to Kate Bergmann since it certainly was high time for her to be heard on the radio given what she'd said in her other letters to Kate when Holiday came up the path with the mail.

"There's a letter from Aunt Miracle," she called out. "That's all. Not even a catalogue."

Prudential's mother, resting on the porch letting the light breeze from the west blow up her skirt between her legs, took the letter.

> Dear Lila,
>
> I had a bad period this last month and lost so much blood I feel like I'm running on water but Moses had to take me to the hospital and the doctor said I could have miscarried so the news wasn't all bad since if I miscarried there had to be a baby started but I don't have much faith in doctors. He did an operation and now I'm in bed for two weeks. Lord knows why but he said what with my pressure and the bleeding, it wouldn't hurt.
>
> We are doing fine. Fixing up the places out back and painting. Aida has been stone sober since February and if she lasts through her birthday, we're going to make her up a dressing table like the one she had when we lived in the main house.
>
> The Fletchers are moving back. They tried to sell the place and no one wanted it so they're coming in July and I hope it works especially with Moses because they are as nice people as would ever live here. Not high and mighty at all. Only Moses is high and mighty.
>
> I'm putting in this article I found about a lady who died of having fifteen children one after another. If a daughter of yours would like to pay a visit this summer, I'd like to have her. I miss Prudential every day.
>
> I heard from her and she seems to be doing fine in New York City but I haven't heard her on the radio yet. Guy has a

new job working at the O'Learys'. Please remember what I said about the vitamins.

Love,
Miracle (May).

"So," Lila Dargon said. "You want to go see Aunt Miracle, Holiday?"

Holiday shook her head. "I want to stay here," she said. "I don't like trips."

"It's not a long trip and you'd have a good time," Lila said. "Maybe Mercury could go too."

"Then who'd you have to help you out with the babies if Mercury's gone too?"

"Prudential."

Prudential stood up and put the bowl of snap beans on the table.

"I want to go," she said quietly.

"But darling, how can you go when you're in New York City?"

"I'll go from New York City there," Prudential said. "I got to New York City from there, after all."

Lila folded the letter, put it in her pocket and stood up.

"I don't like lying to my sister about you being in New York when you're standing right here beside me and sleeping in your own bed with Holiday and have been here since February."

"I went to New York to make something of myself," she said. "It didn't work. That's why I don't want Miracle to know."

"What is it to Miracle? She knows you're only thirteen years old."

"She got attached to my dreams," Prudential said. "She's never going to New York. She's never going to leave Vienna, Virginia."

She carried the beans into the kitchen and cut up carrots.

"I'll tell you what," she said to her mother. "If you let me go take care of Miracle right now, tomorrow on the seven-thirty bus, I'll tell her the gospel truth about New York City first thing."

Lila shook her head.

"I don't understand you, Prudential Dargon. You've got too many side paths in your brain for me to follow."

Prudential dumped the carrots and snap beans into the pot of beef stock bubbling on the stove.

"What do you think, Mama? You think this doctor could help make Miracle have a baby?"

Lila shook her head.

"Babies come from God, not doctors, Prudential, as you very well know."

"That's not what I heard."

"You get too much bad news from those magazines you read at Willoughby's."

"I didn't find out about babies by reading magazines, Mama. I found out about babies by minding my own business in my own house in Okrakan, South Carolina."

And she fled from the kitchen, out the back door, across the field and into the woods at the end of the farm, weeping for the first time. For her own dead baby and for Miracle and for knowing too much at thirteen years old to hold in a long slight body without any pockets of flesh for protection.

The next morning she left on the seven-thirty bus for Virginia pleased for the chance to take care of Miracle.

Maybe, she thought on the long trip north, she would move to Washington, D.C., where President Roosevelt lived. Certainly the President of the United States would not live in a city where terrible things can happen to children.

July Fourth, 1943

In the end, Lara went with Charley back to Skunk Farm, early in the morning of the Fourth of July.

The day was hazy, sprinkled with gray altering the shapes of things in the distance. When they turned the corner onto Route 7, the large white house seemed suspended in air, separated from the land on which it sat.

"The elms have been cut," Lara said.

"They look worse than they did before," Charley said.

"We'll take them out and plant young trees," Lara said.

"You said that the first time we moved here," Kate said.

"Well this time we'll do it," Charley said.

"If we stay," Lara said.

"Of course," Charley agreed. "If we stay."

Closer, the house looked different than Charley had remembered when he had driven this road before lifted by the sight of it around the bend. Now it was smaller as places from childhood will seem when you return to them. The paint on the front windows was peeling and there were several tiles gone from the roof. The long row of short fat elm stumps gave the place a transitional appearance, a sense of being on the decline.

"Prudential is here," Kate announced from the backseat as if her statement was news. Everyone knew Prudential had come all the way from New York to take care of Miracle. They even expected her to be by the willow tree waiting for their arrival but she was not there. No one seemed to be around at all.

"Where do you expect Moses is?" Charley asked.

Lara's chest tightened. "It's a holiday."

"I had forgotten," Charley said.

They parked the car next to the patio. Lara lifted Sam, sticky with chocolate ice cream on his fingers and his trousers, and went in the back door, which was as always unlocked. The house smelled damp and musty, sealed from the outside, and she went around the downstairs opening all the windows and french doors.

There were no flowers. She had been so accustomed to the flowers Miracle kept everywhere that the absence of them made the house unfamiliar as if the furniture belonged to someone else. When she opened the door of the icebox and saw that it was empty, her eyes filled.

"Charley?"

He was behind her.

"There is no food."

He laughed. "We've been away for quite a long time."

She sat down on a kitchen chair with Sam, licked the end of a Kleenex and washed his face and fingers with it.

"Nothing to eat," Kate said, looking in the icebox after her mother. "And it's a holiday."

"They knew we were coming, didn't they, Charley?" she asked as he brought the suitcases from the car. "You talked to Moses, didn't you?"

"I've talked to him several times. They knew."

He let the screen door shut behind him.

"I'm surprised they forgot to get food," she said.

What surprised her more as she thought about it, carrying Sam upstairs to wash him in the sink and change his diapers, was her deep hurt that there were no provisions. How quickly she had adjusted to their lives at Skunk Farm. How easily she had depended.

It made her cross. Not at the Bellowses but at her own presumptions.

She picked up the telephone and called Vruels'. Doc Vruels said he would be open until noon.

"I heard you'd moved back to Minneapolis," he said.

"From whom?"

"I think it was from Moses."

"Well I didn't," Lara said.

"And you're moving to Elm Grove for good."

"We're here for now," Lara said. "I'll be over soon for supplies."

Out back, she noticed the cottages had been painted a sunny yellow and Guy's cottage had a new roof. The barn door had been replaced and the fields were already high in wheat, and as she turned from the window, she saw Moses come from the cottages into the clearing carrying something long—a rake perhaps or a shotgun.

In the Bellows cottage that morning, preparations were underway for Aida's birthday party. Ever since Guy and Aida were married, the Bellowses had celebrated Aida's birthday. It was the only family birthday taken into account, because it fell on a holiday, and early on they decided it would have to stand for all of the birthdays in the family. Moses didn't even know what day his birthday was —either the 3rd or 4th or 5th of November—and his father never had known either the month or the year. So Aida's birthday was it for the whole family. Cousins close by would come, aunts and uncles—their friends were all related. Most summers, if it wasn't too hot, they roasted a pig behind the cottages and the party went on all day, into the night with dancing and singing, too much eating and drinking. By nightfall, everyone, even the women, had sunk into a deep slumber and for a few days afterward they paid for their merriment, but it was once a year and worth the price. So this morning, not too hot for roasting a pig, everybody in the Bellows cottage was about his business.

Guy had butchered and was preparing the pig, which would cook all day over the fire. Prudential cleaned chickens on the kitchen table. Upstairs, Miracle was dressing. Her blood pressure was down and she had lost weight, flesh off her hips and belly. Her face showed the bones and she was feeling young for the first time in months and months. Moses came into the bedroom from the top field where the lambs were and kissed her.

"I don't know why Aida needs a birthday party this year since her bad sense almost ruined our lives," he said without temper.

"We always have a party for Aida."

"And we have to do what we've always done."

"That's right," Miracle said.

He took her around the waist, pulled her down on the bed with him, and they lay there very still, listening to the banter in the kitchen where Aida and Prudential were cooking.

"Miracle." He took her face in his hands. "I want you to tell me the truth."

She looked at him.

"I want you to tell me whether you ever did see John Spencer, actually see him in the flesh."

Miracle considered. She looked into Moses' black eyes and smiled.

"I see what I want to see," she said. "And I don't want to see him just now."

Prudential called up to say one of the chickens had a smell to it and should she cook it anyway. Miracle said she'd be right down to check it out but a new-killed chicken ought not to have a smell. So she put on her dress and shoes to go downstairs.

"The Fletchers will be here around noon," she said. "I spoke to Mr. Fletcher yesterday."

"I spoke to him too."

"I forgot to bring in food," she said. "It's been so long since anyone has been there."

"Doc Vruels' is open."

"They could come down to have some chicken with us." Moses grunted.

"I don't necessarily want to have the Fletchers for Aida's birthday," Moses said. "It's bad enough having Aida's birthday all by itself."

"That's what we should do," she said. "Or carry up some chicken to them."

Moses changed shirts, went into the bathroom to wash his hands and face.

"I'm going to see if they have arrived," he called to Miracle as he left.

He wanted to see Lara Fletcher, he thought to himself. He wanted to see what the sight of her would do to him. This time, however, he knew better than to open up the shutters and let in too much light. There were as he had always known invisible boundaries between people that ran in the blood and they had to be considered.

On the way past Guy's cottage, he took his brother's shotgun from underneath the rocking chair on the front porch just for safekeeping. He did not expect trouble.

Kate was sitting on the kitchen table waiting for Prudential when Moses came in the back door. Not that there was any sign Prudential would be coming, although surely she knew that the Fletchers had arrived and without too much trouble could even see the car from the front porch of the Bellows cottage—unless for some reason she didn't care to see Kate or New York City had changed her completely or out of the blue their friendship had come to an end. Kate didn't want to be the one to make the first move, especially since her stomach was rioting with nerves as it was doing and the dampness was bursting on her brow as if she were going to be sick.

"Maybe she has found another friend like me in New York," Kate said to her mother, but Lara said that was unlikely. Friends didn't come easily in life and attractions like theirs held glue-firm forever.

"Where's Prudential?" she asked Moses before she even said hello.

"She's working in the kitchen at the cottage," Moses said. "Doing the chickens for Aida's birthday party." He tousled her hair. "And how are you, Miss Kate, besides thin as wire?"

"Terrible," Kate said, getting up to leave by the back door. "Just absolutely terrible."

Kate saw Prudential first. She was standing on the railings of the Bellows cottage in her bare feet lost in a blue-flowered house dress of Miracle's which hung loose as curtains on her body hanging up a sign which said HAPPY BIRTHDAY AIDA SUE. Kate had gone down the path out back barefoot so as not to make a sound, and there Prudential was thinner than she'd been in February with her hair done in ribbons like a birthday present.

"Hello," Kate said quietly.

Prudential looked down at her from the railing, cocky, combative.

"I left that pink dress in my apartment in New York if you were wondering why I didn't have it on."

"I wasn't wondering that," Kate said in a thin voice, wretched at her longing for Prudential's friendship. "I was wondering why you didn't come up to see me when I arrived."

"Because I'm busy, as you can see." Prudential tacked up the sign. "We're having a party for Aida's birthday and I've got things to do." She jumped down.

"I could help," Kate said.

Prudential brushed off her shorts.

"Suit yourself."

Miracle hugged Kate when she went into the kitchen with Prudential, took her face in her hands and said she looked weary from the troubles and living in a hotel so long and needed to be fattened up. Aida, apprehensive but not unfriendly, laid a fresh-killed chicken on the table and told Kate to pluck its feathers if she'd a mind to. Prudential sat down beside her with her own chicken whose feathers deep in the leathery skin came easily in Prudential's hands.

"So I see you're stuck up since you moved to New York City," Kate said when Miracle and Aida went out to help Guy turn the pig on the spit.

"I have a lot of responsibilities there," Prudential said.

"Like the radio," Kate said. "I haven't heard you on the radio."

Prudential hesitated.

"I don't actually start until next month. Next month, you'll hear me on *Forever Tomorrow*. You listen to that?"

"I did when we lived in the hotel," Kate said.

Prudential finished her chicken, rinsed him out in the sink, took out his innards and dumped them in the stock pot bubbling on the stove.

"I'll be a new character in *Forever Tomorrow*," Prudential said. "I die of cancer in the show." She lied with such marvelous ease that there was no chance for disbelief. Not even her own.

She took a butcher knife and cut the legs and wings, split the breast down the center. Then she rolled the pieces in flour and cornmeal and put them in a bowl ready to fry.

"I'll help you finish," she said to Kate.

"I can do my own," Kate said, cross at her slowness.

But Prudential sat down anyway and pulled the feathers off the chicken's thigh and breast, her hands moving like lightning, humming out loud, pushing away the chance for serious conversation in the air.

"Why aren't we friends?" Kate asked finally.

"Who says we're not?"

"We're not enemies," Kate said. "I'm just dead to you, that's all."

Miracle came back into the kitchen. She put oil in the frying pan and lit the stove. She salted and peppered the pieces of chicken and laid them in the hot oil one at a time. Then she turned down the fire, washed off the counter, put her hand on top of Kate's head. "Cat got your tongue?" she asked and went upstairs.

When she left, Kate grabbed Prudential's wrist and squeezed it hard. "I wish you didn't have my secrets," she said.

"Who am I going to tell your secrets to?" Prudential asked.

"Your boyfriend."

"I don't have a boyfriend any longer."

"You could tell them to anybody. Everybody you meet in New York."

"I wouldn't do that," Prudential said.

"How do I know?" Kate asked.

"You have to believe me."

For a moment, Prudential thought she would tell Kate all the secrets right away. They would go up to her old room, close the door, sit on the bed up against the wall and whisper. Just the memory of it warmed her inside. But instead she said, "I go home tomorrow."

"To New York."

"No," Prudential said. "Tomorrow I go home to Okrakan."

"What about the radio?" Kate asked, confused.

"I promised Mama I'd come home."

"I see."

Kate didn't ask any more questions. She knew she had been told a story but she didn't understand its meaning. She took the butcher knife and cut up her chicken, rolled it in flour and cornmeal and put it in the frying pan spitting with fat.

"See you later," Prudential said as Kate was finishing. "If you come to the party." And she ran upstairs to change.

At home in her own room, Kate opened the suitcase, took out her clothes, hung them in the closet or put them in the dresser drawer. She took her letters from her father, from her friends in Minneapolis, from Prudential, all written to the Mayflower Hotel. She had never looked at the postmark on Prudential's letters to her and she didn't look now or wish to see "Okrakan, S.C." in the circle next to the cancelled stamp.

Moses had just put Guy's gun on the top shelf in the mudroom when Lara flew down the back stairs and sensing his presence there, sensing him looking at her, rushed through the kitchen in a flutter to avoid their reunion.

"Hello, Mrs. Fletcher," Moses said, stopping her.

"Oh, Moses, hello," she said as if he were the last person she expected to see in her kitchen. "I'm on my way to Vruels' for groceries." Her face was flushed. She opened the cupboards to check supplies although she was too unsettled to remember that she needed mustard and mayonnaise and Campbell's Soup. "There's hardly anything." She put her purse over her shoulder and opened the screen door.

"I just came over to welcome you home," Moses said.

She was out of breath.

"Thank you," she said, trying to breathe evenly so the pounding in her chest would stop. "How are you? I didn't even think to ask."

He smiled his wonderful wide irreverent smile.

"Fine. We are all fine," he said. "I hope you're home to stay."

"I don't know," Lara said. "I don't know how long we'll stay."

The car wouldn't start. It was always the same—she drove so little that she flooded the engine whenever she was in a hurry and now there was Moses coming out the kitchen door, across the patio.

"Flooded," she said crossly. "There's something the matter with this model of car."

She got out, left the door open and paced waiting for the gasoline to settle.

He got in the car, turned the key in the ignition, and the engine caught. "We're having a party tonight for Aida's birthday and the Fourth of July. You're welcome to come down and eat," he said.

She watched him in her rearview mirror behind her—regal as he was, with a straight and certain walk, a sense of dominance. Now they had met, she thought, relieved that it was over. There had been an ordinary exchange between them. Perhaps they had even survived their dangerous trespasses on one another's life.

The party started at four. It started quietly—everybody sitting on the porch of the Bellows cottage with beers, and plates of fried chicken, and pork and potato salad. The cousins and other relations kept coming, some in cars, others on foot over the back field, and by six the party was in swing. Then the Fletchers decided that yes they would go out back, in spite of the fact that Guy had surely been drinking, in spite of their deep uneasiness. They had after all come home to Skunk Farm to make a life there with the Bellowses living out back and that life had to begin sometime, not as a large family for they were not a large family, not either in their own houses separated by a gulf too wide for passage by men and women.

Aida was dancing on the table in bare feet, her bright yellow skirt flapping, holding on to Moses, who danced on the floor of the kitchen beside her. Prudential in the pink dress she had not left behind danced with a girl cousin in the living room and everywhere the Bellowses were outsinging the radio.

236

When the Fletchers arrived, the dancing stopped, the radio was turned down, Aida jumped off the table and put on her shoes. Moses asked them to please come in and have some dinner which they did do and met the relatives and talked to Guy and Aida who stood with their arms folded across their chests, subdued.

Later, Moses sat on the porch railing with Charley Fletcher and talked about the farm, what was planted for autumn, how the animals were, what new animals had been born that spring. At one point Guy came out on the porch. He had in mind to say something to Charley Fletcher, to thank him for his gesture of protection, but there were no words which came to lay to rest the history of their short violent lives together except the words which rushed into Guy Bellows' mind spoken from the Bible at the Baptist church services for the dead in the roaring voice of the preacher: "Dust to dust and ashes to ashes."

And that's what he said, softened by whiskey and the spirit of celebration, warmed by this gathering of relatives.

"Dust to dust is what I say to you, Mr. Fletcher," and he reached out to shake Charley Fletcher's hand.

The Fletchers did not stay long. Charley knew their arrival had interrupted the party, so when they were finished eating, even before the firecrackers, they said goodbye.

Arm in arm, Kate carrying Sam, they walked the path home. Behind them, the Bellows celebration exploded on the quiet summer night with laughter, the gay drumbeat of dancing feet on hard wood floors.

"We don't belong," Kate said, leaning her head against her mother's shoulder.

"Nobody belongs," Charley said, his voice clear in the soft night air.

Charley Fletcher had wanted to make a village like the villages of the old world at Skunk Farm. A place of safety where strangers, even Lara and himself, estranged by culture and language and the mysteries of the heart, could live secure, inextricably bound as if by blood, sufficient unto themselves, protected by a history spun out of the air. He wanted, tucked into the pocket of Virginia hills, America as it was first dreamed up—a refuge where everyone is safe in everyone else's house, where the spirit is free to soar like gulls out over the water, blown home by a benevolent wind. And his deep wish was not at the heart of it a matter of principle with the Bellowses but came rather from the inevitable birthright in a country of strangers, of loneliness and isolation and a longing to walk in the company of friends.

Miracle was singing now, her rich extravagant voice in the air around them. They walked across the patio, into the kitchen, turning out the lights in the hall, in the living room, in the study as they went upstairs in darkness.

Later, when the fireworks started they lay under the net canopy of John Spencer's four-poster bed and watched the sky light up in the bursts of yellow streamers or crack the darkness with a single orange circle or a child's splendid picture of the sun with long gold threads drawn to the corners of the heavens.

Out back, after the relatives had driven home, Moses went upstairs where Miracle was sleeping, took off his trousers and shirt and lay across her, burying his head in the soft flesh of her belly.

"Miracle darling," he whispered. "You awake?"

"Uh huh."

"I come upstairs to wish you a happy Independence Day and good night."

"Good night, Moses," she said, "and put your head up here on the pillow where it belongs."

Behind the cottage, Aida sat on the back steps with Guy, watching the row of sparklers in front of them burn to ash.

"We have a skyrocket," she said. "I hid it under the steps so we could light it together after Moses went to bed."

She reached under the bottom step, set the skyrocket on the ground in front of them. Guy took the matches out of his pocket and lit the wick.

"So happy birthday, pretty woman." He ran his finger lightly over her painted lips.

And in the main house, Charley and Lara Fletcher lay on Lara's side of the bed, embroidered by the shadows of the canopy, under the soft sheet lifted as if by the magic of a light wind, luminous to one another in the spectacular light that filled the sky out back.